CH|

TH

MAGIC MIRROR

CHRISTOPHER BUSH was born Charlie Christmas Bush in Norfolk in 1885. His father was a farm labourer and his mother a milliner. In the early years of his childhood he lived with his aunt and uncle in London before returning to Norfolk aged seven, later winning a scholarship to Thetford Grammar School.

As an adult, Bush worked as a schoolmaster for 27 years, pausing only to fight in World War One, until retiring aged 46 in 1931 to be a full-time novelist. His first novel featuring the eccentric Ludovic Travers was published in 1926, and was followed by 62 additional Travers mysteries. These are all to be republished by Dean Street Press.

Christopher Bush fought again in World War Two, and was elected a member of the prestigious Detection Club. He died in 1973.

THE LUDOVIC TRAVERS MYSTERIES
Available from Dean Street Press

CHRISTOPHER BUSH

THE CASE OF THE MAGIC MIRROR

With an introduction
by Curtis Evans

DEAN STREET PRESS

INTRODUCTION

WINDING DOWN THE WAR AND TAKING A NEW TURN

CHRISTOPHER BUSH'S LUDOVIC TRAVERS MYSTERIES, 1943 TO 1946

HAVING SENT his series sleuth Ludovic "Ludo" Travers, in the third and fourth years of the Second World War, around England to meet murder at a variety of newly-created army installations—a prisoner-of-war camp (*The Case of the Murdered Major*, 1941), a guard base (*The Case of the Kidnapped Colonel*, 1942) and an instructor school (*The Case of the Fighting Soldier*, 1942)--Christopher Bush finally released Travers from military engagements in *The Case of the Magic Mirror* (1943), a unique retrospective affair which takes place before the outbreak of the Second World War. In the remaining four Travers wartime mysteries--*The Case of the Running Mouse* (1944), *The Case of the Platinum Blonde* (1944), *The Case of the Corporal's Leave* (1945) and *The Case of the Missing Men* (1946)--Bush frees his sleuth to investigate private criminal problems. Although the war is mentioned in these novels, it plays far less of a role in events, doubtlessly giving contemporary readers a sense that the world conflagration which at one point had threatened to consume the British Empire was winding down for good. Yet even without the "novelty" of the war as a major plot element, these Christopher Bush mysteries offer readers some of the most intriguing conundrums in the Ludo Travers detection canon.

The Case of the Magic Mirror (1943)

"Phil Marlowe," he said, "the shop-soiled Sir Galahad."
—*The High Window* (1942), Raymond Chandler

"You were always a bit of a Galahad—a trifle shop-soiled, perhaps, but always very pi [i.e., pious]."

—*The Case of the Magic Mirror* (1943),
Christopher Bush

THAT WITHIN ONE YEAR of each other crime writers Christopher Bush and Raymond Chandler would coincidentally refer to their series sleuths as "shop-soiled Sir Galahads" passes belief. Chandler used the term first, in his third detective novel *The High Window*, and it is, indeed, one of the most celebrated turns of phrase of the many such that are found in the hard-boiled author's canon. It seems fair to surmise that Bush read *The High Window* and borrowed the memorable image of the slightly tarnished knight when that same year he was writing *The Case of the Magic Mirror*. Certainly Bush would not have been the lone Forties British crime writer Chandler influenced. James Hadley Chase, author of the notoriously violent *No Orchids for Miss Blandish* (which ripped off another American book, William Faulkner's controversial *Sanctuary*, and was famously denounced for its sadism by a fastidious George Orwell), was compelled to apologize for partially plagiarizing Chandler's first detective novel, the landmark *The Big Sleep* (1939), in his own *Blonde's Requiem* (1945). The extremely popular British author Peter Cheyney also was hugely influenced in his crime writing by American pulp fiction, likely including Chandler short stories, though Cheyney inaugurated both his Lemmy Caution and Slim Callaghan novel series a few years before *The Big Sleep* was published. While Christopher Bush certainly never transitioned into a full hard-boiled writer like Chase and Cheyney, he nevertheless with *The Case of the Magic Mirror* clearly began to show some influence in his work of the American tough school, with its reliance on first person narration by the sleuth and its settings rife with the dissolute rich and scheming *femmes fatales*. *Mirror* in particular is notable for having probably the most formidable female antagonist that his series sleuth Ludovic "Ludo" Travers was ever to encounter.

The novel opens with Travers explaining that what he calls *The Case of the Magic Mirror* actually took place in 1939, but that he only wrote an account of it in the spring of 1942 during convalescence from an operation to remove a "lump of shrapnel from a premature bomb." We quickly learn that the *Mirror* case arose out of an earlier criminal affair, the 1937 trial of several men charged with having engaged in a bookie swindling scheme. The men prosecuted and convicted for the crimes were Charles Rogerley, a racehorse trainer; Lenny Harper, a heavyweight boxer; Patrick Silvey, chauffeur to Joseph Passman, wealthy owner of a string of chain stores in northern England; and Rupert Craigne, a vainglorious stage actor married to Passman's alluring stepdaughter Charlotte (*née* Vallants).

Charlotte Craigne's late mother, with creditors pounding on the door of her charming Suffolk country house, Brazenoak Manor (which comes complete with a faithful old butler, Matthews, by the by, and the "most perfect Adam mirror" Travers has ever seen), deemed it expedient to wed the wealthy if socially dubious Joe Passman. It was Passman's later testimony in the bookie-swindling case, along with that of his stepson-in-law Rupert Craigne, which sealed the fate of Patrick Silvey, prompting the latter man dramatically to vow vengeance upon Passman and Craigne as he was being dragged from the courtroom. ("You fat swine! By God, I'll get you if it's the last thing I do! You too, you bloody lying swine!") In 1939 some who had been involved with the case, like Ludo's friend Superintendent George Wharton of the Yard, still suspect that Joe Passman in fact masterminded the whole swindle. Now Rupert Craigne has been released from jail and he is making a public exhibition of himself, loudly protesting his incarceration and insisting upon his innocence. Will Silvey, for his part, seek his promised revenge against Craigne and Passman when he shortly gets outside of prison walls again?

This is the situation when Ludo Travers, at the behest of his wife Bernice, who is on her way to a month's visit with friends in France, meets with Charlotte to see what he can do to help reconcile Charlotte's husband, Rupert Craigne, to whom she is still devoted, with her stepfather, Joe Passman, upon whom she remains dependent. But Travers learns that Charlotte has more than a mere reconciliation in mind, heartwarming as that might be. Rather, she announces that she wants Ludo to dig up dirt on Joe, in connection with the bookie swindling affair, which she then can use to blackmail her stepfather into financially bailing out the now-penniless Rupert. When Travers balks at this underhanded behavior, however, Charlotte--who, unknown to Bernice, once carried on a torrid three-year affair with Ludo --proceeds to blackmail her ex-lover, producing a photo of a young boy and proclaiming that the lad is her and Ludo's son. Disbelieving Charlotte's claim but fearing Bernice's possible reaction to it, Ludo assents to Charlotte's command, but he plans in reality to dig up dirt on her rather than Joe, with the intention of blackmailing Charlotte into relenting her scheme. "If Charlotte could double-cross, so could I," Ludo explains, "and blackmail was very much of a boomerang."

This criss-crossed conundrum makes a stupendous noir scenario that would have done any of the hard-boiled American masters proud. As in classic noir, the protagonist is pulled down into dubious doings through a past transgression with an unvirtuous woman, one who still holds a powerful sexual hold over him, despite the fact that she simultaneously repels him. And Charlotte's hold over Ludo is of the sort which could well prove fatal. "I don't know if a rabbit admires a particularly attractive stoat while he cowers and waits," Ludo mordantly observes, "but the comparison is the only one I can make, for I found myself watching her every movement and gesture, fascinated as ever, but more and more scared as the minutes went by."

It is hard not to discern in this sticky and somewhat sordid fictional situation an allusion to a long-ago scandal from Christopher Bush's own past life, Bush in 1920 having fathered an out-of-wedlock son (the future composer Geoffrey Bush) with Winifred Chart, a mathematics teacher at the co-educational Wood Green School in Oxfordshire, where Bush himself then taught. Evidence from *Mirror* and other Bush novels suggests that he may have felt "entrapped" by the news of Winifred's pregnancy—or even, possibly, that he may have doubted that Geoffrey was indeed his son. (Never in his life did Bush acknowledge Geoffrey as such.)

Whatever was the truth of the matter in Bush's own life, Ludo Travers is adamant that "the kid's not my son" (to quote the late Michael Jackson) and that he "shan't have that damnable woman round my neck for the rest of my life" (to quote Ludo). Yet as Travers strives to escape from Charlotte's clutches he finds himself confronting first one mysterious murder, then another, and yet another. It is one bloody slay ride that Ludo has let himself in for this time, and his and Charlotte's final destination is shocking indeed.

Curtis Evans

I
THE MUSIC GOES ROUND

CHAPTER I
CHELMSFORD ASSIZES

I DON'T KNOW why I should call this case that of the Magic Mirror for there's nothing in it reminiscent of "Snow White and the Seven Dwarfs," even if the mirror did do a certain amount of magical revelation. I suppose I might have called the book anything: "The Case of the Engine-driver's Nephew," for instance, since Harper's uncle was an engine-driver.

As a matter of fact the title is my obstinate own, and I'm unconcerned as to whether or not you find it apposite. This book, you see, is my own peculiar property in various unusual ways. In the first place, of the many murder cases with which I have been officially connected, this one which I am about to relate was easily the most unusual. On the face of it one could at first hardly call it a case at all, for its solution presented no difficulties. Then curious doubts arose, and the obvious was far from what it seemed, and finally the whole thing seemed incapable of any solution at all. Then when the solution did come, it was so absurdly simple that one doubted one's sanity for not having seen it from the very first.

Now if you are a connoisseur in murder stories you will say that there is nothing unusual in all I have said, since I have merely repeated the pattern of every intriguing case. If you do say that, then I must try to give additional proof of my statements, and the easiest way is to issue a challenge. This is it. In the following paragraph is the germ of that simple solution; enough material, in fact, to allow you to solve the whole thing well before the last page and to prove yourself more agile in deduction than those of us whose professional job it was to do the solving. Here is the paragraph, then, and remember, *one paragraph only*.

This is the year 1943, and this book will deal with events that took place mainly in 1939. In the spring of 1942 I had an accident at the Camp where I hold a War Office appointment of sorts—nothing very serious beyond a lump of shrapnel from a premature bomb, but there had to be an operation and then two months' convalescence. To pass the time I thought I would do some writing, and it was this particular case about which I at last made up my mind to write, and for this main reason. In spite of the war and various financial shocks I am lucky enough to be still very far from destitute, but nevertheless I am a cantankerous person in many ways where money is concerned. I hate seeing good money go down the drain, and more than once I had thought ruefully of the perfectly good money I had spent over the solving of that case. That is why I had quite a thrill when I decided to write this book and get some at least of the money back.

So much for that, except that it involves some new explanation. Since you have probably studied that last paragraph with a certain care you will wonder why I hesitated about writing the book. There are various reasons, and none redound to my credit. For the first time in any murder case I had to run with the hare and hunt with the hounds, which meant that I had to double-cross George Wharton. I had to submit to blackmail, and I persisted in being a moral coward. In fact, in the hackneyed words of the poet, I knew what a tangled web we weave when first we practise to deceive. The more I became involved, the harder it was to disentangle myself, and from certain dry comments which my wife occasionally lets fall, I doubt if I have wholly disentangled myself even at this date. All of which goes to prove what I said at the beginning, that the case was the most unusual in my reasonably large experience, and I will further add that I hope to heaven it will be a long time before I get myself involved in one that even remotely resembles it.

One last thing that made me decide to write this book, or rather seemed to set me free to write it, was that when I was tottering on the verge of decision I saw in a casualty list from Libya that Frank Tarling was missing, believed killed. Not that there is anything that redounds to Frank's discredit. Far from it, for he was as good a man at his job as I am ever likely to see.

The story really begins before my marriage, but that piece of hectic revelation had better be deferred till Charlotte appears in person. The vital beginning was in the autumn of 1937, at Chelmsford Assizes, with Sivley's scream from the dock when he heard his sentence. Before he was hustled below he got out no more than two or three sentences, but they were enough to set the murder train in motion.

I was at the Assizes and with George Wharton—Superintendent Wharton of Scotland Yard, where both awe and affection have nicknamed him the Old General. George figures very largely in this story, so in case you do not know him, here is a brief description. About his outward appearance everything is contradictory, and no man could look less like one of what is popularly known as the Big Four. He is tall and burly, but disguises that with something of a stoop. His huge walrus moustache and his antiquated spectacles give him the look of a harassed paterfamilias, or a hawker of vacuum cleaners with whom trade could not conceivably be worse. All that is part of his technique, for his back can be ramrod straight when wrath or indignation or excitement makes him forget the pose, and since he can read the smallest print with the best of us, the spectacles are donned for his own obscure and deceptive purposes.

For George is a showman who is the master of his art. His sleeves are crammed with innumerable tricks and his personality vivid with innumerable disguises to be assumed on each apt occasion.

George was going to Chelmsford Assizes to hold a special watching brief; not that the Jupiter Case, as the public knew it, was any new development in crime. It was merely a slightly new twist to a very old trick—that of swindling the bookies by faking the times of telegrams. George told me that he was going and I suddenly decided to go too, though that was on the last day of a trial that had lasted three days. He called for me at my flat in St. Martin's Chambers and it was in my car that we drove.

"Why exactly did you want to come along to-day?" George asked mildly, and then with a sarcastic pursing of his lips:

"Wanted a little cheap excitement—eh? Been reading the popular papers."

"Maybe, George," I said. "But there's a lot more in it than that."

As he badgered me I told him some of the reasons, and they were all connected with only one of the four accused—Rupert Craigne, or "Jupiter" Craigne, as he was nicknamed after the smashing success of *Trouble on Olympus*. But two things I did not tell George—the main reason why I was going and the reason why I had not been present on the previous two days.

"Craigne and I were at school together," I began.

"You were!" said George incredulously. "What was he like there? As full of swank and conceit?"

"Not excessively," I said. "He was extraordinarily clever in a meretricious kind of way, and I never quite trusted him. He was erratic and very much out for self. Even in those days he hogged the limelight. Not that he had any need to, for he was a born actor."

I told George how Rupert Craigne and I had met frequently after the war, and how I had put a considerable sum into one of his early shows, and had done well out of it. I had had the chance of putting money into *Trouble on Olympus* but had not taken it.

"Not like you, missing a chance like that?" George said. "You'd have made a packet. That play ran two years, didn't it?"

"It did," I said, "but I'm not sorry. You see, I didn't like the way Craigne was shaping, even then. His mannerisms happened to fit that play and his Jupiter, of course, was really superb. but he'd begun to live far above his means and he'd got in with the wrong set. If he made a penny out of *Trouble on Olympus,* he made a clear fifteen thousand pounds. Not bad money for two years, and yet you know, as I know, that he was always hard up."

"Well, it's all over with him now," was George's opinion.

"I read the accounts in the Press, but what's your personal view of his defence? You were there, and you know how differently things read in print."

"Pitiful," George said. "And despicable. Tried to make out he was the tool of others, and, above all, of Sivley. Said he didn't know the scheme was other than genuine. And that for a man who kept a racehorse or two."

"What an attraction the turf has," I couldn't help saying. "As soon as a certain class of people make money, they get hold of a horse or two and before they know it they're in it up to the neck. Nineteen times out of twenty they burn their fingers good and proper."

"Flashy," George said. "That's them, and that's Craigne all over. Spending money like water. The best of everything for himself and his pals. Two thousand guineas for a colt that was knocked down last March for a couple of hundred. All his bets in hundreds, so I'm told. Only one good thing about him, so they say. He didn't run any women. Stuck to his wife, though they say she's left him. Handsome woman. She was in court yesterday. Someone pointed her out to me."

I hope I didn't blush, but I did change the conversation.

"By the way, what's your special interest in this affair, George?"

He slipped adroitly down one or two side turnings before I got him back to that main question. Then he hinted that there were ramifications in the case and things that mightn't come out in court. The fraud was bigger than the public imagined and those in the dock mightn't be the real principals. When I pestered him to enlarge on that, all I could induce him to confide was that the Law had an eye on Joseph Passman. You may have heard of Passman. His money was made out of chain stores in the North. I knew him well. The breezy type who boasts of being self-made and talks about "the brass." Passman also had the homely trick of referring to himself as Joe, or old Joe. "Old Joe's too fly a bird for that," he told me with a wink when I hinted there was money in backing Craigne in the early days. That was before Craigne married Charlotte, who was Joe's stepdaughter.

"But wait a minute, George," I suddenly said. "Didn't I read that Joe Passman gave evidence against Sivley? It was his evidence that proved Sivley was a rogue. No one else said a word against him—except Craigne."

"Maybe," George said airily. "The fact that Passman gave evidence against an old employee doesn't prove very much. He might have been ingratiating himself with the powers-that-be. He's the plausible sort I can smell a mile off." He gave a grunt. "Besides, there's been some private tipping off. And we know he's paying for Craigne's defence."

"Why shouldn't his wife be paying for it?"

"Because she hasn't a bean but what Passman allows her," George told me curtly.

Before stepping into the Assize Court you might like to have a look at the four prisoners who stood in the dock, charged with conspiring to cheat and defraud. If also at any time you may be tempted to try any variation of that scheme to swindle the book-ies, it might deter you to learn what that particular scheme was, and how it fared.

A bookmaker, as you may know, will accept a telegram timed before the result of a race. If, therefore, you can learn a result and then fake the time of the telegram, the bookmaker will pay you your winnings. But that faking has been done in many forms and the post office is alive to every variation. As soon as a telegram is sent from a sub-post office to a main post office, it is checked as to time. Suppose, for instance, you have the result of the 2.30 at 2.33, and you wire a hundred pounds on the winner, inducing the postmaster of the sub-office to put the time as 2.27. When that telegram is checked, two questions are put to the sub-postmaster. "Why did you accept the telegram? Why the delay in our receiving it, since the time is now 2.35?" If the answers are not satisfactory, the telegram is held back.

There is another safeguard. The character of a sub-postmas-ter and his financial standing are most strictly inquired into before he is allowed to function. There is also the best safeguard of all—the fact that a bookmaker will not part with a considera-ble sum of money won on a telephoned commission unless he is sure of its genuineness and the integrity of his client. How then did this particular gang try to circumvent all the safeguards?

The answer is that they banked heavily on the integrity of the parties concerned, and they mixed the two swindling bets with a loser or two and a couple of bets that were undoubtedly genuine. The rest of the scheme can be learned from a look at the men themselves, and a brief study of their biographies.

PATRICK SIVLEY. Head chauffeur to Joseph Passman for some years, and then chauffeur to Rupert Craigne. He claimed to have saved a considerable sum of money and in the spring of 1937 retired and purchased the village shop of Gadsford, ten miles from Newmarket, and took over the sub-post office. The post office department that inquired into his character admitted that it relied principally on a glowing testimonial from Craigne. Sivley's financial standing was impeccable, but at the trial the prosecution proved that early in 1937 he owed money everywhere, and it also endeavoured to prove that the money for the purchase of the shop had been put up by the other three accused. The prosecution sprang a surprise on the second day by putting Joseph Passman in the box to prove that Sivley did not leave his service voluntarily, but was dismissed when a long series of frauds came to light.

CHARLES ROGERLEY. Racehorse trainer who had been warned off the course in 1911 and later reinstated. He trained for two owners, each of good standing and character, and he also trained for Rupert Craigne when that famous actor owned a couple of horses. It was horses from Rogerley's small stable that won the two races on which the genuine bets were made, and the prosecution claimed that this was his chief role in the gang, to create confidence with the bookmakers concerned. Both horses started at reasonably short prices, and the winnings by telephoned commission amounted to less than four figures in all.

LENNY HARPER. Better known as Lyddite Len, the heavyweight boxer. Had an up-and-down career in the ring, though his detractors claimed that it was more down than up. The *mot* about him was that though he wasn't dead, he *would* lie down. Made considerable sums of money in his time but spent too much on the horses. At the time of arrest he was in training for the biggest fight of his career, and his training camp was at the Royal Swan at Gadsford. He sent the telegrams which Sivley pre-timed. The gang actually made £3,000 over the first telegram, but set against the previous transactions and ground-bait losses, this was a net gain of just over £2,000. On the second telegram they had no less than £7,000 to come.

RUPERT CRAIGNE. His career has been referred to, and it should be added that for his celebrated part of Jupiter in *Trouble on Olympus* he grew a beard of golden brown, and this he afterwards retained. A curious megalomania that authors should be expected to write him future parts to fit an Olympian beard and a head of curly golden hair, however superb the two might be! His role in the swindle, according to the prosecution, was to appear in Gadsford post office—he had taken a furnished house in the district—about five minutes before the advertised time of the starting of the race chosen for the big swindle, and to send off two normal telegrams. While these were being dispatched by Sivley, Harper would appear. He had the result of the race, and would hand in the fraudulent telegram. Since Craigne's telegrams would have taken some time to send, their sending made ample excuse for the delay in dispatching Harper's. Craigne's standing was supposed to allay suspicion, and on the first occasion it apparently did so.

The personal appearance of the accused is rather important. Rogerley was a ferret-faced, undersized man of sixty-five who had begun life as a jockey and had become head man to a trainer when no longer able to make the weights. Harper was a giant of six foot three—just about my own height—but whereas I am only a hundred and fifty pounds, Harper scaled at least seventy-five more. His shoulders were immensely broad, and when he stood still on his pins he had a curious swaying motion. His features showed few marks of his bouts and his voice was strangely gentle, but he had the shiftiest eyes I have ever seen.

Sivley surprised me, for I had expected to see a ferret-faced customer like Rogerley, but put him in black with a wing collar and you'd have taken him for a professional man of good standing. In height he was just under six foot, which was Craigne's height, and he was not unlike him in build. But there the resemblance ended, for his hair was a jet black with just a touch of grey at the temples. His manner in court, till that unexpected outburst, was quiet and deferential, but his hooked nose gave his face an alertness.

As for Craigne, you know what his personal appearance was, and all I should add is that he had a nervous trick which is not too common, of twitching his head round quickly as if he were rubbing something off his collar with his chin. He only did it once that day in court and I gathered, as I told Wharton, that he had largely grown out of it.

Now since that trial is preliminary to the main story, there is no necessity to drag you through the whole of that last day's events. The judge was Mr. Justice Carre (Sir Humbold Carre) and the court presented the usual appearance. The public seats were crowded and the Press seats uncommonly full, but Wharton and I had special seats just off the well of the court, where we could see everything without being too conspicuous.

When I took my first look round, whom should I see to the far left of the front row of the public seats but Charlotte Craigne, and I turned my head hastily away and swivelled round in my chair. It was two years since I had seen her, and it was curious how my face flushed and my heart began to race. A guilty conscience was dimly behind all that, for Charlotte had been my life's one indiscretion, and all that day she was somewhere at the back of my mind as an uneasiness and a depression. Yet for the life of me I couldn't help taking more than one furtive peep at her, and wondering a considerable number of things.

I had known Charlotte Vallants most of my life, for she had been at school with a sister of mine, but I had not become really aware of her till some seven years before my marriage. But I heard about her from time to time, for hers was the kind of personality that few people, and certainly not my sister, would be likely to forget. I knew her people well, though they were not quite my kind and belonged to that racing-cum-theatrical clique which bores me beyond tears. Brazenoak, their place in Suffolk, was one of the most charming houses I have ever known, but when Colonel Vallants died the creditors descended and the place was sold. Mabel Vallants, to the amazement of all and the consternation of most, married Joe Passman, and he bought the property back. When Mabel died, Charlotte made Brazenoak a *pied-à-terre,* and with an allowance from Joe, installed herself in town. Joe and she were on admirable terms and the two would often be seen trotting round. The world's most incongruous couple, as you will know when you meet Charlotte again.

It was in 1936 when she married Rupert Craigne. That he was the only man with whom she had ever been really in love I was perfectly well aware, and for the life of me I couldn't help thinking that she was in love with him still, in spite of what Wharton had said about her leaving him and the rumours which I myself had heard. Perhaps you see the other complications. Joe Passman had come to hate Craigne like hell. What Joe couldn't stand was the way Craigne squandered the brass; he himself had been forced to clear up more than one financial mess. So, as I saw things, there was Charlotte dependent on Joe, as madly in love with her husband as ever, and yet having to cut herself adrift. And knuckling down to circumstances wasn't Charlotte's way. She was always the sort to flout circumstance and go through hell and high water for what often seemed to be the mere whim of being different.

During the lunch interval I asked George how he thought things were going.

"Rogerley'll swing clear," he said. "Bet you a new hat."

"No, you don't," I told him. "But what about the others?"

"A couple of years apiece," he said, but more tentatively. "Craigne may get less."

"Why?"

"Well, if he only got six months he'd be damned," he pointed out. "Whatever he gets, his career's over. Only one thing left for him to do, and that's to go abroad, or blow out his brains."

"If he does that, he'll take care to have a good audience," I said. "It'll be the most spectacular suicide you and I've ever known. Craigne's the perfect fit for Chesterton's description of the famous novelist—always at the head of the procession, beating an outsize in drums and with a sunflower in his buttonhole."

Just before the judge's summing-up I saw Joe Passman sidle into an extra seat alongside Charlotte, and he stayed there from then on. George's prediction turned out to be amazingly accurate, for the jury found Rogerley not guilty, and he was discharged by the judge.

To Craigne the judge spoke with considerable pity, as to a man who had been his own enemy. There was a slight curl of the lip as he reviewed his extravagances and the madness of self-adulation that had ruined a great and honourable career. Craigne had fallen like Lucifer, but from high Olympus, he said, and a rustle ran through the court at that apt allusion. No punishment that the Law could give would equal the devastating completeness of that fall.

Two years was the sentence. I glanced quickly up at Charlotte Craigne, and she made never a gesture, but I did see that she had drawn a veil down from her black hat and over her face. To Harper the judge spoke in something of the same terms, and he too got two years. To Sivley the comments were more biting and almost vindictive, and he was given two years on the major charge, and six months on a minor one, the sentences to run concurrently.

The warders made a movement and then came Sivley's outburst. His eyes must have fallen on Passman, the man whose evidence had shattered his whole defence. His voice was a sudden scream, and in the deadly silence of that court, it was as terrifying a sound as ever I heard.

"You fat swine! By God, I'll get you if it's the last thing I do."

He was shaking his fist at Passman, and then like a lightning flash he was hurling himself across the dock. Harper was brushed aside as if he were a featherweight, and he was making for Craigne.

"You too, you bloody lying swine!"

Then the warders had him and mouthing and yelling he was carried below. When I looked up again, Charlotte Craigne had gone, and Passman too. I came out at once to the street for a breath of air, and was in time to see Joe ushering her into that big Rolls of his, and that was the last I was to see of Charlotte Craigne for the best part of two years.

Wharton stayed on for quite a time, and when we were driving back to town I asked him if he had gathered anything from the day's observations.

"If you mean Passman," he said, "then I wouldn't like to say. If he was in it, then he's covered up his tracks. Not that we mightn't find something yet."

Some months later, when George and I were together on a certain case, I asked him much the same question, and the answer was quite a different one, in fact it was in George's best vein. He glared at me indignantly.

"Passman? Who said he had anything to do with it!"

I was so taken aback that I couldn't make even the feeblest retort. What I did gather, however, was that either the police had been barking up the wrong tree—misled perhaps by the anonymous communication to which George had referred—or that Passman had been wilier than ever and had only too effectively covered up his tracks.

CHAPTER II
INTERVIEW WITH CHARLOTTE

GEORGE WHARTON was not immediately right about Rupert Craigne's reactions after release, for he neither went abroad nor committed suicide. Prison life appeared to have made of him more of a megalomaniac than ever, though his actions seemed the result of months of calculation. He had not made a nuisance of himself in jail, for instance, but had earned full remission marks, and it can be assumed, therefore, that he was solacing himself with the thoughts of a grandiose rehabilitation. His idea was to proclaim himself a victim of a gross miscarriage of justice, and to my mind there was no doubt that he had genuinely convinced himself that he was the victim he proclaimed himself.

A week after being released he threw a brick through the window of Chelmsford police station, and harangued the crowd—it was market day—before he was taken into custody. The burden of his tirade, both then and before the Bench, was that he was the innocent victim of a conspiracy and the unconscious tool of those higher up. Pressed to name these latter, he could only hint at revelation at some more suitable moment, and he made vague accusations against the inefficiency of the authorities whose job and duty it had been to discover the brains and money behind the swindling scheme in which he had inadvertently taken part. I should add that his manners—as they often could be—were charming throughout, with apologies to the Bench for his taking what seemed to him the only way to call attention to his very real grievances.

His fine was paid for him, and by whom was not divulged. After that he lay doggo for some weeks, and then one afternoon he hurled another brick, this time through the window of a famous Regent Street store You can imagine the scene, women shoppers by the hundred swarming round. Craigne haranguing them, his Olympian beard grown again and his hatless head making the golden curls an oriflamme. And so to the same court scene, the same tirade, and the same fine paid for him.

A week or two went by and as I saw no further escapade in the papers, I guessed that Craigne was again lying doggo and planning the next outbreak. That he was not being taken very seriously was obvious. Certain of the popular papers had letters from ex-fans and credulous women saying that something ought to be done on Craigne's behalf, but no Member of Parliament had as yet been sufficiently interested to ask questions in the House. And then all at once I was dragged into the affair, which was probably the last thing on earth that I wanted.

My wife was going away for a month, joining some old friends at Grasse, in the South of France. The evening before she left she sprang the mine at the dinner-table.

"Darling, there's something you must do. I've been so rushed this last day or two that I only this minute remembered it. It's about Charlotte Craigne."

My mind went blank. I think I was in such a sudden panic that my nerves were not functioning, for my face didn't flush.

"I've seen her once or twice recently," Bernice was going on, "and I told her I was sure you'd help. It's about Rupert. She's in terrible distress and doesn't know which way to turn for the best. She has to be so discreet, too."

"But how can I help?" I managed to ask.

"But you were a friend of his."

"I know," I said. "That's the very point. I did happen to be what one might call friendly with Craigne, but that was long ago. I loathe the fellow and in any case I don't see what I could do to help."

"Darling, don't be Pharisaical. I don't like you when you talk like that. It's Charlotte I want you to help, not him."

"But why should I help Charlotte?" I asked warily.

"But you knew her, didn't you?" Another quick panic on my part, and then at the next words it went. "I mean, you must have known her if you knew Rupert. Besides, she said she was sure you'd help her. It was she who suggested it. Besides, I like Charlotte, and I'm sorry for her, so it'll really be helping me. And I do think there's something in what Rupert Craigne claims."

There was the chance of a lifetime to make a clean breast of everything, but I was too much of a moral coward to take it. Are you married? If not, skip these next few words which may make you wince. For what I should have said to Bernice was something like this.

"Darling, I want to talk over something with you. You know that you're the only woman in the world as far as I'm concerned. There isn't a woman living who could make me look at her twice. The most marvellous thing that ever happened to me was when you said you'd marry me, and there isn't a day when I don't tell myself how lucky I am, and how marvellous you are. All the same, a man who doesn't marry till forty must have had all sorts of experiences—I mean if he is normally constituted. What I'm trying to get at is that Charlotte Craigne and I used to be very friendly once. . . ."

There might have been the tiniest storm in the teacup, and even tears, and yet I'm perfectly convinced at this moment that I should have heard no more about Charlotte Craigne. What I did say was something very different.

"My dear, you can't possibly be serious! Rupert Craigne's trial was perfectly fair and there wasn't a shadow of doubt about his guilt. He's just a *poseur,* and a dangerous one. All his life he's flourished on flattery and conceit, and he has the flaunting impudence to make a public play of himself. The only decent thing he could do would be to disappear."

I suddenly felt the atmosphere becoming exceedingly chilly.

"All the same, I'd do anything to help you, as you know, if you feel your own way about it. But why should Charlotte Craigne imagine I could help?"

The question was intended as a deft turning aside, and it served its purpose. Bernice definitely thawed.

"But, darling, she knew you were connected with Scotland Yard. Everybody knows."

I gave a Whartonian grunt. I am *not* connected with Scotland Yard, as I have patiently pointed out to Bernice before. There are certain things I am supposed to know rather well and at various times the Yard—and it is no false modesty to say that I always wonder why—pays for the knowledge and the time employed.

"I'm very busy, as you know," I said, "much as I'd like to help. What is Charlotte Craigne proposing to do about it—or about me? Is she going to write?"

"She's going to telephone, darling. She's making use of a friend's flat, somewhere in Knightsbridge, and she thought you might spare her a few minutes to talk things over. I told her you'd love to."

Now I had an idea that when Bernice came back from her holiday she'd have forgotten all about the Craignes, so as soon as I got back from Victoria the next morning after seeing her off, I gave my man Palmer very careful and confidential orders about the telephone. He was to answer all calls and if a voice resembling that of Charlotte Craigne asked for me, then I was out and the time of my return unknown. One or two fruitless calls, I thought, and Charlotte would give me up as inaccessible, or something might happen to make her regard me as no longer useful for whatever scheme she had in her mind.

Then absent-mindedness proved my undoing. Scarcely had I finished than the phone went and I lifted the receiver.

"Hallo?" I said, and the one word was enough.

"It's you, Ludo, darling!" said the well-remembered voice. "Has Bernice told you about everything?"

"Depends what you mean," I said guardedly. And then in the same moment I made up my mind. There would be no use in trying to put her off, so why not see her and get the whole thing over? Maybe there would be nothing after all that a few words couldn't settle.

"Something about wanting to see me," I went on.

"Don't be so despondent, darling," she said. Her voice had that husky quality that had always made the most trivial remark into part of an intimacy.

Two minutes later I had the address of the flat and a quarter of an hour after that I was in a taxi.

It was some years since I had seen her closely, but those years had stood more still with her than with me. Thirty-five can be an alluring age with most women, and it was most magnificently so in the case of Charlotte Craigne. She looked not a day older, and all the attractiveness was there, and the mannerisms. I don't know if a rabbit ever admires a particularly attractive stoat while he cowers and waits, but the comparison is the only one I can make, for I found myself watching her every movement and gesture, fascinated as ever, but more and more scared as the minutes went by.

She was the most flagrant and the most graceful of liars. Yet I could never make her admit it, for her explanations and excuses were always so dexterous, ingenuous or even amusing, and so bolstered up by a new series of fabrications with fresh wiles and artifices expended on them, that suspicion seemed treachery and protestation sheer brutality. She could be witty, mordantly malicious, and utterly unscrupulous; fabulously generous and then incredibly selfish, intensely loyal in all sorts of things and wholly unreliable in the rest.

She was not handsome. Her mouth was too big and the jaw-bones too prominent, but when she smiled, and that was often, you thought hers the most expressive mouth you had ever seen, and as for the hardness of jaw-bones and chin, they gave an arrogant, patrician poise to the head. Her eyes were lovely and she had the most beautiful head of hair, which she would mass and curl in what I'd call a tomboy fashion, and as her nose was the least bit *retroussé,* the whole effect was roguish and altogether charming. I should call her neither a man's nor a woman's woman, but the sole property of Charlotte—at least till she became infatuated with Craigne. As for the sexual side of life, it had no real attraction for her and was merely one more mood.

You will pardon me for having dwelt at such length on Charlotte Craigne, and yet I wish I had said more, for she is not only the most important character in this tale, but almost the tale itself. And if you wonder how I could have become involved with such a woman, or have stood her for three years—and it was she who left me and not the other way about—I can only plead that in those years between wars and before the army took me mercifully again in hand, I was something of a prim intellectual. I have said Charlotte was my life's one indiscretion, and I add that for the sole reason that she was the only woman who ever attempted to exert any wiles on me or tried to prove to me that I had attractions very remote from the scholarly, In fact, she was the perfect antithesis, and we had just that one point in common which was needed to stay as flux—a perpetual urge to thumb our noses at convention. With me it had been an abstract wish, for in public I had been timid in my manifestations, but when I was in Charlotte's company, all the inhibitions were released. Jekyll and Hyde again, though a Hyde with considerable reservations.

"Here you are, and how lovely to see you," she said. She was taking my hat and gloves, but suddenly was turning back to me.

Her hands went to my shoulders, and I feared she was going to kiss me, or rather that I should have to kiss her. "You're older, you know."

"Of course I'm older," I said. "The amazing thing is that you're not. Hitler doesn't seem to worry you a bit."

"Come and sit here," she told me soothingly, and patted a cushion in the angle of the chesterfield. "And don't look so portentous, darling. I haven't brought you here to seduce you."

"A few years too late," I said with an attempt at flippancy.

She laughed, or rather gurgled, which was the nearest she ever could come to a full-blooded laugh.

"That's much better. Cigarette? Or would you rather have your pipe. But, darling!" She was taking the pipe out of my hand. "I do believe it's one of those I gave you and you've been saving it up till now." She smiled endearingly. "Now I know you're going to be friendly."

"And why shouldn't I be friendly?"

"Every reason, darling." Now she was picking dropped petals off the side-table. "Did Bernice go this morning?"

"Oh, yes. You knew all about her trip?"

"Of course," she said, and sat in the chesterfield angle to face me. As she lighted herself a cigarette I noticed that her finger-nails were the old shade of maroon, and they matched the buckle thing that held the low V of the black frock. I'd always told her she looked her best in black with a touch of red.

"Did you ever tell Bernice about us?" she suddenly asked.

"I didn't," I said curtly. "But what's Bernice to do with us at this moment? I mean, I'm waiting to hear why it was you wanted to see me so urgently."

She flicked the ash from the cigarette and got to her feet.

"Bernice may have quite a lot to do with it. And don't look so glum, darling. I knew you hadn't told her. A woman can always tell. And perhaps we shan't have to bother poor Bernice after all."

"Keep Bernice out of it," I told her angrily. "And let me tell you, Lotta, that I'm an uncommonly busy man. I wish you'd come to the point. What is it you want me to do?"

"Help me and Rupert," she said. "What do you think of him? Since he came out, I mean—if that's what they call it."

"You want a frank answer?"

"Why not?"

"Then he's doing himself an incredible amount of harm. He was guilty as hell, whatever he may have induced you to believe, and so, if you've still any influence with him, for the love of God get him out of the country."

"That *is* frank, isn't it?"

"You asked me to be," I said. "And now you tell me something. Did you and do you believe that yarn of his about being an innocent victim of some mysterious person higher up?"

She patted a cushion for herself, and once more sat facing me in that opposite angle of the chesterfield.

"I trust you, Ludo," she said, and I couldn't help a little curl of the lip at the pathetic smile she gave me.

"You're up to some trick, Lotta. Please don't go round in circles. It's so tiring. What is it you want?"

She refused to smile. "If I hadn't trusted you, I wouldn't be speaking to you now. That's why I don't scruple to tell you that I'm a pretty desperate woman, and I've made up my mind to play a dangerous game." She smiled. "Sounds like something out of Ouida. But it isn't funny at all, darling. It's something damnably dirty, but you're going to help me all the same."

"Oh?"

"Yes, darling. You're going to help me."

She reached for an ashtray and stubbed out the cigarette. Then she was on her feet again, marking time for the next move.

"You see the position I'm in. Joe's making me an allowance." She always alluded to her stepfather as Joe, or our Joe. "It's on condition that I have nothing whatever to do with Rupert—"

"Just a minute, Lotta. There's something I'd like to know. You're just as much in love with Rupert as ever?"

"Heaps more," she said soberly. "After all, I helped to spend his money and land him in the mess, and now it's up to me to get us both out."

"Good," I said relievedly. "And the position is that you can't help him because of Joe."

"Yes. I daren't even see him. I believe Joe's perfectly capable of having me watched. What I'm going to do, therefore, is to get some hold over Joe. Frankly, I propose to blackmail him."

"Good God!"

She gurgled. "Don't be shocked, darling. I mean every word I say. And what you don't know is that Rupert isn't half as mad as you take him to be. There *was* someone higher up, as you called it, and that someone was our Joe."

I raised my eyebrows.

"I can't prove it," she went on. "It's intuition and a whole lot of odds and ends, such as the way he reacts when I drop hints, and the way he occasionally avoids a conversation. Also he's afraid of me. To a very minor extent I can blackmail him already, but that's nothing to what I propose to do. And that's where you're going to help me."

"I?"

"Darling, don't be obtuse. You're going to get the proofs, and you're the only one I can trust. Bernice told me all the perfectly marvellous things you've done since I saw you, and I always did think you had the most marvellous brain—"

"Now, now, Lotta," I had to cut in. "If you don't mind I'd rather not hear any more about it. Even if I were disposed to do what you suggest, which I'm most certainly not, I'm far too busy to give up the time." Then I was shaking my head exasperatedly. "But why discuss it? It's too preposterous for words. If you're serious—then you're—you're—"

"Mad, darling. Is that the word? But I'm not mad. I've thought it out and I don't give a hoot in hell what happens. I'm desperate, and I'm prepared to be utterly unscrupulous."

"With whom?"

"With you, if necessary."

I stared. "With me? But how? And why?"

She came over and sat by me again. "Look at me," she said. "Don't be squeamish. I'm not going to mesmerise you. You always said you could tell from my eyes if I was serious or not. Very well, am I serious now?"

"Don't blether so much," I told her annoyedly. "Get on with what you were saying. Why are you going to be unscrupulous about me?"

"I'm not, if you listen to reason. If you get me the evidence, then we're friends. If not, then I tell Bernice all about us."

"Tell her and be damned," I said, and began getting to my feet.

Her hand held me back. "Don't be impulsive, Ludo. You don't know all I may have to tell her."

"And why don't I?"

"Because you don't know it yourself." She frowned. "At least I don't think you do. Sometimes I thought you had me followed"—she smiled—"what a quaint word! I mean, you knew where I'd gone and why. When we decided to end things and I had a long holiday abroad."

"As far as I'm concerned you're talking Greek."

"Good," she said. "That gives me all the more hold over you. And please don't be shocked, darling, when I tell you what I was really doing. Actually I was having a baby. Isn't it all frightfully domestic!"

I had stared and gaped. Then my lip curled. "What a delicious story. Who is it this time? Mrs. Henry Wood?"

"I wouldn't laugh, darling," she told me. "I happen to have all the proofs, including the best proof of all. The boy's marvellously like you."

"You're lying," I told her amusedly, but somewhere inside I was not so sure.

"Have it your own stupid way," she told me, and shrugged her shoulders. "But don't blame me when I have to be vindictive. The position is this and you can't laugh your way out of it. Either you do what I've asked, or I write to Bernice this very night, and I send her the proofs, with photographs of the boy. I have her address."

"Write and be damned," I told her again. "Or, if you like, let me see these proofs."

She smiled. "Oh, no. I popped them into my bank just before you came. They're far too precious."

"Proofs! There aren't any proofs." I got to my feet and was making for my hat. "The story's so melodramatic that I can't even congratulate you on its composition."

"Very well, darling. Have it your own way." Then she was opening her bag and handing me a snapshot. It was of a small boy, and somewhere in the south of France or Italy, for there were mimosas for a background and terraces of young vines. I had a good look at it and then shrugged my shoulders.

"A fine-looking boy, but might have been fathered by anybody. How much did it cost you?"

She wasn't at all annoyed, and that was a bad sign. "It's what it may cost *you*, Ludo darling. Bernice will see a resemblance soon enough. A sherry? Or is it too early?"

"Nothing, thanks," I said frigidly, and picked up my hat and gloves. "Now I'm going, I'd like to tell you this. You can do what you damn please. I came here prepared to help you in any reasonable way, but I'll not be mixed up in blackmail, and, what's more, I'm damned if I'll be driven or submit to blackmail myself."

"How pious of you, darling!" A touch of annoyance was in her tone for the first time. "You were always a bit of a Galahad—a trifle shop-soiled, perhaps, but always very pi."

She shook her head, then smiled with what was meant to be contrition.

"Sorry, darling. That was a hateful thing to say. All the same, I'm very much in earnest. I shall give you till eight o'clock: and then I shall write the letter. If you change your mind, then you shall take me to that little place in Chelsea. It's still there. Bernice and I had tea there only the day before yesterday."

I ignored all that. "Well, good-bye, Lotta. If ever you can talk sensibly at any time and would like me to help you in any other way—well, I'll do what I can."

"How sweet of you," she said, and before I could stop her was on tiptoe and kissing the tip of my upturned chin. "That's till to-night, darling. Ring me well before eight. I loathe having to hurry."

I made my way downstairs with all the dignity I could muster, but, busy as I was, I didn't hurry back to my flat, but sat for at least an hour in the Park. My thoughts whirled so fast and so chaotically that for the first half-hour they were more of a waking nightmare.

I knew she was lying; at least I would know it for five minutes only, and then for five seconds I would have my doubts, and, knowing me, those five seconds carried more weight than the five minutes. But whether she was lying or telling the sober truth, one tact remained. The effect of her letter on Bernice would be more than disastrous. Charlotte had wheedled her way into Bernice's trust. Bernice mightn't even need any proofs, and there I wished to God I'd taken that photograph. Perhaps the boy resembled me after all. How the hell could I tell whether he did or didn't? But Bernice would see a resemblance. She had trusted me so implicitly that the shock would be overwhelming, and though she might still try to tell herself that the letter must be wrong, yet there was always the old adage that where smoke is there must be fire. And God knows what lies Charlotte would add to bolster up the main charge. She might even say that no sooner was Bernice's back turned than I came to the Knightsbridge flat and made a whole series of new suggestions. And what worried me most was the thing that damned me most— that I had never owned to Bernice that Charlotte and I had been friendly; even that euphemism would have been enough.

All that afternoon my thoughts went round in the same maddening circles, and then at last I thought I saw a way out. If Charlotte could double-cross, so could I, and blackmail was very much of a boomerang. But it was not till early in the evening that I had my own scheme fully prepared. It was, in fact, about half-past six when I rang up Charlotte, and shortly before eight o'clock we were beginning our dinner in that out-of-the-way Chelsea restaurant.

CHAPTER III
COUNTERSTROKES

THE FOOD SEEMED the most insipid I had ever tasted, but I suppose it was good enough if I hadn't lost all my appetite through worry and excitement. There was one good thing about the meal, however—Charlotte didn't crow over her triumph. She assumed for the occasion one of her matey moods; all womanly, and full of anxious, sympathetic questions about myself and my work.

It's a rather recherché little place, even if it is a bit off the map. There was quite a good quartet playing light music, and you could buy practically anything in the way of drink, and I remember who had kümmels with our coffee.

"Here's to the old bad, sad days," Lotta said before taking a sip.

"May they rest in peace," I said, and then was putting a slip of paper in front of her. "Since we've got to talk business some time or other, why not now? Here's my pen for you to sign on the dotted line."

"I, Charlotte Marion Craigne, married woman, of Brazenoak in the county of Suffolk, do hereby declare that I have asked Ludovic Travers of St. Martin's Chambers, London, to obtain for me certain information concerning my stepfather, Joseph Abram Passman, of Brazenoak as above. This information is needed solely in order to remove an injustice caused to my husband, Rupert Alan Craigne, by the said Joseph Passman, and I exonerate the said Ludovic Travers from any consequences that may arise from any other use I may make of it."

She frowned as she read it and then looked rather blankly at me. Alfredo, the proprietor, was nearby and I called him over. He seemed delighted to witness the lady's signature, and he absolutely scurried to his office to fetch blotting-paper.

"Well, that's that," I said off-handedly as I put the document in my pocket. I don't suppose it had any official value at all, and

I had thought of it only as I was leaving my flat. Perhaps if I had had time I'd have drafted it differently, but it read to me good enough to put some kind of brake on Charlotte who had always been terrified of anything official.

"But, my dear, what's it all mean?" she asked me.

"Just this," I told her. "It's proof that I'm not being black-mailed, and if you use any evidence for blackmailing Joe, and land yourself in a mess, then you're in it alone."

"But, darling, I never wanted you to do anything but get me the evidence." she expostulated.

"Splendid," I said. "That makes us both happy about everything. And while I'm talking I'd better say this and get it over. I know you're lying and bluffing, but since you can make a considerable amount of trouble for me if I call the bluff, I've decided that it'll be easier to do what you ask. I'm not being blackmailed at all. I'm just as anxious as you, or any other good citizen, to see Passman convicted, if he's guilty, and that's why I'll try to get evidence against him."

"Darling, what a marvellous speech!"

"Glad you liked it," I said, and I hope it was amusedly. "But I'm not going to get you this evidence myself. I'm going to compromise."

She frowned.

"Don't be alarmed," I said. "I definitely can't spare the time, and I doubt if I've the means or the ability. But I'll find a good man for you. A private detective from a first-class firm. I hope he doesn't cost you too much money."

She leaned forward anxiously. "How much would he cost?"

"Depends on the speed with which he can get to work and get results. It might cost fifty pounds if he's lucky, and it might cost a couple of hundred—or more."

She smiled relievedly. "I can manage that. I thought you were going to say thousands."

"If I find the right man, am I to give him his instructions, or will you? I won't agree to any partnership. Either I handle the whole thing, or you do."

"But of course you'll do it. And it's perfectly sweet of you."

"Well, I told you I wanted to help you, didn't I?" I told her with an air of gentle reprimand. "If you'd handled me the right way we might have made a start by now."

"How forgiving you are, darling!"

"I don't know about that," I said with the necessary gruff deprecation. "But wait a minute. I knew there was something important I wanted to ask you. If you try blackmailing Joe, won't you stand to lose? I mean, won't he cut you out of his will?"

"Of course he will," she said amusedly. "But when I commit blackmail I do it in style. The lump sum I shall make Joe fork out will be ample consolation, darling. It'll keep me and Rupert till bye-bye time."

"Does Rupert know about this scheme?"

She looked horrified. "But of course not! It's going to be his big surprise."

"You haven't seen him since he came out?"

"I simply daren't. I believe Joe's even capable of having me watched. I don't know when I shall see him. All I've managed to do is get a letter to him." She smiled wanly. "You know. All the wifely things. Keep your chin up and watch for the silver lining."

"Well, everything's settled, then," I said. "There's only one thing to do. You said you had certain evidence against Joe. You must tell me what it is so that I can pass it on to our man. It doesn't matter how intuitive it was."

Then she became vague. That was a good sign, because when she was in her happiest mendacious vein she was always very voluble. Two things only seemed of use. Lotta said she had recently taxed Joe with being in the swindle, doing it playfully and expecting him to take it the same way. He had been very annoyed, but later that day had given her a cheque for a hundred and told her to buy herself some clothes. The other thing was that Joe was going to employ Harper. Lotta said she thought Harper was starting work for him almost at once, but what the work was she had no idea. But it certainly looked as if Joe had some reason for keeping Harper's mouth shut.

"Well, I'll pass all that on", I said. "But there's one other thing I had to mention. Sivley's due out soon, and that was a damnably vicious attack he made on Rupert in the dock. Do you think he was serious when he threatened to do Rupert in?"

She shook her head quickly. "What a swine that Sivley was. I hated the beast even when he was Rupert's chauffeur, but Rupert never would listen to me. I think that man's capable of anything. My God, I could have killed him!"

Her eyes were blazing and her voice had risen.'

"There're some people looking at us," I said quietly. "And, by the way, there's a man I rather promised to see at ten, and it's near that now. Do you mind if we go?"

In the taxi on the way to Knightsbridge she suddenly snuggled against me and put her hand touchingly in mine.

"Ludo, I've been the most despicable beast."

"I wouldn't say that," I told her flippantly. "A bit reminiscent of some of the old days, perhaps."

"And you, darling, you've been simply sweet. I'd do anything in the world for you." She shook me gently. "Tell me what I can do."

I had a sudden brainwave.

"Well," I began, and then stammered artistically. "Well . . . I mean . . . I mean it doesn't matter."

She nudged me again. "Go on, darling. What was it you wanted to say?"

"Well . . . I suppose it's rather abrupt of me, really. I mean, you're a grass widow and I'm a grass widower, and I don't really want to see that man very particularly to-night."

She gurgled deliciously. "Darling, how sweet of you! I'd have loved it." She sighed. "Some time soon, perhaps. To-night you'd be awfully disappointed."

She snuggled even more closely, and I took the bad luck in good part. Then I told her I'd ring her up as soon as I'd fixed up with the detective. Where was it to be?

She said she would be in town for two more days and Joe was coming up on the last day. I jotted down the Knightsbridge number again, and by that time it was journey's end. We said good-night in the taxi.

Now I had two reasons for making that amorous proposition. One was to induce her to believe that I was putty in her hands, and the other reason you will see. For as soon as the taxi was round the corner, I hopped out. It was a lovely June night and dusk was in the sky and I didn't find it at all irksome standing in the square beneath the trees and keeping the flat under observation. It was eleven o'clock almost to the tick when a taxi drew up. A man got out, but the light was too bad for me to recognise him, though I did see him pay the driver and run up the steps as if in some haste. Or it might have been because he feared recognition.

I fairly sprinted round the near corner and just managed to hail the same taxi. When I paid the driver off at Trafalgar Square, I put an innocent question.

"That fare you dropped at Knightsbridge. I think it was a friend of mine. George Clark. A biggish chap with a heavy black moustache."

"He was a biggish chap all right, sir," the driver told me. "But he hadn't no black moustache." He chuckled. "As a matter of fact, sir, he had a yellow one, and a beard. I saw it under the muffler thing he had on."

So Rupert was spending the night at the flat, as I had guessed. That made me think a bit, but it didn't make me go hot and cold all over as when I wondered what I should have done if I had guessed wrongly, and Charlotte had accepted my timid proposal.

The next morning I went round to see Prince and Holloway, who'd done certain small jobs for me before. They were a first-class firm with a very good connection indeed, and I wasn't any too happy about blurting out every side of the business about which I had come. Henry Prince saw me and the version I gave him was sufficiently near the truth, for Henry was discretion itself. He agreed that the business was a ticklish one and likely to be lengthy. I said that since a lot of the work would be for me, I'd guarantee and settle all accounts. I didn't want him to be lavish, but I did want the job done well. Also the particular employee who handled the affair would have to be exceptionally competent and tactful.

"I'm not worrying about that," he said. "I already have the man in mind. I don't think you know him, but he's a nephew of John Holloway. He's exceptionally keen, and I think you'll find him most able. He's not available at the moment or I'd bring him in now."

He consulted a pad, and then was asking if it'd be convenient for this man to see me at St. Martin's Chambers early that evening. I suggested six o'clock. He'd be there, he said, and the name was Tarling, Frank Tarling.

"A charming fellow in some ways," he said. "I hope you'll find him just what you want."

I said I was sure I should, and that was that. All the afternoon I was so busy that when Palmer announced a Mr. Tarling, I had to pull myself together before I remembered.

I don't quite know the kind of man I expected to see, but I think it was someone on the earnest side; hook-nosed, perhaps, and lean. What I did see was a young fellow of under thirty, about five foot eight in height, and with a face that reminded me at once of Franchot Tone, with eyes that had a perpetual and ironic amusement.

He was at home from the moment he entered the door. He gave me a comfortable and comforting feeling. He didn't talk a lot, but what he said was apt.

"I always hankered after your job when I was a boy," I said. "I think it was after reading *Kim*."

"It's a great life," he said, and nodded to himself. "I never put on a false moustache without getting a kick out of it."

He gave me a queer ironic look and I wondered if he were pulling my leg. Then he had a look at the point of his pencil and we got down to business. I told him in great detail the Passman side of the affair.

"The best thing I can do is to look up the Press files," he said. "Especially the Chelmsford ones. Looks as if I ought to get that trial pretty pat."

"I agree," I said. "Above all, study Passman's evidence against Sivley and decide where exactly it fits in."

"What's he worth, this Passman?" he said, looking up from his notes.

"Don't know. Anything from a quarter to a half million. You were going to say something?"

He shook his head. "Maybe I was, Mr. Travers. Guess I'd rather wait and hear anything else that's coming."

Well, I told him all about Charlotte, and when I say all, I mean all. He was to be trusted, and it would have been unfair to him to keep anything heck. He didn't bat an eyelid, but went on with his notes. He did smile to himself when I described my own bit of detective work the previous night.

"Here's the position, then," I concluded. "I'm double-crossing her for all I'm worth. You'll have two jobs to do, and of course you'll have to use one or two men. The first is to get any possible evidence against Passman, and, frankly, all we need that for is to string Charlotte Craigne along. The main job is to find out what truth there was in that sob-story of the baby. Here's the actual date when I last saw her, and I believe it was understood she was going somewhere on the French or Italian Riviera."

"She had a maid?"

"A good question," I said. "I remember a maid called—wait a minute—Butler. No, not Butler. Bullen. That's it—Bullen. I never saw her though. And what I must keep perpetually reminding you of is, what a diabolical liar the woman is. Take my experience last night, for example. Swore blind she didn't know when she'd see her husband again, and all the time she knew he was coming to the flat."

He nodded, closed the book and hooked a leg over the side of the low chair.

"Mind if I put a question or two, Mr. Travers? This Passman, for instance. With all his dough, why should he take a hell of a risk, for a thousand or two?"

"That's what I've been wondering," I said. "Joe's fond of the brass, as he calls it, but I doubt if he's all that fond."

"I suppose he hasn't any police record?"

"Our Joe?" I said, almost shocked. "Not he. And there's nothing of the slippery financier about him. It seems to me," I said, "that there are no easy answers to your question. Charlotte Craigne's lying for some reason of her own and Passman never had the least thing to do with that swindle. On the other hand, there may have been more in the swindle than ever appeared, and he was in it because it was going ultimately to be worth the risk. That's what I'd like you to find out."

"So much for Passman," he said. "And now one other thing, Mr. Travers. Everything that Rupert Craigne's doing seems to me to be deliberate. All that window-smashing is only to give him the chance of getting into the papers, so that everybody can read that he's claiming to be the victim of some big shot. I know that's obvious, but the point I'd like to make is this. I think he's trying to work on Passman's nerves. His wife wants the evidence against Passman, and she's sort of following up his good work. The whole thing's a carefully co-ordinated scheme."

"I admit it," I said. "I'd say Charlotte's been in touch with Rupert ever since he came out. The whole thing's been carefully planned."

"Then why?" he was asking with a humorous despair. "It doesn't add up right. Why should those two work on his nerves if he isn't guilty? Rupert Craigne can't be making a mistake. He must know if Passman had a hand in the game, or not. Very well, then. Am I right in saying there aren't two answers to your question after all? I mean, Passman *must* be guilty. Either that or the two Craignes are playing a mighty deep game with you."

"But why?"

He shrugged his shoulders. "That's what you're paying to find out."

I glanced up at the clock. My dinner hour had long since gone, so I rang for Palmer to fetch us two of the service meals and some more beer. We went on talking till the meal was ready, and we talked all the way through it.

"Would you let me take a liberty?" he asked, "You're an older man than I, Mr. Travers, and you're an older hand at this game than I am. But your official cases aren't concerned with yourself, if I may say so. If you sum my job up, it's to protect your interests."

"Granted."

"Then I think that Charlotte Craigne's the most important factor. It's her side that's dangerous. That's why I'd like you to fall in with every suggestion she makes to you, provided, of course, it doesn't compromise you in any way."

"I get you," I said. "Every new suggestion she makes will be part of the main scheme. A new clue to what her real object is. I use my own wits and I also report to you."

"That's great." he said, and grinned. "You and I are going to enjoy all this, Mr. Travers."

"Let's hope so," I told him fervently.

Then he asked what kind of reports I'd like—detailed, or just the hard facts. I said I'd like them detailed. Two heads were always better than one and, though I very much doubted it, there was just the chance that I might read into his reports some vital clue that had been missed.

"You're dead right, Mr. Travers," he said. "Also, I take it you'd like two sets of reports: one for your private eye and the other to send on to the lady."

"A capital idea," I said. "Her report can be as bare as you like and it needn't necessarily be true."

"I'm going to enjoy this case," he told me with another grin.

"What's more," I said, "I'm taking good care of it she doesn't come into contact with you. I'm going to do a bit of useful lying for once. What we're handling, at least from my point of view, isn't dynamite; it's fulminate of mercury. One scratch and up she goes."

Well, we concocted a kind of code. Tarling was to be alluded to as Harold, for instance, and Passman was to be The Professor. I was to be Uncle Tom, but all those aliases were only for Charlotte's reports, as mine were unlikely to fall into the wrong hands. After that we went to the garage in Long Acre where I kept my car. Charlotte, or Rupert, or both, would make no bones about watching my flat, so if it was urgently necessary, Tarling and I would meet at the garage. Charlie Cross, the manager, was

there, and he said it'd be okay by him, and for me to receive letters care of his office. When I asked if I might use the telephone
he told me to go ahead.

"You stand by and listen," I told Tarling. "The lady mayn't be
at home and on the other hand she may."

She was at home, and apparently alone, for she talked freely.

"I've got your man for you, Lotta," I said. "Oh, yes, he's absolutely first-class, and incredibly discreet . . . No, I think it
best for all concerned if you don't see him. You know what we
agreed and we can't have him confused with two sets of instructions. What's he like? My dear, you couldn't miss him. The sort
of sleuth you see on the films. About forty-five, hatchet-faced,
piercing eyes—absolutely Sherlocky, in fact. And if you see him
sleuthing about, for the love of heaven don't recognise him."

"Something I've thought of, darling," she said, and I was motioning to Tarling to get his ear up close.

"I think you should run down to Brazenoak and see Joe.
We're going back together to-morrow evening. Have you a good
excuse or shall we compose one now?"

"I'll find an excuse," I said. "Leave that to me, and if I do turn
up, don't for the love of heaven fail to look surprised. But that
isn't the point. Why should I have to see Joe?"

"My dear, what a question. Surely if you talk to him. . . .
Don't be silly, darling. I know you can't mention certain matters. But you're so frightfully clever that he's bound to give himself away over something or other. . . . Oh, about lunch-time, I
think. There's a cricket week at Trimport, and he'll love to spend
his afternoons there."

That was the gist of the conversation. When I hung up I
asked Tarling what impressions he'd had of her.

"She sounds a mighty attractive dame to me, Mr. Travers;"
he said, and, curiously enough, he said it soberly. "But that
Trimport she was talking about. I only got back from the States
in the fall, so I'm rather rusty about things. Isn't it that swagger
bathing resort in Suffolk?"

"That's it," I said. "It's the haunt of the theatrical and stockbroking fraternities. The men are down principally at week-

ends and holidays. They're the kind you meet in the compartment of a golf train. As for the women, you'll hear more 'Darlings!' on Trimport beach to the acre than in any other square mile in the country."

"You don't like the set."

"I don't," I said. "I hate snobbism and cheap display and loud women and complacent men. Perhaps that makes me a snob too. But there's something you might like. What about a rough map of the country down there? You can make a better map of your own later on."

He said that'd be the very thing, so I drew it on a piece of Charlie's notepaper.

"Gadsford's where the swindle was worked," I said, "and where Craigne had a country cottage. He also used to have a house at Trimport, in his affluent days. The distances are in miles, but the roads aren't main ones. They're only minor roads or lanes for the most part. Chelmsford, as you know, is in Essex, farther south. The trial was held there and not at, say, Ipswich, because the Assizes there happened to fit in."

There was just time for a quick one in the private bar of the Golden Eagle, in Mattley Street. He insisted on standing the drinks, which wouldn't appear on the expense account, and we drank to the success of the enterprise.

When we said a final good-night I was calling him Frank.

CHAPTER IV
PASSMAN AT HOME

THE FOLLOWING DAY was a Sunday, and as I had been working very heavily for some days compiling a financial report for a certain corporation, I decided to take things easy. But though I lolled over newspapers and crosswords, the day was about as uneasy mentally as it possibly could be, for at intervals I would keep thinking of that conclusion at which Frank and myself had both confidently arrived, that Charlotte and Rupert were working on a co-ordinated plan, and that I was to play a considerable, though as yet wholly undisclosed part in their scheme.

It is not a comfortable feeling to know that two people of the Craigne sort are working behind your back.

Then there was Bernice. I claim no special marital virtues but I would have fought like a tiger if her peace of mind was to be threatened, and Charlotte's threat was directed against us both. Above all I writhed when I thought of the sheer insolence of the blackmailing business, and the flippant coolness with which Charlotte had broached it.

That was why I was quite a different man when I started off for Brazenoak early the next morning, for I was doing something at last, and the day might bring all sorts of disclosures and reliefs. I drove to Ipswich first, by the way, and saw a man whom I need not necessarily have seen, but that call gave me a good excuse for calling on Joe Passman. So well did I time things that the clock on the stable tower of the manor was striking twelve as I parked the car in the shade of the trees.

Brazenoak Manor was a sprawling timbered house that had once been surrounded by a moat. Some of this had been reopened for a lily-pond and the rest narrowed to a trickle of water between deep sloping banks that in spring were smothered with polyanthuses, and now were gay with blue and yellow irises. Fine elms bordered the quarter of a mile of drive, and the beauty of the place could make a stranger gasp at any season of the year.

In the old Colonel's time the gardens, had had the beauty of untidiness, but Joe's money had been lavishly poured and whenever a weed now dared to appear, one of a dozen gardeners would pounce on it. Matthews, who had been butler in the old days, seemed glad to see me, and while we were having a word or two, Joe appeared. Stick a thimble on the stalk end of a fat pear and two short matches in its base and you have his figure. When I first knew him, in his climbing days, he wore a goatee, but for some years he had been clean-shaven. I don't know why he was always so respectful to me, for he had never made any money out of me and was unlikely to, but I was always respectful to him because he loved respect for one thing, but principally because he had once represented big interests of which I might at any time wish to make use.

"Ah, Mr. Travers," he said heartily, and was coming on with outstretched hand. "How are you, sir."

"Very well, Mr. Passman," I said, and took the soft, clammy hand. "You're looking uncommonly well too."

"Joe's good for a few years yet," he told me with a chuckle. "But come along in, sir. Have, some sherry. I've got some fine stuff. Hollis's best. Matthews! Matthews! Where the devil's the man got to. You'll stay to lunch, Mr. Travers? Duck and green peas, and a drop of good stuff."

Little boastings like that were Joe's speciality, amusing but making him in a way rather likeable, that is if you knew what lay behind them. There was in them always the perpetual wonder that he, who had left school at ten to work as an errand boy, should not only own the best but have had the discrimination to buy it. I should tell you, too, that though most of his business interests had been in the North, he was a Londoner by birth, and his accent was cockney-cum-Yorkshire.

We went to his study, where he always spent his mornings reading the financial papers and writing his own letters. It was a corner room with french windows opening south and east, and had the most glorious view across the valley. I had a sherry and it was as good as Joe had claimed. Then I broached my business. Was he inclined to part with certain shares he held? A friend of mine wanted them for sentimental reasons, but none had come on the market. Joe found me a paragraph in that morning's *Financial Times* referring hopefully to those same shares, and I felt a bit of a fool, for I still don't think he believed me when I assured him I'd had no time to read the papers. However, he said he'd think the matter over and let me know.

Lunch was at one, and as it was five minutes to, Joe escorted me to a new downstair cloak-room he'd had installed. The way was along a short corridor and I particularly want you to get the lie of it into your head. Imagine it as a rake with three teeth. One tooth emerged from the study. Half-way along, a tooth went backwards to kitchens and servants' quarters, and at the far end the third tooth entered the dining-room. The new cloak-room lay half-way along the first two teeth I have mentioned, and the corridor was lighted by windows at each end, though the light on a dull day would have been pretty dim.

No sooner had I stepped into the corridor than among the sporting and other prints on the walls I noticed the most perfect Adam mirror I've ever seen. It was a handy size, and quality was in every inch of it. I was attracted by it not only because I am a collector in a small way but because Bernice had been looking for a period mirror, and I had promised to keep my eyes open.

Now collectors are cunning people, and I was dealing with a remarkably astute individual, so I pretended to be interested in a print.

"Rather nice, this," I said, and polished my horn-rims for a closer look.

Joe peered at it. "What's it worth?"

"A ten-pun note," I said, and then appeared suddenly to become aware of the mirror. "That's a nice little mirror. My wife could do with one like that. She wanted to buy one the other day."

"What's it worth?" fired Joe again.

"A fiver," I said, and shrugged my shoulders.

"Make it ten and it's yours," Joe snapped at once.

"Oh, no," I said. "I'll think it over." Then I was moving on, for though that mirror was worth forty guineas, I knew Joe was a man of his word. At any time I could have it for ten pounds, and some day I certainly would have it, and before Bernice returned. Meanwhile it should be an excellent excuse for another visit.

While we were having a wash I put a question as off-handedly as I could.

"How's that extraordinary stepson of yours these days? He hasn't pestered you at all?"

"He's a bloody scoundrel!" Joe told me, and glared. Then he was shaking his head. "I'm sorry, Mr. Travers, but I can't bear to hear that blackguard's name mentioned. What do you think of him?"

"As little as I can," I said, trying to make a joke. "I wouldn't let him get on your nerves. He isn't worth it."

"Let him get in my way and I'll crush him like that." He closed the fingers of his threatening fist. Then his voice lowered. "You know Charlotte? My stepdaughter?"

"I do know her," I said. "My wife knows her better. How's she taking all these antics of his?"

"On the whole, very well," he said. "She's got sense, that girl. But he's a cunning scoundrel, Mr. Travers. And a plausible one."

Charlotte was already in the dining-room. When I appeared she showed a superb surprise.

"Well, if it isn't Ludovic Travers! It must be years since I saw you."

"Unhappily, yes," I said gallantly.

"Mr. Travers will sit there, Matthews," she said. "I like people to be opposite me when I talk."

"What's that smell?" Joe said, and sniffed. "It's those damn pinks again. Makes the place smell like a pickle factory. Close that damn door, Matthews."

Charlotte and I prattled through most of that meal. Joe was what I'd call an attentive eater, and rarely made a remark, though I do remember that when we were wading into duckling and green peas, he remarked with a wink: "Not bad stuff, this—eh?"

"Isn't he quaint?" Charlotte said, and when Joe bridled, leaned across and patted his cheek endearingly. "Joe's a darling, and he's going to be the sole comfort of my old age. Aren't you, precious?"

"Damnation," said Joe angrily. "I wish you wouldn't call me Joe in public. No respect nowadays, Mr. Travers. It's bad in front of the servants."

"You and I have got used to that sort of thing, Mr. Passman," I said tactfully. "All standards are different from what they were in our young days."

"More's the pity."

"Now, darling, get on with your lunch," Charlotte told him maternally, and then to me: "Talking of servants, you'd never guess who's Joe's new chauffeur."

Joe froze stiff, knife and fork in the air, but before he could speak she was going on.

"So generous of him, and such a kind heart. It's Harper, who was in that dreadful business with poor Rupert."

There was such a husky sadness in her voice that Joe stared, open-mouthed. He scowled, shook his head, and the fork went to his mouth.

"What if I do choose to be generous? Whose business is it but mine?"

"Nobody's, of course, darling." She patted his cheek again. "But it's very awkward for me. Here am I, trying so hard to forget poor Rupert, and remembering him every time I see Harper."

Joe growled an inaudible something. But there was no indication so far as I could see during that meal that he was afraid of her in the way she had suggested at the restaurant that night. His only fear, and the chief bond of his attachment, was that she represented a class into which he had once hoped to insinuate himself. She gave a distinction to that highly expensive establishment, and she was value for money. Also I do think Joe, in some curious way, had a furtive but very considerable affection for her.

After the meal she disappeared, but she had warned me that Joe always took a brief nap after lunch, and that at two-thirty the Rolls was ordered for Trimport. Joe told me he loved watching cricket, though the Trimport week would be gutless stuff compared with the Yorkshire League games he had generally contrived to watch on a Saturday afternoon. Charlotte wasn't accompanying him and he asked me to make a day of it and come back with him for dinner. I pleaded pressure of work, and in any case I wouldn't keep him from his nap. He walked with me to where I had left my car and we had a very friendly parting. I couldn't help smiling at his final remark.

"You oughtn't to drive a car and smoke a cigar like that. Three and six apiece they cost me."

"And worth every inch of it," I told him as I waved a cheery hand in farewell, and he called after me that he might change his mind about those shares after all.

I drove slowly along the drive, drawing on the last third of Joe's magnificent cigar and craning my neck to see the last of the gardens. As I turned into the leafy lane there was a sudden flash of colour and there was Charlotte coming from the shadow of the trees to the edge of the grass verge. As I slowed down she was opening the door, and in a moment was seated alongside me.

"Am I not a lovely surprise for you, darling?" she asked me with a gay impudence.

"Both lovely and a surprise," I told her flatteringly. "I don't know that I've ever seen you looking better. That frock thing suits you."

For once she said nothing, at least about that. What she did tell me was to drive a couple of hundred yards on to where I could draw under some trees, though in any case she'd have to hurry back and see Joe off to Trimport. Then she was asking me anxiously if I'd learned anything. I said I'd picked up one or two things, but I'd rather not mention them till I saw just where they led. I did say that Joe was very bitter against Rupert and she had better be careful if she was double-crossing him and seeing Rupert secretly.

"My dear, as if I should!" she said indignantly. "All the same I did manage to get in touch with him yesterday. I can't tell you how, but I did. The poor darling's simply in despair. What do you think? Joe's made him an offer of a lump sum if he'll give me grounds for divorce! Poor Rupert was practically in tears. He actually said it might be better if he dropped out." She smiled. "I cheered him up. I mean, I hope I did. Poor darling, he was so dreadfully down. And, you see, I could only hint at a big surprise. And it will be a big surprise, won't it, darling?"

I was busy drawing the car up on the grass beneath the trees, but I mumbled that it undoubtedly would. There was a stile just where we were and she told me it was a short cut back to the Manor.

"In a minute I must fly," she said, "but I must give you the rest of the news. Sivley's out! It's all over the; village."

"He's coming to Brazenoak?"

"But, of course! It's his home. They say he's going to stay at the cottage with his mother. She's an old hag if ever there was one."

"And you still think that threat of his was all hot air?"

"I don't know," she said, and suddenly looked worried. "I did until now. Perhaps I thought he never would come out, though that was silly of me." She gave a little shiver. "Now I'm the least bit frightened."

"That's foolish of you," I said, and then suddenly she was clutching my arm. "That man. I don't want him to see me."

I peered along the shadowed lane and there was a man just coming into sight.

"Who is he?" I asked as she pushed out her legs and shuffled well down in the seat.

"An American," she said. "Says his grandfather came from Brazenoak. He's writing a book about manor-houses, but, my dear, his camera! A simply marvellous one. Tell me when he's gone."

I picked up a touring guide and pretended to be absorbed in it. It was not till the stranger was abreast of the car that I spotted him for Frank, though I should have guessed. Our eyes met for a moment, and half a minute later I was giving Charlotte the all-clear.

"A typical American," was my fatuous comment "A nice-looking young fellow, though."

"Joe loved him," she said, and took a look back to see if he'd really gone. "He's promised to take the most elaborate pictures of the Manor." She suddenly gave a look of dismay. "My dear, I must fly and head him off. He mustn't take the pictures till the morning. Joe'll be simply desolated if he isn't allowed to pose in every one of them."

Nothing happened till the Wednesday, and then, at about half-past nine in the morning, Charlotte rang me up. She said she had driven her car to a village three miles from Brazenoak as she daren't use the Manor telephone.

"I'm desperately worried about Rupert," she said. "I've heard from him again, and what do you think that beast Joe has done? Told him that if he doesn't give me immediate grounds for divorce he'll virtually kick me out. Isn't it caddish? I feel I could strangle him."

"There's a certain amount of sense in what Joe's doing," I told her with the courage of distance. "If you did break with Rupert it'd be better for both of you. It might straighten him up."

"Don't be pious, darling." Her voice was frigid. "Are you on my side or Joe's?"

"On yours, of course."

"Then you've got to stand by to help. I'm sure Rupert's going to do something desperate. Where will you be this week-end?"

"Knocking around here," I said. "The sooner I can finish the job I'm on, the sooner I get a holiday."

"I'm relying on you," she said earnestly. "You don't know how much. Rupert frightens me. Everything frightens me. And that man of yours. Why doesn't he do something?"

"You can't hurry such people," I told her testily. "You've got to be reasonable, Lotta. He's got little or nothing to go on. All the same I will urge him to do the best he can. It'll cost you more. You realise that."

"My dear, what do I care about the money," she told me with a fierce impatience. "I tell you we simply must do something." The voice softened. "Not that you haven't been perfectly sweet."

"That's all right," I said lamely. "I'm just doing my best."

Nothing happened during the rest of that day, and I was in the same fog and the same impatience. Had I known that before another week had gone there would be two dead men to account for, perhaps I'd have been less anxious for action. Then the following morning there was the first report from Frank. He said he didn't want to use my valuable time over three reports, for there was always a precis to send to the firm, so would I send to Queenie—as he called Charlotte—any extracts I thought suitable. If I typed it she wouldn't know any different, and he sent two specimens of his pseudo-signature for me to forge. This is what he wrote.

DEAR MR. TRAVERS

I didn't speak on Monday because I didn't know who might be about, and I gathered you didn't want to speak to me.

Things are going better than I expected at this early stage. I got those Press files dug out and a fine set of photographs, and I reckon I've practically every detail off by heart. With regard to P's evidence in court against S., I must say it looks genuine to me, and makes the case against himself flimsier than ever. He needn't have given that evidence unless he wanted to, so why get himself in bad with his own gang? It doesn't add up right.

I arrived here on Sunday night as Edward Franks, Jr., and am staying at the Oak (Tel. Br. 215). At Chelmsford one of the newspaper men lent me a History of Suffolk, late eighteenth century, giving a list of the principal characters—landowners, farmers, tradesmen and such—in each town and village. Under BRAZENOAK I found a farmer named Franks. As soon as I got to the Oak—a grand little pub—I wanted to know if there were any Frankses in those parts, and I was told there weren't now but had been once. The village sexton said if I called on the vicar he'd show me the parish register so that I could read all about the births, deaths and marriages of the Frankses. The village had its biggest sensation since a certain famous trial when I announced that my grandfather was the last of the Frankses to live there, and he'd emigrated to the States, and now I, his grandson, had come all the way from Hollywood to see the old home. It was reckoned that my grandad had lived at Pennygate Farm.

In the morning I called at the Manor, spinning the same yarn. My first reactions to P. were most favourable, even if he does spread himself good and proper, though I must say that he's got plenty to spread himself about. He took me all over the place, but unfortunately I had only two films left—so I said—in my last roll so I could take only a couple of pictures. I wanted plenty of excuse for some more visits.

A funny thing happened. I took the first picture which was from the rose garden with the old boy posing against a sundial and the house as background. He was pleased as Punch and wanted to know how many pictures I'd finally be taking. I said about a hundred or so for my book—I'm supposed to be writing a book on English manor-houses as a reference work for Hollywood—and at least a dozen would be of his place. He said would I be staying in B. for any length of time. I said that B. was what I'd crossed the Atlantic to see, and I'd be in B. off and on for a goodish time.

He's a lascivious old goat and yet the more I see of him the more I like him. What a character!

Queenie and I have been getting on fine this week. I'm supposed to be pretty well-off, and that didn't make a bad introduction. Everything about me is class. I'm buying a new wardrobe in Bond Street—imaginary, so don't think it's going on the bill—and I've a valet I hired in town who's now at the Oak with me. One of our best men, by the way. And don't think I'm acting the goat myself or posing as the louder type of American tourist. At the Oak I'm being treated with enormous respect. Elsewhere Queenie said to me this morning when I happened to meet her in the village: "What lovely manners you have, Mr. Franks!" I blushed, for I honestly think she was serious. On Saturday afternoon I'm supposed to accompany P. to Trimport so that I can watch some English cricket. A bit of a trial for a lad who played for the eleven!

Now to something more definite in the way of value for your money. On Monday evening I strolled along to Pennygate Farm, home of my ancestors. The farmer, Donald Widger, was still hay-making with his men, but his wife was at home. Who do you think she is? May

Bullen, who used to be maid to Queenie. And listen to this. Sivley put her in the family way and there was a girl. Widger married her nevertheless, but I learned later, in the Oak, that Widger had said that if S. had the nerve to come back to B. when he came out of jail, he'd run him out of the village. Hot air, because S. *is* back. He's living in a cottage just behind the church with his mother, but he hasn't appeared in public yet.

But about May Bullen. I think you'll agree there's no point in hurrying matters. If she were suspicious she might report something to Q, and then the fat'd be in the fire. What I do know is this.

a. M. hasn't much use for Q., but she's a strong supporter of R. C.

b. She left Q's service because of that trip abroad that Q. was taking, and, I deduced from the little girl's age, because she knew herself pregnant. Q. was *not* going to the French or Italian Riviera. She was going to the Austrian Tyrol with some people whose name M. will have remembered by the end of the week—I hope. It was something like Kravnik, and she's trying to think back because I once met some people in the Austrian Tyrol with a name like that.

c. M. is very bitter against Sivley.

The best news is that M. says Q. was back at B. within three months of going away. I hope to trace all that down and to find out just what happened abroad as soon as I get the name of the people and the spot where she stayed. I hope Q. herself will fill in some of the gaps. I'm hoping to spend the early winter in Austria, I shall disclose, so she may give me some tips.

That's about all. The firm's not supposed to predict success or failure, but you're different, and I don't mind telling you that I think you'll cease to be a parent in a fortnight's time. All the same, I don't think I'd stiffen my attitude towards Q. till the right moment comes, or till you and I have had a chance of a talk.

I hope you didn't find this brief report too free and easy. Believe me it contains everything of importance that's happened so far. If you want to telephone me, one o'clock and four-thirty are the best times.

Watch your step with Q. I don't know much about her yet but I know enough to think you considerably understated her possibilities. I wouldn't trust her as far as I can throw a battleship.

Yours.

F. T.

P.S.—Two stop press pieces of news while I was waiting to put this in the post. S. hired the Oak car this evening to take him to the cross-roads four miles away, where be caught the Ipswich bus. He was travelling light, with only a handbag.

The other news is that Rogerley is coming down here to-morrow and has booked a room by phone at the Oak. Can't say it looks like the eagles gathering round the carcass, but since H. is now employed by P., two of the four will be in B. to-morrow. Three if S. returns. Wonder why he should depart before R.'s arrival?

That report cheered me enormously, especially as I remembered something that Charlotte had once let fall. The de Karnoviks were the people with whom she had stayed in Austria on a previous occasion, and Marie de Karnovik was an Englishwoman who had been at school with both Charlotte and my sister. The de Karnoviks had a place in Munich as well as a chalet in the Tyrol, and I distinctly recalled that Charlotte had mentioned travelling via Ostend, Brussels, and Stuttgart.

To make sure, I rang up my sister, pretending I thought I'd heard someone say Marie de Karnovik was in England. I was marvellously lucky, for I learned the name of the village where the chalet was—Hasserbruch. Then at one o'clock I rang Frank at Brazenoak.

"Great work!" he said. "I'll have a man on his way there to-night. Anything else new at your end?"

"Nothing," I said, "except that Queenie expects some sort of balloon to go up this week-end, so keep your eyes open. As usual it's her yarn and not mine. A pity, by the way, that you didn't have a man on Sivley's tail."

"I did," he said. "I had my own man but only as far as the Ipswich bus. I can always find out where he went from there. But why are you worried about him?"

"I'm not," I said. "I just wondered, like you. A man like Sivley ought to stay put and not go gadding about. That's how it struck me. And, as you said, it was curious he should leave just when Rogerley was turning up. Was Sivley bolting so as to avoid him?"

Well, Friday came and nothing else happened. That evening I wrote to Bernice and told her about the mirror. I said I'd had occasion to go to Brazenoak in order to help Charlotte as Bernice had asked. There was nothing in it except that Charlotte was worried about Rupert, and since the only help I could give was financial, and I certainly wasn't going to offer that, it looked as if I shouldn't be wanted after all. Which was all to the good, I said, as far as I was concerned, for I didn't trust Charlotte very far; besides, my flirtatious days were long since over.

Those last seven words were the operative ones, as they say, and I thought them highly ingenious. Bernice would write back and say that surely Charlotte wasn't trying to flirt with me, and why should she? My answering letter could reveal just a bit more, and by the time Bernice arrived home, most of the murky past would have been revealed.

And so to that Saturday morning. I was up early for me—at half-past seven, in fact—and at a quarter past eight I was just finishing breakfast. That was when the telephone bell went, and with eyes still on *The Times*, which was propped against the cof-fee-pot, I reached as usually for the receiver.

CHAPTER V
BIG DRUM AND SUNFLOWER

"LUDO! IS THAT YOU, LUDO?"

"Morning. Lotta," I said with an assured heartiness, and then before I could say another word she was cutting in, and her voice had a fierce intensity.

"Can you hear me?"

"Just," I said.

"Listen, my dear. I daren't speak above a whisper. I'm telephoning from the Manor and Joe might be down at any moment. You must come at once. Do you hear me? You must come at once."

"Yes, but—"

"Don't argue, darling, please! How soon can you be here?"

I thought it over quickly. "Ten-thirty, but it'll be quick going."

"Make it earlier. My dear, you must. And wait for me where we stopped the other day. Against the stile." A moment's hesitation and her tone miraculously changed. "Darling, I think I'm going to cry. Just relief, that's all. Bless you, darling."

There was a little sob in her voice as she hung up. I began polishing my glasses, which is a trick of mine when I'm confronted by an unusual situation or am momentarily taken aback. Then I remembered to holler to Palmer to rush the car round from the garage.

By half-past eight I was on the move.

It was a gorgeous morning and I suddenly remembered we were in July. The scent of new hay was everywhere, and the countryside incredibly green, and soon I was actually enjoying that drive, especially when I recalled Frank's assurances that soon I'd be out of Charlotte's clutches. As I came near a roadhouse I looked at the dashboard clock and found I was ahead of time, so I halted for a coffee, and while I drank it I took the precaution of jotting down every word of the morning telephone conversation. That was to be of tremendous consequence, but I take no credit for it since my nature is to be careful over things like that. When I moved on again I was just a little behind time, but when I drew the car in on that grass verge by the stile, it was exactly ten minutes past ten.

But Charlotte was not there. I waited for a quarter of an hour, and then was so furious with her that the least further flicker of annoyance would have made me go straight back to town. Then all at once she was at the stile, breathless but full of apologies.

"My dear, I'm sorry I was late but I just couldn't get rid of Joe." She was beckoning, so I locked the car and mounted the stile.

"Just along here," she said, "and then we shan't be over-heard."

We went along the path for a hundred yards, then she cut through a gap into the wood and along a scarcely visible path to behind a holly tree.

"Darling, we haven't a moment," she said as soon as she'd halted. "It's Rupert. He's doing something desperate and he's got to be stopped."

I nodded and waited.

"The letter came this morning," she said, and then as I raised my eyebrows. "Oh, it's perfectly safe about letters. Joe's never up till long after they've come. Besides, Matthews would do anything in the world for me."

Her fingers went to the low neck of the frock and the letter was produced.

DARLING,

"This may be the last letter you get from me, I don't know yet. I've decided to accept that swine's offer, but by God everybody shall know about it. I'm told he's been at Trimport all this week, his fat belly in a deck-chair, watching the cricket and throwing his weight about. Well, I'm going to Trimport to-morrow morning and I'm going to collect a crowd and tell them a few things. If he turns up there in the afternoon, he'll find the place too hot to hold him. And I'm not afraid of scaring him off his bargain. He'll cough up all right, but by God I'll have something in return.

"God bless, and keep your pecker up whatever happens.

"R.

"P.S.—I don't think I can wait for your unexpected surprise."

I grunted as I returned it, and as she took it her eyes were anxiously on me.

"He's madder than ever," I said. "If he's decided to accept Joe's offer, why the devil can't he do it gracefully?"

"Is that all you can say?" she asked helplessly, and then with a sudden anger: "Don't you see he's trying to screw his courage to—to—" She broke off with a shake of the head, "I can't bear to think of it."

"If you think he's going to take Joe's money and then do himself in, then I don't think you need worry," I told her. "I honestly don't think Rupert's heroic enough for that."

"Sometimes I hate you." she said, and stamped her foot exasperatedly. "Don't I know him? You, talking about knowing him when you know nothing about him at all!"

It was on the tip of my tongue to say that I knew plenty. But least said, soonest mended. Then her hand was almost timidly on my arm.

"Sorry, darling. I oughtn't to have said that to you." She shook her head wearily. "My nerves are all shot to pieces. But about Rupert. He mustn't be allowed to do what he says at Trimport. We've got to stop him."

I let out a breath. "I doubt if I've any influence with him."

"Perhaps not, darling, but you'll help. Look at the risk *I'm* taking. Joe's bound to be told by somebody and he'll be furious with me."

I didn't like it. The last thing I wanted was to get in bad with Joe; but before I could put into words just what I was thinking, she was asking how long it would take us to get to Trimport. I told her forty minutes, considering the narrow roads.

"Then I must fly, darling," she said. "You wait in the car for me."

What was meant to be a brave smile and she was gone. As I strolled back to the car I wondered if the smile had been really brave. Experience of Charlotte had taught me to suspect every word and gesture, yet I was ready to acknowledge that this time she had good enough reason to be scared, for Rupert was about to make the most tremendous fool of himself, and this is why.

I have told you that he had a house at Trimport; indeed he only disposed of the house when the great scandal broke. At Trimport he was full in the swim, and his was the most elaborate and gaudy beach hut, and the largest, and his were the most highly coloured of beach umbrellas, and he entertained a lot, though generally the most notorious of the celebrities. But even at Trimport, Mecca of notoriety seekers, of loud women and fatuous-faced though astute enough men, Rupert was just a bit too conspicuous and hogged too much limelight. In fact he was most damnably unpopular, and only a man of his utter egotism and self-adulation would have been unaware of the fact. When the great scandal broke, Trimport shrieked with delight, though there was an undercurrent of annoyance that he had brought disgrace on the place through its close association with the theatrical and stockbroking professions.

Now that particular Saturday was Trimport's great day. It was the culmination of the cricket week, and there was to be a dance and firework display in the evening. All the men would be down from town for the week-end, and if Rupert Craigne tried to collect a crowd he'd be only too successful. But what made me wince to think of it was the reception he would get. And as I thought of it and of him as the world's most besotted of fools, I glanced at the dashboard clock again and saw that Charlotte had already been gone a quarter of an hour, and again I was annoyed. All that talk about haste, and—

But there she was, breathless again, and saying that once more it was Joe who had kept her.

"I thought I'd never get away," she said as I moved the car on. "And I was trying so hard to get him to change his mind about going to Trimport this afternoon. He's arranged to take that wretched American, and I simply shudder at what he'll be like when he finds out."

There wasn't any talking, for the lanes were narrow and I had to tell her she mustn't distract the man at the wheel. But once she snuggled up against me and told me how comforting I was, I gently eased her away and got on with the job. It was precisely eleven-thirty—remember that—when we breasted the slight rise and came in sight of Trimport.

We had come in by the west road, so that the little town lay to our left. Before us lay the bay and its semi-circle of beach, like a lunatic's rainbow with its huts, kiosks, and umbrellas. Bathing was safe enough inshore, but farther out there were treacherous currents, and only really good swimmers went beyond the two-hundred-yard mark, which was clearly outlined with posts and flags, and was known as the Bar.

But something unusual was happening out there, and I drew the car to a half. Then I saw what it was, and at the same time Charlotte was clutching my arm.

"My God, it's Rupert!" She gave a little moan. "We're too late."

We were too late, but I rushed the car on and then drew it to a screeching halt again on a little hill not a hundred yards from the beach. What we saw and heard was amazing. There, in a small boat just beyond that demarcation line, was Rupert Craigne. His golden hair and beard flared in the full sun, and he was wearing a bathing-suit of the most vivid emerald. In the sea were scores and scores of people, mostly men, but women and children were crowded at the water's edge. In the air was the most terrifying noise: men yelling, laughing to each other, hooting and cat-calling, and there was Rupert, defiantly at the prow of the boat, yelling his own defiances or it might have been his defence, for so loud was the nearer din that I heard no sound of his but saw only his gestures.

Charlotte clutched my arm again. She was crying into her handkerchief and her voice was a moan.

"You've got to stop him. Ludo, you must!"

"My God, how can I stop him!" I told her furiously. "He was a bloody fool, and . . ." Then I let out a breath. "We'd better get away from here before we're seen. It's too late to help now."

Then I was looking out again, for the din had suddenly lessened. Rupert was making frantic gestures for silence, and then in that comparative quiet there was another sound. A crack! Like the letting off of a gun. Where the sound came from I don't know, for sounds play queer tricks across water, but I was not worrying about the sound, at least after that second of quick wonder, for something else was happening. Rupert stood for a moment or two as if balancing on the edge of the boat, and his hands were strangely at his breast. Then he fell backwards, and that was the last I saw of him, for the boat hid him.

"My God! Someone's shot him!" I said, and was scrambling out of the car.

In the same moment the noise was deafening again. It was some new stunt to attract attention, and the cat-calls and hoots were worse than ever. Perhaps the hooting bathers had not heard the crack of that gun, for they were nearer to their own noise, and it had come more clearly to me up the rise. And then people began to wonder. The noise hushed as if by a miracle and there was a deathly silence. Men were swimming towards the boat. For a moment I thought I saw a flash of that emerald bathing-suit as the body rose for a moment to the surface, but it might have been a trick of sunlight on sea. But if it had been there it was now gone, and that was the end of Rupert Craigne, for minutes had gone too, and it was impossible that he should be alive.

There was a little moan and Charlotte slid sideways. A woman was coming down the slope and I called:

"Please, please! This lady's fainted. Will you stay with her for a minute?"

Then I ran. On the beach was an excited crowd, and such babble and chatter as you never heard. Far out a man was standing in the boat, and another clambered up and the two began rowing more out to sea. Other men were in the water beyond the demarcation line, and one or two were diving for the body, which was a pretty hopeless game in spite of the heroics. Then I halted, for why I was running, and what to do, I had no idea. Then I was sheepishly polishing my glasses and wondering just what I ought to do.

The boat was coming towards the shore and I made for it. All round me was the babble of voices, and nurses were calling to excited children who doubtless thought the show had been put on for their benefit, but I heard nothing as I hurried towards the boat. Others were hurrying too, and I had to force my way through the crowd. I was lucky, for one of the men in the boat was Jim Mason, the stockbroker, a level-headed, oldish man and a bad misfit for Trimport. His eyebrows lifted at the sight of me.

The other man was telling the crowd to get back and if they didn't he'd put the boat out to sea again. Another voice was heard.

"That's my boat, sir, and I think I'd better take it."

It was a fisherman, Quadling by name, who also had boats for hire. The crowd pressed closer, and on a sudden impulse I splashed through the water and got into the boat. Quadling got in too and took over the oars, and had the boat coming towards the far town.

"You'd better keep out of the way of that, Travers," Mason said, and pointed.

That was a drop of blood.

I was staring, and Mason's voice came soberly again. "What's all this to do with you?"

"With me?" I said feebly. "Oh, I just happened to see him shot. I mean, I thought he was shot. It took me a minute to recognise the crack of that gun."

"Better keep off-shore a bit, Tom," he told Quadling. "When we get to the gap, you fetch the police."

"A hell of a business this," he said to me. "Made me sick to hear those bloody people."

"Yes, but who did the shooting?" I said.

"No use worrying about that now," he told me mildly. "That'll be for the police to find out. You bet your life he got clean away. Everybody was staring out to sea and he fired from the shore. Probably from one of those back bathing-huts. By the time we began to guess what'd happened, he'd made his getaway."

Well, we got the boat ashore, though at least a score of busybodies had followed along the beach. I said there was no point in my walking there, for I could give no evidence that a hundred others couldn't give. Mason agreed and I went with Quadling. We were hurrying, but I did manage to ask how Craigne had got hold of the boat.

"I had a letter from him yesterday," he said, "asking me to have a boat ready at about eleven. He was a good customer of mine in the old days and I wanted to oblige him. Couldn't help wondering, though, what he was up to."

"But didn't everybody spot him at once?" I said. "I mean even before he got into the boat?"

"I had orders to have it ready a goodish bit along," he said. "Besides, he had on a jacket and sports trousers and the bathing-suit under it, so you didn't notice. It's down on the beach where he left it. He tore it off and chucked it down to me there just after he got in the boat. And he gave me a ten-bob note."

We were nearing the main street, so I made an excuse to turn off. I didn't quite know where I was, but I judged that if I kept on the way I was going I should come to the car. Then I lost my way and it was some minutes before I was put right again. Perhaps I went wrong because I was so busy with my thoughts. Was it up to me, I kept thinking, to see the local police and tell them about Sivley—or rather remind them? Then I decided that they oughtn't to need any reminding. In any case I was skating over exceedingly thin ice, and I didn't want to be mixed up in the business at all. Then I wondered if Mason would put the police on to me, and I hoped he wouldn't be such an interfering fool. Or was it I who had been the interfering fool?

When I came in sight of the car I thought that Charlotte must have gone down to the beach in search of news, for there was no sign of her. The woman wasn't there either, but when I came nearer there was Charlotte sitting in the back. Her eyes were red and at the sight of me she was whipping out her vanity case from her bag.

"Don't look at me, Ludo," she told me harshly.

I stared, then with a shake of the head took my seat at the wheel. The clock said twelve-thirty, and I had no idea it was so late.

"Shall we be getting back?" I said as sympathetically as I could. "There's nothing to wait for now."

She didn't speak so I put the car in reverse. When we moved forward I caught a glimpse of her in the driving mirror, and she was putting the case away again.

"I was a fool to faint," she said. "I don't think I've ever done such a thing before. Who was the woman, Ludo?"

"Don't know," I said. "Just some passer-by."

"She was very kind," she said, and after that there was a silence while I drove a couple of miles.

"Have they found Rupert's body?" she suddenly asked at last.

I shook my head.

"They mayn't find it for days, if at all. That's a job for the police and everybody. Don't talk about it, Lotta. What you've got to remember is that the police will notify you officially as soon as they know where you are. You'll have to have all sorts of answers ready."

"Did they get Sivley?"

"Sivley?" I said after a moment or two. "Why should it have been Sivley?"

"Are you mad?" In the mirror I could see her staring eyes. "Of course it was Sivley. You know it was Sivley. Why did you pretend it wasn't?"

"Whoever it was, they haven't got him," I said, resignedly. "But why do you keep on talking about it? It only distresses you."

"Distresses me!" She began to laugh. The laugh seemed high-pitched and hysterical and I jammed on the brakes. "My God, you infuriate me. You and your pious platitudes! Rupert's been killed and you say it distresses me! Blast you, Ludo—blast you!"

"Now, now, now!" I said placatingly. "Sorry I annoyed you. Perhaps it *was* a fatuous thing to say."

I heard her let out a breath. "No, it wasn't," she said wearily. "I'm just all nerves. I can't think it really happened."

I let the car pick up again. "You forget it was a shock to me too," I said, and: "Sorry. Perhaps that's fatuous too."

"Sivley," she was saying as if to herself. "I'll see him hung if it costs me every penny in the world. If the police don't get him, then I'll get him myself. Funny, isn't it? I never could kill anything, even a fly. But I'd love to kill Sivley. I'd like to pull him in bits, limb from limb."

I said nothing, but let her talk on. I thought it would ease her mind, and I didn't want my own thoughts and eyes taken off that tricky road.

"What made you say it wasn't Sivley?" she was suddenly asking.

"Well, how could Sivley possibly have known that Rupert would be at Trimport?"

"He must have had ways and means," she said. "Who else could have killed him?"

"Someone who had a grudge against him and shot him on the spur of the moment. A whole lot of people lost jobs when Rupert—well when he got himself in that mess. Isn't that so?"

"A ridiculous motive!"

"Very well, then. Perhaps some fool at Trimport got fed up with his talking and thought he'd scare him with that gun. He didn't mean to hit him, but he did. But what's the use of arguing? For all we know Sivley may be at Brazenoak, and with a first-class alibi."

She gave a little sneer of derision.

"In any case, Lotta, you and I can't do anything about it. And I wish you wouldn't make me talk," I said, as I just braked in time to pass a tradesman's van. "Sit back and relax. There'll be plenty of talking to do when you see Joe. Perhaps you'd better think out what you're going to say."

"You'll come with me?"

I thought for a moment and then said I would. After all, there was that Adam mirror for excuse, and if I didn't go there was no telling what lies she'd tell Joe about me.

"Very well," I said. "I'll say I was coming to see Joe and met you by chance, and on the spur of the moment you decided you'd like me to drive you round. As for being late, we can blame the car."

After that she was quiet till we were about a mile from Brazenoak, and by then it was getting on for half-past one, for I had been taking things easy.

"Stop a minute, Ludo," she suddenly said. "I must powder my nose again. I'd hate Joe to see me like this."

"Good," I said. "Perhaps it would be better, if we're going to spin that yarn. Where shall we have been to? Ipswich?"

"Yes, Ipswich," she said, rubbing rouge into her cheek.

We moved on again, and I don't know why, but my heart began to race. I think it was at the thought of having to tell Joe those white lies, and to wonder if he'd be annoyed at our being late for lunch. But Charlotte, as I knew, could handle him pretty well.

As we came out from beneath the woods towards the main gate I suddenly saw a uniformed constable standing there as if on duty. My foot went to the brakes.

"Get ready, Lotta," I called quietly back. "The Trimport police are here already. You'd better think quick what to say. Probably Joe knows already."

The constable's hand went up and I stopped the car.

"Yes, officer?" I said.

"Sorry, but you can't come in here, sir."

"But why not? I'm lunching here."

He smiled. "Sorry, sir, but it's orders."

"But this is Mr. Passman's niece. And what's the idea of holding us up?"

But he was turning to Charlotte. "Are you Mrs. Craigne, lady?"

"Yes," she said, and was staring bewilderedly.

"Sorry, then, Mrs. Craigne, but I've some bad news for you."

I almost smiled, knowing what he was going to say. But that wasn't at all what he said.

"Yes, Mrs. Craigne," he was going heavily on, "your uncle's— well, he's dead, lady. Sorry to be so abrupt."

"Dead!" I said. "Why, he was sound as a bell!"

"Not for what killed him, sir," he told me dismally. "To tell the truth, sir, he was murdered."

"Good God!" I was staring like a lunatic. "Murdered, you say? When?"

"Less than half an hour ago, sir."

"Good God!" I said again. But the constable was not paying any attention to me. He was making for the rear door, and I looked round to see that Charlotte had once more slithered to the car floor.

CHAPTER VI
OCCUPATION GONE

ANOTHER CONSTABLE was patrolling between the front and study doors as I drew the car up. As soon as I'd given him some quick explanations I was in the hall and hollering for Mrs. Day, the house-keeper. Matthews appeared and he gave a faint smile of relief at the sight of me.

"Fetch Mrs. Day, quick," I told him. "Mrs. Craigne's in the car outside. She's faint."

I picked Charlotte up but she was too heavy for me. The constable lent a hand and we carried her into the hall. Mrs. Day, wide-eyed and flustered, was already there.

"She's coming round," I said. "It was the shock of hearing about Mr. Passman."

"The poor dear!" she said. "And what a morning, sir! Never, never did I—"

I cut her moaning short. "Shall we carry her up to her room?"

We went on up, Mrs. Day fluttered behind. When I came down a man was at the foot of the stairs. He was giving me an inquiring look before I reached the bottom, but I had some cards on me and I handed him one.

"I seem to know your name, sir," he said.

I told him a little about myself, and then he remembered me and a certain case that George Wharton and I had been on.

"I'm Venter," he said. "Inspector Venter of Bury St. Edmunds, Perhaps you remember me, sir."

I said I did, and then I told him what I was doing at Brazenoak, through the version was a carefully edited one. Then I asked where the body was, and he was taking me along to the study.

Joe Passman lay at right angles to the front door of the study with his head towards it. His face was sideways, and there was on it an expression of either horror or tremendous surprise. Venter stooped and turned the body slightly over, and I saw a knife driven right home in the left breast. It was a sturdy, black-handled knife of the kind a butcher might use, and there must have been a vicious strength behind it.

"Your doctor seen him?" I said.

"Yes, and he's gone," Venter said. "There wasn't a thing he could do."

"Prints on the knife?"

"None."

"Anything missing from his pockets?"

He smiled and shook his head. "Not as far as we know, sir. But we're not worrying about details like that. We know who did it."

My eyebrows lifted inquiringly.

"Sivley," he said. "He was actually seen in the grounds making his getaway."

"Then the hue and cry's out?"

"Yes," he said. "I've just rushed a description to the Yard. The whole country'll be on the look-out for him before the afternoon's gone."

The telephone went and he picked up the receiver.

"Hallo? . . . Sorry, sir, but you can't speak to Mr. Passman. Well, sir, he's dead. . . . Yes, that's right, sir. . . . And who is it speaking, please?"

There were nods and grunts and the latter were all that I could hear.

"I understand, sir," Venter resumed. "Yes, sir; Mrs. Craigne's very upset, but she's standing it well on the whole. . . . No, sorry, sir, I'm afraid you can't come here, not at present. . . . I will, sir. Good-bye."

"An American gentleman staying at the Oak," he said. "Says he was going to Trimport with Mr. Passman this afternoon. In fact they should have started ten minutes ago, that's why he rang up."

"Mrs. Craigne mentioned him to me," I said. "A very nice fellow, I believe, and very well-to-do. But about this business, Venter. What's this about Sivley being seen?"

"An under gardener saw him cutting away through the woods just across there," he said. "He spotted him at once. He should have knocked off at twelve, but was doing something in those glass-houses. He hollered to Sivley to know what he wanted, but Sivley was out of sight like a shot. Another minute and this gardener heard the sound of a motor-bike."

I nodded and was running an eye round the room. "Passman was reading his paper," I said. "Matthews brought him a tankard of beer—"

"At twelve-thirty," interrupted Venter with a dry smile.

"And Passman had half finished it," I went on with a nod of thanks. "Sivley came through that side-door. Passman heard a sound and looked round. Sivley whipped out the knife and had it in him as he hoisted himself from the chair. Passman fell where he is now, and he didn't feel a thing. Sivley must have had the nerve to bolt out at this front door."

"That's how I worked it out too," he said. "That shrubbery gave him cover to reach that side-door except for a ten-yard dash."

"And now I'll tell you something," I said, and I made his eyes pop when he heard what had happened that morning.

"My God!" he said. "He did what he said he'd do. Were you in court when he made that threat?"

"I was," I said, "and it's something I'll never forget. All the same, I took it for so much hot air."

"To tell the truth, so did I," he said. "I've heard that sort of stuff before. But the nerve of him, sir! Doing Mr. Craigne in and calmly getting on that motor-bike and doing the other one in before the news got through."

"Yes." I said, "and I'm open to make a bet with you. I don't think you'll get him again. He'll have sense to know he can't get clear and he'll do himself in."

"I won't bet," he said, "but I don't think you'll be right."

Then he was asking to be excused. He'd have to get Trimport it once, and there'd be endless other telephoning to do. The ambulance was coming and a photographer and another print man.

"I don't think I'll worry Matthews for a meal," I said. "I'll get something at the Oak. I'll be there if you should happen to want me. And do you mind if I have a word with Mrs. Craigne, if she's well enough?"

Charlotte was seated in an easy-chair before the open window, and she gave me a wan smile as I came in. Mrs. Day was kneeling by the chair and had evidently been in the act of coaxing her into eating something. She scrambled to her feet as I came in.

"Feeling better?" I said to Charlotte.

"Much better. You were so good."

"Well, I won't worry you now," I said. "I'll come back later in the afternoon. I'm going on to the Oak now to get a bite of lunch. Better than worrying everybody here, And, by the way, I told Inspector Venter, who's in charge here, *exactly* what happened this morning, word for word."

Her eyes narrowed momentarily, but she was smiling as she nodded.

"Make her eat something, Mrs. Day," I said. "And take care you eat it, Charlotte. See you later, then."

A nod and a smile and I was gone. As I drove to the Oak I ought to have been a gratified man, and for many reasons, and yet I wasn't. The morning had been too ghastly, perhaps, and I was like a man placed before a mouth-watering meal but with no appetite to eat.

As I drew up before the Oak I caught sight of Frank sitting at ease on the side lawn, a spot that gave strategic views of the cross-roads. He made signs for me to go in the front way, and in a minute he was with me.

"Well, well, well," he said. "You got my letter then?"

"How could I be here if I hadn't?" I said. "You got mine, too?"

"Sure," he said, and then was seizing my hand again. "Well, if it isn't great to see you. What about a drink?"

"I don't think I will," I said. All this, by the way, was for the benefit of the landlady. "What I would like is a bite of something to eat. Eight o'clock this morning was my last meal."

"Sure", he said. "Mrs. Porter, could you send Smith up with a tray of something to my room? And a tankard? Make it two tankards."

We had the best room in the place and again with a strategic view each way along the road. The clock tower at the Manor was just visible through a gap in the trees.

"We shan't be overheard," he said, and in his natural voice.

"As an American you're terrific," I told him. "Just exactly right. Familiar, but far from gaudy."

"Cut out the Polonius stuff", he grinned. "You're in a taxi now and the clock's ticking. What's the lowdown on Passman?"

"I was at the Manor when you rang up just now," I said. "There's an Inspector Venter on the job, and I happen to know him."

"Yes," he said impatiently, "but what's this about Passman being dead? All I've heard is village rumours. That's why I rang."

"You tell me the rumours," I said.

"A police car dashed up to old Mrs. Sivley's cottage and everybody said Sivley was being arrested again. Then someone saw a copper at the Manor gate and everyone was saying Sivley had killed Passman, just as he threatened. When I say everyone, I mean talk in the pub. The place has been seething with excitement. They could hardly clear the bar at closing time."

My lunch tray came in—cold beef and ham, salad, and a slab of gooseberry tart. The man who brought it didn't look like a waiter.

"Put it over here, Smith," Frank said. "And put my beer here. This is my man. Answering to the name of Smith."

Smith was well-trained, for he didn't even look at me. I had a look at him, and for all his quietness he seemed a hard-boiled customer. He had a simian upper lip, two chins and goggling eyes of blue that seemed perpetually startled, and his short crisp hair was the kind that comes low down on the forehead and gives a beetling look.

"That all, sir?" he asked Frank, and at the same time gave me a quick look.

"Just a minute," I said. "It might be as well if Smith listened to what I've got to say."

Smith peered from the door and then turned the key. I talked between bites, and I went over the events of the morning from the moment Charlotte rang me up till the moment I'd entered the Oak. The others made no comment. The story was dramatic enough in all conscience, and I don't see what questions they could have asked. In fact it was I who asked the first question.

"You followed Sivley to the Ipswich bus, didn't you, Smith?"

"Yes, sir."

"What clothes was he wearing?"

"Tweed cap, black and white check, biscuit-coloured sports coat, grey flannel trousers and brown boots," he told me promptly.

"How big was the case he carried?"

"A large-sized attaché-case. About so big. Enough to hold pyjamas and toilet things. Maybe a bit more. It was light enough, by the way he carried it."

"What's the idea?" Frank asked me. "You want to hand over that description to Venter?"

"Lord, no!" I said. "The police have their own description, which they got from that under-gardener. At least, I guess that's where they got it from. It'd be bang up-to-the-minute as regards clothes. But hadn't Smith better be taking that tray down? It might seem funny if he's away too long."

Smith began clearing the table at once.

"But this is the real point," I said. "Is Rogerley still here?"

"He was this morning," Frank said. "We've been keeping a quiet eye on him. Wait a minute." He got out his small note-book. "Nothing important for to-day. He went out at ten and carried a stick as if he was going for a walk."

"He called on old Mrs. Sivley," put in Smith.

"You didn't tell me?"

"Never had a chance, sir," Smith told him calmly. "I only learnt it just now. He went round the back of the church way and called as I said. He wasn't there two minutes, and then he went along the Ipswich road for a walk. He didn't get in to lunch till five past one."

"This is what I'd like to have done," I said. "Don't ask me why, because I don't know, except that I'm a curious bloke, and I can't for the life of me think why Rogerley came down here. I'd like Smith, or you, Frank, to tell Rogerley the Passman news. Just about being stabbed, and Sivley being seen will do. Watch his reactions."

"You get on with it," Frank told Smith, "but mind you don't tell him too much."

When Smith had gone I let out a breath. "Well, there we are, then."

"And Othello's occupation almost gone," Frank said, and his grin was a bit rueful. "A pity. I like it down here. You ought to see the village grandfathers flicking their forelocks to me. Now Passman's dead I'll bet there's a rumour that I'm buying the Manor."

"Don't be too sudden," I said. "I don't think Othello'll be back on the dole. You heard what I said about Charlotte's love for Sivley? What's the betting she doesn't ask to have her private sleuth transferred to tracking Sivley down?"

"But the police'll do that."

"In her present mood she wants Sivley badly," I said. "She won't be interested in the police. You don't know her as I do. When she's in a mood she's no use for logic or common sense."

He didn't look particularly cheerful for all that. Then his face lighted with an idea, but it was only a variation of the dismals.

"By the way, we've a man already on the way to Austria. Left this morning. Would you like us to recall him and save you the expense?"

I had to think hard for a moment or two before I caught up with him. "You mean that as both Rupert and Joe are dead, there can't be any more pressure put on me?"

"Why, yes."

I smiled and shook my head. "Let your man carry on. The idea was to clip the lady's claws, and clipped they're going to be. You see," I explained patiently, "you never know when she might break loose again for some quite different reason. I want permanent protection."

"I think you're right," he said, and his face brightened a bit. "But how're you feeling about things, Mr. Travers?"

"Not what I should be," I said, "and that's what I can't quite fathom. I ought to be sitting on top of the world, but I'm not. I've got an uneasy feeling that everything isn't so pretty. I know it's callous and all that. Sitting here and gloating over a couple of corpses, but there's no inhibition like that in it. I ought to be damn pleased that Charlotte's got to abandon that blasted scheme of hers. And yet I don't feel cheerful inside. How do you account for that?"

"I'll tell you," he said. "It's because we never quite believed that she was making use of you solely to get some hold over poor old Passman. She may have been, mind you. All the same, the more I saw of Joe the less I was convinced that he'd been mixed up in that cheap swindle. Very well, then. What's worrying both of us is what her real idea was in trying to blackmail you, and whether what's happened to-day is going to make any difference."

"I shall be seeing her between tea and dinner and I'll talk to her damn straight." I said grimly.

He grinned. "You may ease your mind, but I doubt if you'll get much satisfaction. All you'll be presented with is a new set of lies." His face sobered. "But I'll put Smith on Sivley's trail straightway. If you like you can tell Queenie you anticipated what you knew would be her wishes. And, by the way, I ought to call and offer condolences. What's the best time?"

"To-morrow afternoon," I said. "Play your cards right and you'll be the mainstay and solace of the next few days."

There was a tap at the door and in came Smith. "I've seen him, sir," he said to Frank, "and he was all of a dither. I wouldn't be surprised if he isn't going to bolt. He's talking with Mrs. Porter now in her room. I thought I'd just let you know."

"Attaboy!" Frank said to him.

"Why should he bolt?" he said to me as the door closed on Smith.

"Ask me another," I said. "Perhaps his occupation's gone too. What did he come here for, if it comes to that."

"We know he came to see Sivley. Perhaps to offer him a job."

"His training stable's near Salisbury," I said. "Why spend money on petrol and this pub when a letter would have done?"

"One man we haven't done much thinking about, and that's Harper," he pointed out.

"I know," I said. "Harper doesn't quite fit in either. Too much generosity about, for my liking. Joe giving the helping hand to Harper, and, if your idea's right, Rogerley giving one to Sivley."

Another quick tap on the door and in slipped Smith again. "He's off!" he said. "Paid his bill and just packing his bag."

Frank shrugged his shoulders. "Well, there's nothing we can do about it. You might find out what petrol he has put in his tank from the pump here. That might tell us if he's making for home. And let everybody know you're spending the week-end with a sister at Norwich. Then see me again. You're following up Sivley's trail on that Ipswich bus. The nearest large garage to the bus stop at Ipswich might help. We know he got hold of a motor-bike somewhere."

*   *   *   *   *

We had a leg stretch before tea; just a stroll round by some field paths and well away from the Manor, for we didn't want to be drawn into talking shop again. I didn't see how Charlotte should learn from the Oak that Frank and I had greeted each other like old friends, but we rigged up a story which I would try to put across later that afternoon.

Just before six o'clock I made my way to the Manor on foot. That would give me an excuse for returning to the Oak and reporting direct to Frank. The constable was at the main gate, but the other had gone from the house front. Venter was still there, in shirt-sleeves and at the telephone.

"Why people want to get murdered on a Saturday beats me," he told me wryly. "Passman's office in town is closed; I can't get his solicitors; and every time I want the Yard there's a quarter of an hour hold-up."

"Nothing new?" I asked.

"No, sir. Someone's due down from the Yard this evening. Some hush-hush business connected with Passman."

"I'm going back to town almost at once," I said. "Here's the telephone number if you should want me by any chance. I'll just say good-bye to Mrs. Craigne and then I'll be off."

Venter had pushed the bell, and Matthews came in.

"Have you a wireless set here?" Venter asked him.

"One in the drawing-room and one in the servants' hall, sir."

"Anyone in the drawing-room?"

"Mrs. Craigne, sir."

"Then I'll come with you and listen to the other one," Venter said.

It was just time for the news and the two went off as soon as Venter had unearthed a man of his to sit at the phone. I made my own way to the drawing-room and found Charlotte lying on the big chesterfield before the open french windows. She was looking herself again. A little more powder on the cheeks and a touch of black under the eyes would have made her more of the interesting convalescent she was trying to appear by her pose. Curious how even at that moment, when I ought to have felt some genuine pity, my thoughts instinctively took that cynical twist.

"Darling, you've been a perfect angel to-day," she told me with a wan smile. "But you're looking tired. Did they give you a dreadful meal?"

"An excellent meal," I said "And, by the way, I met that American friend of yours. What a charming fellow he is! We had a stroll together before tea."

"He is rather a dear," she said. "I think I shall get him to use his influence to find me a job in Hollywood."

"Good Lord, why?"

"My dear"—the gesture was one of grief and resignation—"I shall have to leave here. Not for a few days, of course. I must see poor old Joe decently buried. And when they recover Rupert's body I shall have him buried here too."

I felt rather ashamed of myself because I couldn't say the suitable thing, but somewhere inside me something was saying that everything didn't ring true. Perhaps I was so used to expecting tricks and scheming that anything genuine had a false ring.

"But why go to Hollywood?" I said. "Joe's bound to have left you comfortably off."

"I just couldn't go on living in England," she said. "People never forget."

That didn't ring true either. If there was one thing I guessed she had been anticipating, it was to cut a dash with Joe's money. However, I heaved a suitable sigh, then cut in with my question.

"Look here, Lotta, I've got to have a few straight words with you now. What I promised to help you in isn't wanted now. Isn't that so?"

"No," she said slowly, and looked away. "I suppose it isn't—really."

"Then what about calling off that private detective?"

"Oh, no," she said quickly. "I've been thinking such a lot, lying here all alone. And, don't you see. Even if Rupert is gone, it's up to me to clear his name. If we can prove that he was a tool of Joe, and Joe let him down, then it's my duty."

"Rather ghoulish, isn't it? I mean, with Joe dead?"

"Don't be pious," she told me, and forgot her pose in a flash of annoyance. "What's Joe's reputation compared with Rupert's?"

"It's your money," I said. "I'll tell him to carry on. He's on a clue of sorts already, by the way."

"No!"

"Yes," I said, "but that's as much as I know. Also," I went hastily on, "I remembered what you said about finding Sivley, so I put him on to that too. Got in touch with him about an hour ago."

"Did you, darling? That was sweet of you."

There was no particular enthusiasm. Indeed, she seemed the least bit taken aback, and I was wondering why.

"One thing you must do," she said. "You must come down here till everything's over. You can stay at the Oak".

"Heavens, Lotta, how can I do that? What about my work?"

"But, darling, you can work just as well at the Oak?"

"Can't be done," I said with finality.

"But, darling, I want you to." There was more than a suspicion of a threat in her voice. "I shall be very, very angry if you don't."

"More blackmail?"

She smiled. "Don't use that word, darling. It's horrid. But I warned you I should be ruthless."

"So may I one of these days."

"What do you mean?" She was actually looking frightened.

"Oh, nothing. But I can be driven so far and no farther."

"Don't let's argue," she said. "And you must really be going now? Do stay and have supper. I told Matthews we might have a quick meal."

"Sorry, but I must get back to town," I said. "See you soon, I hope."

"To-morrow, darling," she told me from the chesterfield. "Bring all your books and everything. You're going to be such a comfort to me."

Out in the hall I damned her under my breath, and myself too for the moral coward I'd been. There had I been, boasting to

Frank of having a final understanding, and all I'd done was to let her twist me round her fingers.

"Mr. Travers, sir." Matthews was coming along the corridor.

"Hallo, Matthews." I said. "This has been the devil of a day for you."

"Yes, sir," he said, and shook his head. A finger went tremblingly to his lips for silence. "May I . . . you wouldn't think it a liberty, sir . . . what I want to say, sir, is could you spare me a private moment some time?"

"Why certainly, Matthews," I said. "When shall it be?"

"Was there something you wanted?" That was Charlotte. She had suddenly appeared at Matthews's elbow and, though she was smiling inquiringly, I knew she must have heard what we had said.

"Oh, no," I said, as Matthew retired with a little bow or two. "I was only sympathizing with Matthews on the terrible day he's had."

A car drew up at the front door. It was Venter's, and when I looked round to say a final good night to Charlotte, she had gone. Venter waited for me outside.

"Still at it?" I said.

"That's right, sir, and I look like being at it for some time."

"Anything on the wireless to-night?"

"The whole issue," he said. "All about both of them. Evening papers full of it. The village is like an ant-heap."

"One thing I wondered," I said. "I suppose I shall see it in the papers, but what sort of clothes was Sivley wearing? The sort of things a man would wear who was riding a motor-bike?"

"Just ordinary clothes," he said. "Sports coat and grey flannels. Between you and me, the same as he left home with. A pair of goggles on, that's all. And do you mind if ask you why you wanted to know?"

"I just wondered," I said. "I thought the motor-bike would help to trace his movements, and so might any special clothes."

He looked disappointed. I changed the conversation, for I knew I was a fool to have put the question at all. Then his man popped out of the study and said he was wanted on the telephone, and I was glad enough to get away.

When I'd thought some more about what sort of a fool I'd been not to have stood up to Charlotte, I began wondering what it was that Matthews wanted to tell me, and why he had been so mysterious about it. What I'd do, I thought, was to ring Palmer up and say I'd be home very late. Then I'd go back to the Manor—back door—when Charlotte was in bed, and have that private talk with Matthews.

But all that was to be knocked cock-eyed. As I came to the village cross-roads and in sight of the Oak, I stepped absent-mindedly into the main road, and at once there was a veritable blast of a hooter behind me. I stepped back remarkably shamefaced, and then my eyes met those of the driver of the car. And he was George Wharton.

CHAPTER VII
BIRTH OF A THEORY

"God Almighty!" Wharton's eyes were bulging.

The car had slithered to a halt to avoid my untimely death, and I promptly opened the near front door.

"Surprise if you like, George, but no blasphemy," I said. "And if it comes to that, what on earth are you doing here?"

"Me? I've got business," he told me resentfully.

"If you're going to the Manor," I said, "you're going the wrong way."

He shot me a look, then his eyes were back on the road again. George was more than a careful driver. I believe he once exceeded forty, and both of his hands always clutch the wheel as if he's perpetually jockeying for position.

"I suppose you're not staying here by any chance?" he asked with what was meant to be sarcasm as he drew the car up in the Oak yard. "Got your car, I see, too."

When his car was run into the garage and he'd got out his bag, we strolled together to the pub.

"To quit the persiflage, George," I said. "I think it might be useful to both of us if we had a quiet talk."

"I've booked a room," he said, "so we might go up there. A spot of grub wouldn't do me any harm either."

There was no sign of Frank, or the beetle-browed Smith. George signed the book as Mr. Wharton, Golders Green.

"Incognito?" I asked as we followed the chambermaid up the stairs.

"Any objections?"

I smiled and said no more. When the girl had gone George had a wash at the bathroom basin, hissing and puffing as if he were rubbing down a horse.

"That's better," he said as he put his coat on again. "And now what were you going to tell me?"

I had no time to waste so I told him that Mrs. Craigne was a friend of my wife and my sister. She had been worried about the antics of her husband and had asked me to do something if I could. After that came the events of the day.

"Right in the thick of it, eh?" George said. "And what sort of a woman is she, this Mrs. Craigne?"

I didn't give anything away, but naturally I did have to put in a considerable amount of truth in order to leaven the lump. After I'd said, for instance, that she was a very attractive woman and of very good family—though George will never admit it he's always a bit of a snob—I divulged that she'd not been behind in helping Craigne get rid of his money, that she hadn't too many moral scruples, and that she'd been playing a double game with Joe Passman.

"You're going to see her?" I asked him.

"Well, I might," he said, and pursed his lips.

"Cough it up, George," I said. "I've been perfectly frank with you. What are you down here for?"

Then the maid was bringing in his supper tray. I was sorry about that interruption for it might give him time to work out some specious tale. But for once he told me the truth, though it must have hurt.

"Just that old business," he told me as he tucked the napkin into his collar. "I've got authority to go right through Passman's papers."

"You think he might have been mixed up in that swindle after all?"

"You never know," he said. "A remarkably funny thing came to light about a month ago. You remember that chap Rogerley?"

"The trainer?" I said, and almost blushed.

"His stable's near Salisbury," George went on. "We got an anonymous letter, post-marked Winchester, saying we might do worse than inquire into the past history of a Mrs. Drawe. There was a bit more to it than that or we shouldn't have sent a man down. When he got there, what do you think he found? She'd just been taken to hospital and she died under an operation two days later."

"And was there anything in it?"

"Only this. She was Rogerley's sister. Her husband died a year before, and the two of them had been largely dependent on Rogerley. The husband was one of those feckless individuals, always suffering from bad luck. I pricked my ears up when I heard that and down to Hampshire I went. What do you think we unearthed? Just before that swindling gang was nabbed, this Mrs. Drawe and her husband were about to take over a village post office near Salisbury!"

My eyebrows lifted.

"And what's more," George went on between bites, "the arrangements were suddenly terminated as soon as the gang was nabbed. Now do you see things?"

"An extension of the original scheme?"

"That's it. Dammit, they'd made their first packet and it went to their heads, so they thought they'd start opening branches! But this is the point. The Drawes hadn't a bean but what Rogerley allowed them, and he's always living from hand to mouth. Now then; we know it wasn't the first winnings that were being invested in the branch concerned because the first winnings hadn't come in when the Drawes began negotiating for the purchase of the shop. Where was the money coming from then? Could it have been Passman?"

"I still can't believe it," I said. "As I told you before, Joe never missed the chance of making a penny, but he wasn't an utter fool."

"Well, I'm having a look at his papers. Checking up on his spendings."

"Why not?" I said. "But what's being done about Rogerley?"

"Nothing," George said. "There's no case against him. What we think is that he was going to work a swindle over his own horses only. But he got out in time and the P.P."—the Public Prosecutor, he meant—"doesn't even see a case for charging him with intent."

He gulped down a last cup of tea, wiped his vast moustache with ample sweeps of his huge handkerchief, and got to his feet.

"Well, I must get along and see Venter. Hell of a day in front of me to-morrow. The managing director of Passman, Ltd., coming down and another director, and the solicitor. Seeing the Chief Constable later—"

"I'm in a hurry, too," I told him. "So just one last tip, George. If you're examining Passman's papers, I'll bet you find some of Mrs. Craignes finger-prints on them. That woman wouldn't let anything stand in the way of curiosity."

We went downstairs together and George said it was a pity in a way that he and I wouldn't be working on a case, for Brazenoak struck him as a nice little spot. Sivley, he said, would be nabbed before Sunday was out.

"Hallo, Frank?" I said, for Frank was at the foot of the stairs and suddenly interested in the face of the grandfather clock.

"Looking at this clock," he said. "What's it worth, Mr. Travers?"

Then he caught sight of Wharton. I did the introductions and made the explanations.

"Glad to meet you, sir," Wharton said. "And what do you think of the ancestral home?"

"It's a great spot," Edward Franks, Jr., told him. "If I had the money I'd like to transplant it."

"Ah, we've still got something to show you people from the other side," chuckled Wharton. Then he was making his excuses and saying he might see him later. I received only a nod. Frank gave me a nod too, but towards the top landing.

From the window of his room we watched George set out for the Manor.

"So that's the great Superintendent Wharton," Frank said.

"You sound disappointed."

"Well, he looks a bit past it."

"Don't you underestimate George Wharton," I told him. "He's crafty as a weasel and if you try any monkey tricks you'll wish you were playing tag with a man eater. Smith's on the trail, is he?"

"He rang me up half an hour ago," he said. "He's found the garage where Sivley bought the motor-bike, and he's got the number. A second-hand machine that cost him twelve quid. When Sivley left Ipswich, which was at once apparently, he took the Felixstowe road. That's all my man knows at present."

"Next time you get in touch with him, tell him Sivley was wearing the same clothes when he killed Passman as he was when he left here that night. By the way, what did he do with his attaché-case when he bought the bike?"

"There was a carrier behind," Frank said. "He strapped it on."

"Smith doesn't forget much," I had to say.

"He's a good man," Frank said with a nod of the head. "If he doesn't beat the police to finding Sivley, then I'm a crooner."

"Wait a minute," I said, and told him what Wharton had divulged about Rogerley.

"That's damn funny," he said, and frowned. "What was Rogerley doing down here then? He wanted to see Sivley and he probably saw Harper. Surely he wasn't thinking of having another crack at beating the bookies?"

"Lord knows," I said. "But let me put this up to you. Rogerley didn't see Sivley, as far as we can judge. What he did do was to run like a jack rabbit as soon as he heard what Sivley had done to Passman, Why?"

"Maybe he thought Sivley had a spare knife for him."

"Sivley made no allusions to Rogerley in the dock," I pointed out. "But what about this? Rogerley bolted for home because he knew Sivley would be waiting for him there."

"Gosh, yes," he said. "You've got something there, Mr. Travers. What do you say to my going down to Rogerley's place and keeping an eye open?"

"Even if you don't go, it'll be something good in theories to put up to the merry widow," I told him. "Let her think her man's gone there. She'll think she's getting value for money. You bet your life Wharton will know Rogerley's been here. You might even tell him yourself. Say it's village gossip and how everyone was talking about the old swindling case. He'll put two and two together just as well as we can. The police'll be hot on Rogerley's trail before tomorrow's out."

Now Frank had no experience of me as a theorist, and I'm afraid he was inclined to regard me as an oracle. George Wharton could sometimes be infuriated at my ability to find an immediate theory to satisfy any circumstances, but he would profit unblushingly from my average of one good thought in four. It was George, by the way, who once remarked bitterly that given a moment to polish my glasses, I could spontaneously produce a theory to account for the eccentricities of the larynx of Balaam's ass and the gullet of Jonah's whale.

"The *merry* widow," Frank said with a grin. "Was she merry?"

"In a subdued way, yes," I said. "She was posing to me as the brave little woman, but I don't think she was altogether dissatisfied. You think that's a queer thing to say?"

"Damned if I know," he said. "Would you mind if I put something forward, Mr. Travers?"

"Why the apologies?"

"Well," he said diffidently, "I don't like putting forward theories without something substantial to go on."

I nodded with never a blush.

"That woman's a rattlesnake," he said. "It isn't what you told me about her that makes me say that, it's something I feel whenever I'm up yonder at the Manor. If she isn't playing some dirty game—and I don't mean blackmailing you—then my name's Adolf. That's all I've got to go on."

"Well, what's the theory?" I said, to help him out, for he still seemed a bit chary of going on.

He lighted himself a cigarette. "This," he said, and nodded. "Your alluding to her as the merry widow just clinched what I've been thinking a goodish part of this evening. Mind if I do a bit of catechising, Mr. Travers?"

"Carry on," I told him.

"She's capable of double-crossing anybody, even her husband?"

"Undoubtedly."

"Then all this talk of sticking to him through thick and thin may be only ballyhoo?"

"It may."

"And you wouldn't regard him as being an asset to her?"

"Well," I said, "I hardly know how to answer that one. Taking everything into account I'd say that while his death wouldn't be necessarily a happy release, it has certain elements of relief."

He grinned. "Mr. Travers, you should have been a lawyer. But I think I can confirm what you've just said. If I'm still here next week I think she'll be making eyes at me. When I saw her yesterday morning she was quite flirtatious. You could almost say she knew she'd soon be a widow, but I'll come to that later."

"Watch your step," I told him. "You—young, wealthy, Hollywood influence."

"She may have to do the watching," he told me enigmatically. "But here's the theory. Sorry to've been so long-winded. But why shouldn't she have been in touch with Sivley? She might have fixed him financially. She might have arranged with Rogerley—she knew Rogerley well enough in the old racing days—to help Sivley's get-away. When you come to think of it," he went on, "she hasn't done so badly out of what's happened today. She's got rid of a lunatic husband and she'll get some of Passman's money."

"It's a hell of a theory," I said and shook my head. "I'm not cribbing at it. What I mean is, there's a hell of a lot in it. And you

say she gave you the impression yesterday of knowing something was going to happen?"

"She sure did. When I got back here I kept saying to myself:
'What the devil's that woman got on her mind?'"

"Well, chew on it a bit," I said. "If you get any further and you
think there's any way to get proofs, then you can act without any
further reference to me."

I had got up to go, but he followed me to the door, hand on
knob. "Just one other thing, Mr. Travers. If my theory's correct,
then we get an explanation of one thing that's puzzled us both—
what her idea was in dragging you into all this."

"And what was it?" I cut in at once.

"To get you ultimately to be on the spot when her husband
was killed. To prove she could have had nothing to do with it, or
with killing Passman. To be able to faint and act the distracted
wife, so that you'd be in a position to testify if she ever needed
your testimony."

I had to give a sideways nod, and then was polishing my
glasses. "I don't know that you're not right. There may be gaps
in the whole theory but there's a devil of a lot of sound spots."

We more or less left things at that. I paid my bill and he saw
me into the car and I said that on the Monday I might be down
again. I added speciously that I was in need of a few days' rest.

It was not till an hour later that I remembered something
that Wharton's arrival and Frank's theory had made me forget—
that I'd intended to go to the Manor and hear what it was that
Matthews had so secretively wanted to tell me.

I slept till late on the Sunday morning for I had reached
home in the early hours, and dog-tired. From the first moment
of waking I had a curious revulsion of feeling. On the Saturday
I had been too close to the actual murders. In seeing the corpses, you might say, I had forgotten the men, but now I couldn't
help thinking of both Rupert Craigne and Joe Passman as I'd
known them.

For Joe I had always had a sneaking regard, and even his
little weaknesses were amiable. Rupert I recalled with less kindly

feelings. There was nothing about Rupert Craigne of which I could think with anything even remotely resembling a chuckle. One thing only I recalled, and there the laugh was against him. He was junior to me at Halstead and I heard the story second-hand. In a German lesson was a fellow called Greenhill, who was a deadly shot with a pellet of chewed blotting-paper propelled with the tongue from a rolled paper. He plugged one at the back of Rupert's neck but at that very second Rupert had one of his twitching fits and caught the pellet in his open mouth. In a moment he was spluttering, to the vast annoyance of the master, who promptly gave him a slab of Goethe to commit to memory. It was curious that in a subsequent lesson Greenhill, who had flourished unsuspected for months, should have been caught out by the same master, who was both bat-eyed and deaf, and it was always suspected that Rupert had ratted. There in embryo, was the man who had ratted on Sivley.

A strange world, I thought, that Rupert, Frank, and myself should all three have been at Halstead, and what divergent ways we had trodden. Then in the midst of those philosophic musings. Palmer brought in the papers. My own two were too heavy to give the goriest details about the murders, so I borrowed Palmer's couple of papers, for he is always partial to the what-the-butler saw type of Sunday reading.

About the actual murders there was nothing that I didn't know. But there was news about Sivley besides his photograph. The police had traced him to Ipswich and from there he had been seen proceeding in the direction of Trimport, the road to which branches off from the Felixstowe Road. It was supposed that he had lain doggo at Trimport till the morning of the murder.

Two things struck me at once, and to one I have already referred. Why did Sivley lie doggo at Trimport when nobody, not even Charlotte Craigne, knew that Rupert would be at Trimport till the Saturday! The answer seemed a startling confirmation of Frank Tarling's theory. Charlotte had been in touch with Sivley, and in closer touch with Rupert than she had made out. She had doubled-crossed Rupert and had dropped a hint to Sivley. It needn't have been anything so fantastic as an injunction to murder and the means with which to commit it. All it need have been was something like this. "I'm sure, if you see Mr. Craigne personally, Sivley, he can clear everything up satisfactorily and remove any misunderstandings. I don't want it known, but I may say in strict confidence that he'll be at Trimport on Saturday morning."

I had a twinge of conscience when I worked that out, because I knew it was my duty to mention it at least to Wharton. But how could I mention that without revealing much of the murky past and the real reason for insinuating myself into the Craigne affairs? As for the second thing that puzzled me about Sivley, it was this. What of the weapon—almost certainly a rifle—which he had used at Trimport? Even the smallest rifle, unless it is stripped, is an awkward thing to carry about. And, as I worked it out, Sivley didn't carry it off with him. He had abandoned it and set off at once on his motorbike to finish the job, and Passman. And for Joe he had used a different weapon and one easy to carry. Then why had not the police found the rifle where Sivley had abandoned it? This was something I could ask Wharton. Even if the police had found the rifle and were keeping it dark for inscrutable reasons, Wharton might tell me what those reasons were.

I settled down to work that day and by evening realised that if I put in as good a day on Monday, the job would be over. There was nothing on the wireless about the twin murders, so I rang up Frank at Brazenoak.

"Anything new your end?" I asked him.

"Nothing much," he said. "I'm pretty friendly with your pal W, if that interests you, but I daren't try picking his brains."

"You saw the papers, about Sivley at Trimport?"

"On the way to Trimport," he corrected me. "Smith had that before the police did. Smith has the trail to within five miles of Trimport, and he can't pick it up. Neither can the police."

"Be a good fellow," I said, "and type a brief report for Queenie. We must justify your existence. Tell her what's been about Sivley, add any old yarn for overweight, and get it posted at Ipswich or near. And for God's sake don't sign it with the wrong name."

He said he'd get it done at once and posted before midnight. I said I'd be down for lunch on the Tuesday unless anything unforeseen happened.

So much for the Sunday. There was nothing in the morning papers about Sivley's movements, and so Wharton's prophecy of a Sunday arrest had been too optimistic. I wondered if he'd as yet thought of the Rogerley end, for there was no mention of Rogerley in the papers either, not that there was any reason why there should have been. The evening papers had nothing new, unless one counts as new the fact that Rupert Craigne's body had not yet been recovered.

By dinner-time my job was finished and I could lie back with a sigh of relief. After the meal I thought it might be as well if I rang Charlotte.

"Darling, I expected you down." That was her gambit and it was an aggressive one.

"Just couldn't find time," I said. "Tomorrow morning, though. But understand this," I went on in a bellicose tone, "if my job hadn't been finished, I shouldn't have been down then."

That somewhat cheap and cowardly defiance was effective, for her tone altered at once.

"But darling, I thought we understood that; I mean, about your work. But you must lunch with me here."

"Sorry, but I shan't be down in time."

"Then you'll miss poor Joe's funeral," she told me accusingly.

"The papers said it was on Wednesday!" I said, suspecting some new trap.

"That was all eye wash, darling, just to keep the curiosity-mongers away. It will actually be a very simple service. Poor darling, he wished to be buried in the grounds here."

"Well, I'll see you to-morrow sometime," I concluded. She must have heard the finality in my voice for she was cutting in at once.

"Don't hang up, darling. I've heaps of things to tell you yet. About Harold. I had a report by the evening post. My dear, he's most thrillingly clever, but I've decided to change my mind after all. I think I'll drop the whole thing."

"Sack him, in other words, and pay him off."

"Crude, darling, but that's what I mean. Thank him most frightfully, of course. And the other thing, darling. It's simply too mysterious. Matthews has gone."

"Gone?"

"Darling, how obtuse you are sometimes! Gone. Disappeared. Simply walked out of the house."

"Good Lord!" I said.

"So you see, darling, I was right when I said you should have been here all the time in case anything happened."

"Have you mentioned it to the police?" I asked.

"I'm sick to death of the police," she said peevishly. "The whole house has been overrun with police. Litters of them, my dear, like ferrets. But really, darling, Matthews isn't a case for the police. But I'll explain when I see you."

That was that and quite enough it was. That there was something uncommonly fishy about the disappearance of Matthews I felt in my bones from the first words she had said, and perhaps the reason why I felt that shiver of suspicion was because of yet another suspicion, and one far more vital.

Charlotte had called off her private tec., and after receiving a report that he was hot on the trail of Sivley. That could mean only one thing, that the last thing she wanted was to have Sivley caught. And if that wasn't further confirmation of Frank's startling theory, then, to use his own words, I was no more than a crooner—and my worst enemy would hardly call me that.

CHAPTER VIII
CONFIRMATIONS

I DROVE STRAIGHT to the manor and timed my arrival for three o'clock. By then, I thought, any funeral guests would have departed and on the other hand it would be too early for me to be asked to tea. There were no signs of the police and a couple of gardeners were going over the side verges of the drive with a motor mower.

A parlourmaid admitted me, and she said she thought Mrs. Craigne was in the gardens. I said I'd find her, and then Mrs. Day happened to appear and I asked her about Matthews.

"It's a mystery, sir, and none of us can understand it," she said.

"Anything strange about him on the Sunday, before he left?" I asked.

"He wasn't himself all the afternoon and evening," she said, and seeing a certain look come over my face; "No, it wasn't the master, sir, though I must say he got really worried when we had the news about Mr. Craigne."

"What was Matthews like? Just uneasy?"

"As though he had something on his mind," she said mysteriously. "Like a cat on hot bricks, as they say. It was just as if he couldn't rest or settle to anything. Gave us all the miserables, he did. But there you are, sir; he wasn't the sort you could say anything to."

"Has he any relatives?"

"Only a sister", she said. "She's a widow and has a little shop at Bury St. Edmunds. A fancy shop it is, right against the Abbey."

Through the hall window I caught sight of Charlotte coming towards the house, so I went to meet her. There were cushions on one of the stone seats in the rose garden, so we sat there. At once I was asking about Matthews. From what Mrs. Day had told me I was more than ever sure that what he had meant to tell me was something not only secret but damnably important.

"My dear, isn't it too mysterious for words!" Charlotte said. She was still in decorous black, though the dress had certain frilly features that were not too funereal. Then she was taking a note from the black and white bag she'd been carrying under her arm. "I actually found this stuck in the mirror of my dressing-table."

Miss Charlotte Madam,

"I regret I must go away for a few days on urgent private business, and I'm very sorry I could not let you know as I have only just realised that I must go at once. A friend is waiting for me and I cannot find you to let you know. I take the liberty of leaving this. Mrs. Day knows what to do and it will be as if I am having my holiday.

"Yours respectfully,
"Wm. Matthews."

"It reads just like old Matthews," I said. "But how's it come to be typed?"

"There's a portable in the study we all use," she said. "It's used for all sorts of things. Typing menus and so on. But the signature's his. I know it by various notices he puts up in the servants' hall, about alterations in meal-times and so on, or visitors, or special orders. And I know why he typed it. He was so upset generally that he couldn't trust himself to write. Mrs. Day says he gave them all the willies."

"What'd he take with him?"

"Darling, are you conducting an inquiry?"

I stared. "But I thought you wanted me to help you?"

"Perhaps I did—then. Now I think it was just ridiculous of me to worry, I expect he'll be writing in a day or two."

"Why couldn't he find you on Saturday night?" I persisted.

"Well, my dear, for one thing I was closeted in the study with a perfect darling of a policeman. Warburton, or some name like that. Then the Venter person wanted a statement from me, as if I were in a police court. After that I literally hid myself in the lower terrace garden and I didn't emerge till long after dark. It was lovely there in the cool." She took a cigarette from her case and leaned forward for my lighter. "Then I went up to bed and there was the note. Nobody knew a thing, except Angela—she's the younger parlourmaid—who said she saw him going across the back lawn and making for the drive. Oh, and carrying a small bag and wearing a raincoat. That was about nine or half-past."

Then she was getting up and saying I must see poor Joe's grave. It was under the cypresses in the lower garden, overlooking the valley, but while we were walking there I wasn't thinking about Joe. It was Matthews who worried me. About the whole business there was something remarkably curious, and it seemed to me that I was to blame. If I'd seen Matthews that evening when he was so anxious to speak to me, then whatever had happened wouldn't have happened. That's how vaguely I felt about things, though one fact did give colour to my fears. Charlotte had talked too much to me about Matthews. She'd tried to explain things, or explain them away, and yet there never was a person more utterly contemptuous of reasons.

I don't think I'd have trusted myself as to what I might have said or done if she'd struck a wrong note while we were standing by Joe's grave. By luck she selected the right mood and she manipulated it well.

"A lovely spot, isn't it. Anybody could lie quietly here."

It was a lovely spot, not only for the beauty that lay around it, for the open valley to the south was lovelier still with the green of trees and the snug red of a farm or two and the haze of distant blue among the far elms.

"There's to be a stone surround, and flowers," she was going on. "Heaps of daffodils in the spring. Poor Joe was very fond of daffodils."

The *poor Joe* grated after what I knew, and it was on the tip of my tongue to ask what she'd made out of the murder. Then I put it a different way.

"What relatives are there?"

There were two nephews, she said; sons of Joe's only and younger sister. He had helped with their education when the parents were killed in an air raid in the last war, and now they were in Ceylon.

"Passman's Celebrated Tea," she said with a suspicion of a sneer. "Surely, darling, you've seen it advertised. Well, they're in charge of it. Quite worthy people. One of them was here about two years ago. On leave I suppose you'd call it."

"One of them gets this place?"

"The elder," she said. "And quite right too, I suppose, even if it was ours for hundreds of years."

"And you?" I asked, as we turned back to the house.

"I get fifty thousand cash, darling, and free of tax. And my pick of the cars. And I must tell you this. An annuity of a thousand a year provided I don't cohabit with Rupert. Poor Joe! He couldn't possibly have foreseen . . ." She hesitated as if that train of thought might involve her in difficulties, then went off at right angles. "What a queer word—cohabit. I suppose you and I actually cohabited, darling? I forgot to say that of course there's heaps of charitable bequests."

"And so you're a wealthy woman," I said with as near to a sneer is I dared venture.

"Oh, but I've learned my lesson, darling. I've changed my mind about everything. I'm not staying here, though of course I could for quite a time. The executors were charming about that. No," she said, all at once the woman of affairs, "I shall go to town and live very quietly and then I shall be going to Hollywood with that delightful Mr. Franks. I think he's quite taken with me, darling."

I couldn't help smiling. She was bending artistically over a rose, and the pose would have enchanted Marcus Stone.

"That will be in the autumn?" I asked ironically.

"The fall, darling. That's the expression. I never could quite understand what falls. Perhaps it's the leaves. But I shall be coming back here every now and again. I promised I'd keep an eye on the house, and, of course, there's Joe's grave. And poor Rupert's body may be found in spite of what they say."

"What about our boy? Taking him with you?"

I just had to say that. At the startled look that she flashed at me, I repented of it, but in a second she'd recovered her poise.

"How sweet of you, darling, to ask that! And too paternal!" A dreamy look round and then she was shaking her head. "Fond as I really am of him, I couldn't take him with me. The resemblance is too startling."

"I thought it was I he resembled."

"He does, darling. It's a kind of shot-silk effect. At one moment he's the very image of you, and then it's me. In the photograph it's you he resembled, darling." A sigh. "Poor Bernice! Wouldn't it have been too devastating a shock. But here we are, darling. Just in time for tea."

"I really won't stay," I said. "Haven't booked a room yet, and heaps of things to do. When do you go to town, by the way?"

"Probably to-morrow, darling. Not later than the day after."

She insisted on putting a carnation in a lapel of my coat. I didn't catch her last words as I drove off, but I think they were something solicitous for my welfare at the Oak. I remember that as soon as I was through the gates I ripped out that damned carnation and threw it to blazes. That eased my mind a bit. I could even smile as I substituted her shoulders for the carnation, and I was shaking the innards out of her, or gripping her down on my knee and the same fingers tingling from the welting I'd given to her flaunting backside.

As I entered the front door of the Oak I caught sight of Wharton. His antiquated spectacles were perched on his nose and with the bundle of letters he was carrying to the outside letter-box he looked just like a commercial traveller who has succeeded in making up his week-end accounts. I booked my room and waited for him in the lobby.

"You here again?" was his greeting.

I told him I'd promised Mrs. Craigne to run down in case she needed any help, which she now didn't. I also said that since I was in Brazenoak I was going to have a few days' holiday.

"I'm due back to-night," George said. "One little job to do and I'll probably push off at once."

"Have tea with me," I said, and promptly gave Mrs. Porter the order. "And where's Mr. Franks?" I said. "He might like to join us."

"He's gone into Ipswich with his car," she said. "There's a picture on that he wanted to see. He said he'd be back to dinner, though."

"I told him he ought to have dinner at the White Horse," George cut in. "A bit of Dickens atmosphere for him to take home with him."

George and I had tea out of doors in the pleasant shade of a pollarded elm, and the time for wasps, thank heaven, hadn't yet come. He was quite genial, even if things hadn't gone the way he'd hoped. Nothing whatever had been found among Joe's papers to connect him with the swindle, and there were no mysterious counterfoils of cheques.

"How did you get on with Mrs. Craigne?" I asked.

"Very well indeed" George said, with heavy emphasis on each word. "I think you must have your knife into her, the way you spoke of her."

"Perhaps I was a bit livery," I told him amusedly.

"I found her what I'd call a real nice lady," George went on. "There's always something in the top-notchers that the parvenus can't get."

"What about Sivley?" I said. "The time-table's gone a bit wrong, hasn't it?"

"There may be some news soon," he told me oracularly, and from what followed that remark I knew Frank had put him on to the Salisbury trail. "Did you know that Rogerley has been down here? Actually staying here in this very pub!"

"No!"

"I give you my word it's true", George said. "And he left on the Saturday just before I got here. Not that there was anything in that," he added rather apologetically.

"Good watercress this," I said, as George reached for the last of the sandwiches.

"They feed you well here." The thought put him in an even better humour. "An old friend of ours is due here at five. Like to be there when I ask him a few questions?"

"An old friend?" I asked puzzledly.

"Harper," he said, and I realised with something of a shock that the ex-boxer had been very much of a forgotten man.

George hadn't forgotten him, for he told me things that I didn't know. For instance, when Joe first employed him, Harper was to sleep above the main garage and have his meals in the house, but Matthews and Mrs. Day organised a staff protest and Joe had to give way. Harper still slept above the cottage but got his meals at the second pub, the Lapwings. A curious name for a pub, but lapwings figured in the arms of the Vallants family.

"He's coming here at five because this pub won't be open and he won't attract attention," George explained. "There isn't much to ask him, but it might be as well if I had a witness."

Harper turned up on time. George solicitously met him in the lobby and conducted him upstairs. Harper looked even burlier, perhaps because he was not in his dark livery, and he also looked decidedly uncomfortable. He cast an uneasy look at me, for George didn't trouble to introduce me, and for all he knew I might have been what George would call one of the Big Bugs.

Harper was duly seated. George was at the table, and he produced those spectacles of his and carefully adjusted them. A glance at some papers and he was peering over the spectacles, and his voice was mild.

"We shan't keep you more than a few minutes, Mr. Harper. Just one or two little things to clear up. Everything in strict confidence of course, and"—the most benign of smiles—"no raking up the past, as they say."

Harper ventured on a smile.

"The man Rogerley was staying here last week," George began. "Did you see him at all?"

"No, sir." The answer was like a shot out of a gun. "Didn't see him, sir, or speak to him."

"And Sivley. Did you speak to him?"

"No, sir. I didn't want to have no truck with either of them."

"Sivley didn't interest you."

That wasn't quite Harper's language, and he cocked a questioning ear.

"The less you had to do with him, the better," Wharton translated.

"That's right, sir. It was him who got me in wrong." He gave a quick reminiscent shake of the head. "To tell the truth, sir, I daren't trust myself with him, and that's a fact."

"The truth's an excellent thing," Wharton pronounced. "But just one other question. Why exactly did the late Mr. Passman take you into his service?"

George's brow furrowed as he peered again from over the tops of the spectacles. Harper's answer again came like a flash.

"I reckon he had a kind heart, sir. He told me he'd seen some of my fights and he'd won money over me. A rare generous gentleman, he was, sir."

George shook a sorrowful head. "You know, Mr. Harper, if you hadn't referred so admirably to the value of truth, I'd be inclined to call you, in blunt terms, a pretty good liar."

Harper's mouth gaped. Then he made as if to get to his feet. "If I was you I wouldn't do that, sir. No one ever called me a liar and got away with it."

Wharton grunted. Then he turned to me.

"A pity, don't you think, that Jimmy Speer didn't call Harper a liar in the ring?"

Harper collapsed as if punctured. George had alluded to Harper's last fight when Speer dropped him in the fourth round.

"But talking of liars," George went on, his eyes on Harper again. "You went to see old Mrs. Sivley and were most anxious to know when her son would be back."

"She's an old liar," Harper burst out. "I did go round, I admit that now, but to see her about something else." I could see from his face that he'd thought of something. "The fact of the matter is, sir, that I'm none too comfortable where I am now, and if Sivley had gone for good, then I thought she might take me in. She's a good cook, they reckon. Then while I was there I just happened to ask after Sivley. Just manners, that's all."

"Ah, well," said George with a sigh. "I suppose there's nothing else we want to ask Mr. Harper, is there?"

He winked at me—the eye that was blind for Harper. I had to guess what he wanted me to do, and to this day I don't know if I guessed right.

"Not unless he'd care to tell us the present whereabouts of Sivley," I said.

Once more George was peering inquiringly at Harper. Harper was spreading his palms.

"How should I know where he is, sir? I know no more'n Adam."

"But if you did, then you'd tell all you knew?"

"I would that, sir. All he's done is to do me out of a good job."

That was news to me.

"Yes," Wharton said reminiscently. "Mrs. Craigne told me she wasn't keeping you on."

"She's a—witch!"

"I beg your pardon?" Wharton looked horrified.

"Sorry, sir. I didn't mean that. It just sort of slipped out."

"You'd better keep a watch over your tongue, my man," Wharton told him severely, and when Wharton liked to be severe he could make a man cower. "You can go now. I've finished with you,"

Then, as Harper reached the door: "If anything should occur to you in the course of the next day or two, you can tell it to this gentleman here. But see it's the truth. Good afternoon to you!"

"So he's lost his man," I said as soon as he'd gone.

"He's got another," Wharton said contemptuously. "At the Lapwings. Handy man, and they're thinking of making his training quarters there if the Board allow him to have another fight."

He glanced at his watch. "Well, time I was going. I'm not like some people I know. Hogging the road at sixty miles an hour."

"Glad to hear it," I told him. "I'm a thoughtful driver too. I'd hate to crawl at thirty and hold up traffic."

I saw him off. His last words were to be sure I remembered him to that Mr. Franks, and I was to remind him that if he was in town he would redeem that offer to show him round the Yard. If George had had the least idea of the circumstances in which he was to meet Frank Tarling in town, he'd have foamed at the mouth, fallen in a fit, and the feet of the young men would have carried him out. Isn't that some sort of quotation, and to do with Ananias, you may ask? Well, if there's a better Ananias than

George, I've still to meet him, though I hope his end won't be the same.

It was at about half-past six when Frank came back, and Smith was with him. I gave him Wharton's messages.

"Gosh!" he said. "If that guy ever finds out!"

"Has Wharton seen Smith?" I asked.

"Never clapped an eye on him. Why'd you ask?"

"I'll tell you later," I said. "And what about a tonic out here in the shade?"

We had a couple of drinks apiece, and I told him what little I'd learned from Wharton. It was in Harper that he was most interested.

"I think I know why Passman engaged Harper," he said, and when I wanted to know the answer, he said if I waived my rights as employer, he'd rather keep it to himself for a bit, and test it out further.

We ordered dinner upstairs in my room to give it a kind of christening. Smith was there, ostensibly waiting at table. It was a job he did remarkably well. Frank made him tell me the last trace he picked up of Sivley.

"I don't know if you know that country, sir," Smith said, "but it's all woods and ups and downs, just like this. About five miles from Trimport it flattens out and there's an old brickfield or two. Outcrop of London clay, I reckon. That's where I picked up an old fellow who told me he was coming home that night when Sivley bought the motor-bike, and as he passed a certain spot right against a side lane, he saw Sivley sitting on the bank and the bike leaning against a tree. It was dusk but the old man was sure it was Sivley. He gave him a good-night and Sivley just grunted something. The old boy's theory was that he was waiting for the dark so as to lie rough. There was a haystack in the field opposite. He says he looked at the stack and he saw where someone had slept there. That was the next day."

"The last of Sivley and the last of us," grinned Frank. "Seems I was right about Othello's occupation."

"Oh, no, you weren't," I said, and told him about Matthews. As for the note that Matthews had left, he didn't seem to think there was anything wrong with it, at least as I described it.

"Why do you think it unusual, Mr. Travers?"

"The whole thing's unusual," I said. "For one thing, I think Matthews would have said something to Mrs. Day. For another I don't think he'd have gone before Passman's funeral, with all the work it must have made. Then there was the hush-hush something he wanted to tell me last Saturday night".

"You think the letter ought to have been in his own handwriting?"

"If you mean it was unusual for the letter to be typed, then let's be fair," I said. "Granted that Queenie might have typed it and forged the signature, it still remains that Matthews's hands were very shaky that night. I doubt if he could have written a legible letter."

"The signature was legible?"

"Now you've got me," I admitted. "To the best of my recollection, it was just about and no more. But the main thing as far as we're concerned is this. Why did he go? In the morning you and I are going to Bury St. Edmunds to see his sister, but I'm open to bet anything up to a fiver that she knows nothing about him."

"You think he knew something?"

"Yes," I said. "I think your theory is working out right every time anything happens. I think he'd seen Queenie and Sivley, or even overheard them. Now he's in hiding so that he can't be questioned by the police till everything's over. Then he'll pop out again. And some other things that help your theory," I went on. "Queenie's changed her mind twice. She sacked you because presumably she doesn't want Sivley found. I saw her this afternoon and she's changed her mind about staying in Brazenoak, and that, mind you, after flagrantly forcing me to come here. She says she's going to town, and only coming down here occasionally. Who wants to be in town, in this sweltering heat?"

"I get you," Frank said. "London's the best place in the country to hide in. Sivley's there and they'll get in touch with each other."

"That's it," I said. "And let me tell you this. I was never so furious with that woman as I was this afternoon. If she's guilty of what you and I think she is, then I'll get her if it's the last thing I do. I don't give a damn for what harm she does to me."

There was approval in his nod.

"She's going to town to-morrow," I went on. "Smith will follow her there and from then on she'll be left neither by day or night. I don't care how many men you have to have or what it costs me. She's got to be watched."

"I'll fix it," Frank said. "And what about her bill to date?"

"There's no question of *her* bill," I said, getting everything off my chest. "Everything to date is to go to her account. If she thinks it steep, then what's her fifty thousand for?"

"I think you're right, Mr. Travers," Frank said. "Even that Austrian end was her fault, so to speak. By the way, we ought to be getting some news from there pretty soon. But we've a job for Smith. What about me?"

"Two jobs for you. You'll be here most of the time, and you'll occasionally go to town. Here you'll keep an eye on Harper, Rogerley—if he comes down again—and Queenie when she comes down. You'll also let me know the minute Matthews appears again. If you can pick up anything else, all to the good. To-morrow you'll see Queenie. Arrange to meet her in town. String her along on that Hollywood business. Get pretty close to her. By the way, she let fall that you're pretty close now."

He grinned, but rather wryly. "If I weren't engaged to a damn fine girl, I'd be sleeping with that dame inside a week."

"Don't have any scruples as far as I'm concerned," I told him.

He grinned again, and without reservations. "Boy, oh boy, am I going to enjoy this job!"

"Maybe you will and maybe you won't," I said. "It's Queenie who may decide all that. But I'll be keeping in touch with her in a minor way myself. All of us can compare notes at frequent intervals."

"What about reports from Smith? You want them regular too?"

"I don't want any report at all unless it's about something really worth while," I said. "You know what I mean, Smith?"

Smith gave me a nod, and if one of his eyelids didn't flicker then I'm a torch singer.

CHAPTER IX
END OF A PHASE

THE MORNING DAWNED clear and by nine o'clock, which was the time at which I had breakfast, the sun was comfortably warm. By midday it would almost certainly be tremendously hot, and Porter, the landlord, said there'd probably be thunder.

"If you don't feel like going to Bury, I can slip over myself," Frank told me.

"I've come down here for a holiday," I said, "and a holiday I'm going to have. And we'll go in my car, which'll be so much petrol off the bill."

We got there at about ten and found the little shop without any trouble. As it sold stationery and cheap editions of books as well as wools and women's oddments. I had a good excuse to go in. Matthews's sister was much younger than he, but I saw a resemblance at once. After I'd paid for a bottle of ink and some notepaper, I mentioned that I had come from Brazenoak and was I right in thinking Matthews was her brother.

"Yes, sir," she said at once, her face lighting. "And you know the Manor, do you?"

"Very well, indeed," I said. "I knew it in the old Colonel's time."

She was suddenly giving me a peering kind of look.

"Forgive me, sir, for asking, but might you be Mr. Travers?"

"I am," I said, and smiled.

"I've heard William mention you," she said, and was shaking her head regressively. "Nothing like the old days when all's said and done, sir. There wasn't so much money but there's nothing like working for real gentry. And only Mrs. Craigne left now."

"Yes," I said, and heaved a sigh.

"William has a great liking for Mrs. Craigne," she went on. "And that reminds me, sir. William's gone for his holidays, as you probably know, sir, and Mrs. Craigne sent over specially yesterday to know if he was here. I can't understand him being so absent-minded as not to leave an address."

"I expect he'll have sent one by now. But of course he isn't here," I added archly.

"Not a whole holiday," she said. "He likes to get right away. He generally goes to the Isle of Wight."

I said it had been a great pleasure to see her, and she said the same about me. It was only a quarter-past ten and Frank looked rather surprised when I said we were going straight back.

"You're going to the Manor this morning to do some reconnaissance work," I told him. "We don't want Queenie slipping away and neither of us knowing where."

He liked it no more than I had done when I told him about her having sent over specially to ask Matthews's sister if her brother was at Bury.

"It certainly makes it look as if his going was *bona fide* after all." Then he cheered up a bit. "I don't know, though. That's just the sort of thing a smart dame like her would think of. She sure knows all the answers. But you'd better watch out, Mr. Travers. Suppose the old girl finds out that you've been making inquiries?"

"Very unlikely," I said. "Even if Queenie gets to hear, then I've only done a perfectly natural thing. I happened to be in Bury—taking you round the place as you wanted to see it—and I happened to remember Matthews's sister."

I didn't tell Frank that I wanted him at the Manor because I had a job to do of my own. What I intended to do was to see Harper, and as I didn't know what might arise from the interview, I preferred to keep it to myself.

The village of Brazenoak is crescent-shaped, and lies curled about the Manor, with the pubs at either end. The Lapwings, quite a nice little pub in its way, was slightly nearer to the Manor than the Oak was, and it had also a field-path running through its meadow that brought the Manor nearer still. I was lucky enough that morning to come across Harper weeding a flower-bed that ran along the pub's south-east wall, and I couldn't help thinking of Hercules among the women.

"Morning, Harper," I said genially.

"Morning, sir." He gave me as apprehensive look his fingers went to his cap.

"Busy?" I smiled. "Or can you spare me a minute? Preferably where we can't be overheard."

He took me through the meadow gate to a large open shed where apparently wood was sawn on wet days. I offered him a cigarette, held the lighter for him, and then stoked my pipe. When I went to sit on the sawing-horse he said he'd take that himself and I'd better have the box, and he dusted the top with his handkerchief. That showed we were getting on fine.

"You don't know me, I expect, Harper?"

"I've been thinking, sir, and perhaps I do. Are you the Mr. Travers who was at the Manor the other day?"

"I am. How'd you know I was there?"

"Well, I didn't see you yourself, sir, but you know how things get about. As a matter of fact one of the gardeners recognised you. He said you'd been there years ago."

"True enough," I said, and then gently applied the screw. "Since then I've been doing a certain amount of work for Scotland Yard. Principally with Superintendent Wharton, who saw you yesterday afternoon."

I heard him shift uneasily but I didn't look at him, and I was smiling as I contemplated the bowl of my pipe.

"But I'm not on that business this morning. All I wanted was one little confidential word with you. Highly confidential, in fact, and it's about something that'll surprise you. Yesterday afternoon I heard you allude to Mrs. Craigne as a—witch, was it? . . . Why?"

He gave a titter, which was queer in so big a man. Then he shook his head and scowled.

"That just sort of slipped out, sir."

"But just between ourselves—you meant it?"

He gave me a quick look, saw I was smiling, and then gave a sheepish smile of his own.

"Perhaps I did, sir."

I nodded, then let my face sober. "I might be able to do you a lot of good, Harper What I'm wondering just now is whether or not I can trust you."

"You can trust me, sir," he told me quickly. "I'll swear to that. Nothing you say to me, sir, will ever go out of this shed."

"Very well then, listen to this. I'm supposed to be a friend of Mrs. Craigne, but like you I have my private opinions. As a matter of fact, when I heard you say what you did, I felt like slipping you a fiver."

He stared, then allowed himself to grin. "I wish to God you had sir."

"Right," I said. "So much for me, and now what about you? Why did you call her that?"

"Because that's what she is, sir. There ain't no dirty trick she wouldn't get up to. And she's what they call a tail-switcher."

I raised my eyebrows.

"Like to go into details?"

His eyes shifted from mine, but he was giving a dour shake of the head.

"I'd rather save it up, sir, if you don't mind. I reckon it might come in handy one of these days. But one thing I will tell you, sir. Do you know Breddley Hall?"

"What's that? A place?"

"About ten miles from here. Admiral Moblick has it, and his son. Commander Moblick, is an old flame of Mrs. C.'s. When he got home on leave just after I got down here, she used to slip out at night and drive that little car of hers over there. I know it wasn't till three o'clock one morning when she got back. And now I'll tell you a funny thing, sir. Last Saturday night I saw her going that way again. Just about dusk it was. What time she came home I don't know, because she'd given me the push and a fortnight's pay in lieu of notice. But this is the funny thing, sir. I happened to make an inquiry or two, and the Commander isn't home on leave. He only had five days, the time I told you about; he's been back a week or more."

"Did you actually see her in the car?"

He hesitated, then shook his head.

"I didn't actually. But I knew the car all right, though. You can spot that little car of hers a mile off. I remember I said to myself: 'Now where the hell are *you* off to?' and then tumbled to it. Only I was wrong."

We had lunch in Frank's room and I was full of my Harper story.

"You think she had Matthews in the car with her?" Frank asked.

"Put it all together and see how it adds up," I said. "Matthews goes at dusk and one of the maids sees him sneaking off—that's all you can call it. Queenie is at pains to tell me that she hid herself in a secluded part of the gardens that night to avoid the police."

He nodded. "She discovered what it was that the old boy wanted to tell you, and she smuggled him away. He'd do anything for her," he went on with a reminiscent gaze at the ceiling, "That means she could string him along just as she liked."

"I know where she took him," I suddenly said. "To the cross-roads to meet the late bus. There's a late one to Ipswich on Saturday nights. That's it for a fiver," I went on. "She couldn't have gone far because she was back questioning Mrs. Day and the maids about him that same night, and I guess that'd be before eleven. So there's a job for you. Two jobs, in fact. Find out when she did question Mrs. Day, and also if Matthews took the late bus."

"I'll do that myself," he said. "Smith's leaving for town after lunch. I want him to be there when Queenie arrives. That'll be better than tailing her there. She might get suspicious. And that reminds me. I must ring our people the first thing after lunch. We might get someone planted where she's going."

"You're getting a bit ahead," I said. "Where *is* she going?"

He grinned. "Sorry. I guess I was anticipating a bit."

Then he told me everything that had happened at the Manor that morning. Queenie must have been up all night packing, he said, for there were stacks of luggage. In accordance with the terms of the will, she had taken over the Rolls, but he doubted if all the bags could be piled inside. She was proposing to leave at about four o'clock that afternoon, after an early tea, and her new address was 14 Aubrey Gate. Kensington, which was one of a series of palatial furnished flats. She'd taken it for three months, with option of renewal.

"Then she paid a pretty stiff price," I said. "I know that block of flats well enough."

"Give me fifty thousand and I'd hire the Ritz," he said. "I'm due at this Aubrey Gate place at the end of the week." He gave his usual cheerful grin. "Got an appointment with my tailors, so I'm ringing her up and taking her out to dinner."

"Then for God's sake don't make it the Ritz," I said. "I'm the lad who's footing the bill. But something I wanted to ask you. What've you been kidding her that she can do in Hollywood?"

"The usual dope." he said. "Film face and all that. Between ourselves I think she'd register pretty well. I've got her absolutely red-hot on it."

"Did she mention me at all this morning?" I asked.

He gave me a quizzical sort of look.

"Come on," I said. "You won't hurt my feelings."

"The employer's always right," he told me with a grin. "It was like this. I had to mention you and she wanted to know what I thought of you. I said you were obviously of good family but a bit on the heavy side. She said you were all that, and that stodgy was a better word than heavy. Inclined to platitudes and occasionally pious was the rest of it, and hardly the sort of company for a fine up-standing young fellow like me."

I had to chuckle, even if the chuckle was a bit ironical.

"Perhaps she wasn't too wide of the mark. As for the stodginess, well, we shall see."

*   *   *   *   *

It was striking three on the stable clock when I reached the Manor door, and I knew at once that Charlotte had intended to double-cross me, for the Rolls, loaded with baggage, was ready to move off, and when Mrs. Day unearthed her, she looked ready to move off too.

"Franks tells me you're going," I said accusingly.

"But, darling, I told you myself!"

"I know you did, but you were very vague. And, frankly, Charlotte, you're not giving me a square deal. You get me down here and then clear out yourself. Trouble and expense—"

"Darling, must you brawl?" she asked pathetically. Then she was taking my arm. "Come in the drawing-room for a moment, and then I must fly."

She laid her bag on a side table and then remembered something.

"Oh, you must have my new address. I'll scribble it down for you. And the telephone number. Just a moment, darling. There's paper in the study."

No sooner had she gone than that bag caught my eye. In a flash I was across at it, not that I hoped that she'd be carrying that boy's photograph about with her. That was too wild a thing to hope, and yet there it was, tacked behind an inner flap. Into my pocket it went and I was back on the chesterfield and glancing at *Punch* when she came in.

"Here we are, darling. Wasn't I lucky to get it? I had a brainwave, and phoned. But, my dear, the price they made me pay!"

"You can afford it," I said curtly.

"Darling, please! Must you be so—so—"

"Truthful?"

"Truthful!" Her lip curled. "Truthful Travers. Darling, what a lovely piece of alliteration! When I get to Hollywood I must induce them to put that into a film."

"Good," I said serenely. "When it comes to England I'll go and see it. But there was something I wanted to mention. Something purely personal. Joe sold me a mirror just before he . . . Sorry, I mean when I called to see him that day." She was looking so blank that I added reminders. "You know, when we had duck and green peas for lunch. When he was going to Trimport."

"I know, I know," she said impatiently. "But a mirror! What an extraordinary thing!"

I patiently explained. I said, too, that the executors would have to take my word for it, but that if there was any fuss, then I'd relinquish my claim.

"But, darling, of course you may have it," she said. "Shall we go and see it?"

I led the way along the corridor, and then when we got to the spot where that mirror had hung, there wasn't a sign of it. I stared blankly.

"But there isn't a mirror here!" she said, and laughed. "Darling, you must have dreamt it."

I shook my head. "It was where this print is. Wait a minute!"

I unhooked the print and there beneath it, large though it was, was the clear outline of where the mirror had hung.

"Darling you were right," she said, and looked at me with what I was supposed to take for bewilderment. Then she said: "I know. Ask Mrs. Day."

Ask was the word, if you know what I mean. There was a bell at hand, just inside the study door. But she didn't push it. She had to go and see Mrs. Day personally, and she told me to wait where I was. That told me what had happened. Joe had mentioned the mirror to her, and as she was a bit of a jackdaw, and aware of his ability as a collector, she had guessed the mirror must be valuable, and one of her first tricks after Joe was dead had been to appropriate that mirror. Doubtless at that very moment it was inside one of the trunks in the Rolls. And since it would be too risky to hang it in the new flat, before another day was out it would be sold to a dealer.

But she was coming back, and Mrs. Day with her.

"Of course I remember the mirror, sir," Mrs. Day told me. "Mabel says it was there when she dusted on Saturday meaning but she can't remember if it was there on Sunday. What an extraordinary thing!"

"I shouldn't bother," Charlotte told her. "It'll probably turn up some time."

"I said that to get rid of her," Charlotte whispered to me as the housekeeper went "But, darling, you were very foolish about that mirror. What you did was to arouse Joe's curiosity. You know what he was like in money matters. He must have taken it somewhere himself. He probably sold it."

A glance at her watch and she was saying that she must simply fly. As I scurried after her she was calling back that I must tell Mrs. Day to give me tea, but I caught her up at the car.

"Lucky woman!" I said.

She smiled and her hand went to the clutch.

"What'll you give me for it?"

"Two palatial for me," I said.

"I'll leave it to you in my will, darling," she told me sweetly, as the car moved off.

Even while I was strolling back to the Oak I was already realising what an emptiness everything had now that that overwhelming personality had gone from the Manor. Then I saw things in a different way—that now the cat had gone the mice could play in peace. By some curious telepathy Frank must have become of the same mind, for I found him dozing in a deck-chair beneath the elm.

"Hi, you," I said, and gave him a shake. "Is this the way you earn my money?"

He blinked a bit, then grinned.

"Don't tell me you just happened to drop off," I said. "Take a look at this instead."

He had a look, grinned more widely than ever, and then was asking how I got it. When I'd told him, he had another and a closer look.

"So this is Junior!" He held it at arm's length, and then was giving a sideways look "There's nothing of you here. The funny thing is there's quite a lot like me."

"Why not make a clean breast?" I said, rather cock-a-hoop with the feat of having got possession of the photograph.

"You haven't a photograph of Mrs. Travers by any chance?" he was asking, seriously enough.

I said I never travelled without one and I fetched it from my room.

"What's the idea?" I said. "It's a photograph of Queenie you want."

"No, I'm quite serious," he said. "I've tried the dodge before and it's worked. Married people definitely do come to resemble each other. But I still can't spot anything of the Travers family. As for Queenie, the boy's got fair hair, and he hasn't got her nose."

Then he was all at once rubbing his chin. "Like me to keep this? I think I can do something with it."

"What sort of something?"

"Well, my girl's private secretary to a she Nosey Parker on one of the fashionable illustrateds. The sort of dame who writes chatty notes about duchesses and knows when Lady So-and-so's Peke has pupped. What about having a copy made and handing it over to her?"

I said I thought it was a good idea. I also said it might be a good idea if Frank went to the Manor and fetched the walking-stick he'd left behind that morning, and so found an excuse to question Mrs. Day about the Matthews business.

The late afternoon post brought me a letter from Bernice which Palmer had forwarded. Bernice was having quite a good time and said of course that the only thing lacking to make it a heavenly time was my presence. At the end, in fact as a postscript, she wrote:

"I couldn't understand your references to C. C. . . . . Don't tell me that you and she were once more friendly than you made out!"

The exclamation mark, of course, was to show that while such a thing might have been possible, it was—in her wifely eyes—far from probable. I struck while the iron was hot and wrote a return letter. There was a brief report of the sensational happenings, news of which had not yet reached her in the Continental editions, and then I added my own postscript:

With regard to your postscript, I was just thinking how funny life is. Since our marriage I've been what one calls so much of an old stager that when you mentioned Charlotte to me that morning I didn't think of her as a possible part of my bachelor days. By the way, she's going to America; another case of The Ghost Goes West.

When I'd posted the letter I was feeling on quite good terms with myself. One more postscript, I told myself, and Bernice would know quite enough of one episode of my past. Perhaps I had been right after all in not making a clean breast of things at the beginning, for that might have spoilt Bernice's holiday. Truth without tears, I told myself, and I recalled an old saying of my nurse: "A penny a time, Master Ludo, the same as they pay for pianos."

Half an hour later I was even more on good terms with myself. The time had passed quickly enough, and I had no idea how late it was. It was actually just past seven o'clock, which was dinner-time, so after a quick freshen up I looked round for Frank. I ran him to earth in Mrs. Porter's room where he was at the telephone. He made frantic signs for me to keep away.

I was half-way through the meal when he appeared.

"Not even a half-bottle?" he said, eyebrows raising.

I looked up at him.

"Don't be a piker," he said. "I've got something for you to celebrate."

"The news first and the bottle later," I told him as he sat down. "What is it? Mrs. D. let out something?"

"Mrs D.? Chicken-feed," he said contemptuously. "Preliminary report from our man in Austria. The firm just telephoned me a *résumé*. Thought you'd like to have it before the full report."

"And it's good"

"Good?" He grinned. "Listen to this. The de Karnoviks, or whatever they call themselves, have left Austria altogether, that Hasserbruch place included. She was English and he was an Anglophile, and apparently they bolted from the Gestapo. Living in Dalmatia now, but that didn't worry our man. He scouted round and found two of the old family servants, still living near Hasserbruch. They remembered Queenie perfectly. What's more, the woman swore by all that's holy that Queenie was no more in the family way than she was. She said she ought to know, because her daughter acted as Queenie's maid, and so she'd seen her in her bath."

I let out a breath. I couldn't make any comment. I just smiled inanely and shook my head.

"What's more," Frank went on, "our man got the statement sworn out before a notary, and he's getting the still more important one from the daughter, who's now in service in Vienna. If that hasn't cooked Queenie's goose, then I'm a eunuch."

"Great news," I said. "I don't know whether to feel pleased or to be blazing mad with that bloody Craigne woman. But we've still got to pick up her trail after she got back to England."

He tapped his skull and gave me an even more expansive grin.

"Listen to this for service. Mrs. Day and I had a real good crack this afternoon. By the way, it was about eleven o'clock when Queenie marched downstairs with Matthews's note. But about the other thing. There were me and Mrs. D. sitting in the study as snug as two bugs in a rug and she telling me all the family history. Then I remembered that little bit about Queenie's return. She remembered it all right. Queenie brought Matthews a beer mug as a present and Mrs. D. an embroidered tea-cloth or something."

He consulted his note-book. "Know any people called Scott-Fenley, or anything like it?"

"Scott-Fennerley?"

"That's probably it," he said. "I daren't ask her to repeat the name and I only guessed it was double-barrelled. Bet those were the people Queenie went with after she got back from Hasserbruch. They have a big yacht apparently, and Queenie and Mrs. Scott-what's-her-name picked it up at Marseilles. Queenie came back six weeks later."

"The Scott-Fennerleys are the big coal people," I said. "She's a fast mover, like Queenie."

"Well, you bet your life Queenie wasn't confined on board that yacht," Frank said. "That's as sure as that I'm sitting here without a drink."

"Well, you've earned your bottle," I said, and looked round for Mrs. Porter. Then I changed my mind.

"Damned if I'll buy you a drink," I said.

"You won't!"

"No," I said. "But next Saturday you can take Queenie to the Ritz after all."

II
—AND AROUND—

CHAPTER X
SHORT INTERVAL

WHEN I LOOK BACK I see that that evening was a very definite end to that part of this story in which the initiative lay in the enemy's hands. Thereafter it passed to us, though not immediately, for we had to wait till he made a false move, or perhaps I should have said *she*. Also there were one or two things to clear up, and they too had a bearing on what was to happen.

Frank came into my bedroom the following morning and found me sitting up and emptying the teapot. By the way, I'd bought a bottle after all, and after that we had thought it as well to patronise the Lapwings, and it was natural that I should wake with a considerable thirst.

"Still thinking of going back to-day?" he wanted to know.

"Either just before lunch or just after," I said. "And did we say farewell last night, or did I dream it?"

"Better draw a veil," he said. "But I'm just off to Ipswich to pick up the Matthews trail."

"Then you'd better put on one of your false moustaches," I told him. "Ipswich isn't too far away and you're a public character."

He grinned. "Don't worry. I'm the original rubber-faced man. If Barnum were still alive I'd be making a fortune." He held out his head. "Good-bye, sir. As soon as there's anything to ring up about, I'll let you have it."

Before I could ask what was the idea of the *sir* business, he had gone. As I began dressing I heard his car move off, and as I followed it in my mind I suddenly thought of something. You know how it is when you get good news, and overnight at that. In the morning you wonder if it is so good after all. So when I suddenly thought of May Bullen, I knew I might do worse than pay her a call, for she might reinforce what Frank had picked up from Mrs. Day about Charlotte's movements after that Austrian trip.

I kept on after breakfast, working out all the questions, and then I heard a car drive up. In a couple of minutes Venter was making for me.

"Hallo, Inspector," I said genially. "How are you?"

"Not too bad, sir," he told me gloomily. "Sorry to worry you, but I wondered if you could give me some information."

"I can try," I said, and was wondering what the devil he wanted to know.

"It's about Matthews, that butler up at the Manor," he said. "I got a statement from him and thought he was our star witness. Then it turned out that he wasn't the one who last saw Mr. Passman alive. It was one of the maids. He rang for her because he found some dust on something."

"Funny," I said, playing for time. "I mean that his last act should have been to worry about a bit of dust."

"Then this Matthews disappears," he went on, ignoring my philosophising, "and there're one or two things I want to ask him. The coroner was very decent about it, but I want him. I wondered if you had any ideas."

"But, my dear fellow," I protested, "why should I have any ideas? I wasn't here for the inquest. Besides, it was all cut and dried, they tell me. Only one possible verdict."

"It isn't exactly that," he said, and apparently hardly knew where to go on. "I wondered if you had any ideas, as I said. Where he might have gone and why. I've been on the telephone to Mrs. Craigne again and she can't help. She's as mystified as everybody else. So's everybody at the Manor."

Well, I thought it best to tell him that I knew. Mrs. Craigne had mentioned the mystification to me, and as I had happened to be in Bury I'd called on the sister.

"I've been there myself," he said, "and she told me you'd inquired. That's what made me wonder if you knew anything. Now I see it doesn't help," he went on regretfully.

"All I can suggest is that you try the Isle of Wight place where he often took his holidays," I said. "But if you're going to ask me why he should decide at that of all moments to take French leave and go for his holiday, all I can say is I haven't a notion." Then a happy theory presented itself. "Unless, of course, he had brainstorm. He's not so young and the day's happenings might have thrown him off his balance."

That cheered him up. He thanked me profusely and off he went, and I was hoping to heaven that Frank would have sufficiently rubber a face to leave behind in Ipswich no possible connection with the wealthy American of the Oak. Change of accent wouldn't be enough, and if Venter found that some unauthorised person had been making inquiries, there'd be a tremendous flutter among the official dovecotes. Frank could always swing clear, but what if anything were traced to me?

The thought made me uneasy, so I got out my car at once and drove the few hundred yards to Pennygate Farm. A worn brick path led to the front door, and as I looked round I saw a movement among some red-currant bushes. Then the picker straightened herself and I guessed she was May Widger.

"Good morning," I said, and made my way across the ruins of what had been a bed of spring cabbage.

"Good morning," she said. "Did you want to buy some currants?"

She was a very fine figure of a woman. A few years before, when she was more in the bud stage, she must have been a real beauty, but now she was the least bit blown. There was no wonder, I thought, that Widger had married her, offspring and all.

"I'm sorry," I said. "I just came along for a little gossip, but you're busy. I'll come some other time."

She looked puzzled as well she might.

"Mr. Franks, the American gentleman who's been staying at the Oak, happened to mention you," I said. "Then I remembered you and I wondered if you remembered me. Also I saw some people the other day who were asking after you. The Scott-Fennerleys."

She set down her basket and came out from the bushes, and she was smiling.

"Really, sir? And how is Mrs. Scott-Fennerley?"

"Very well indeed," I said. "You're looking well too. I never actually saw you but I used to hear Mrs. Craigne mention you in the old days."

Suddenly her face flushed. A look that might have been called brazen came over it, but I knew afterwards that it had been a kind of heroic facing up to the fact that there were things that I must know.

"Excuse me, sir, but are you Mr. Travers?"

I nodded and smiled.

"I ought to have guessed you were," she said, and looked away.

"Well, it's nice to have found you looking so well," I said. "I'll tell Mrs. Scott-Fennerley about you. By the way, there's something I'm wondering. Mr. Franks and I were having an argument the other night. You remember Mrs. Craigne coming back from a visit to Austria. The last one she made, not long before her marriage?"

She remembered.

"Well," I said, "she went off again almost at once, and with the Scott-Fennerleys. A cruise in the Mediterranean, I think it was."

At once she was confirming the whole thing. Her face colour-ed again as she said she wasn't in Mrs. Craigne's service at the time, but in Brazenoak, where she always had all the Manor news. I beamed and said that confirmation would cost Mr. Franks a half-crown. Then she was referring to the tragedies connected with the Manor, and I couldn't help noticing that she touched very lightly on the Rupert Craigne side, and she didn't mention Sivley. I didn't either, for I didn't want to hurt her feel-ings, and I somehow felt I was being a pretty considerable sort of swine as it was.

I did ask for her husband, and she said I'd passed him on the field by the pond. He was just clearing up the last of the hay, but the season hadn't been any too good. We smiled at each other like old friends as we shook hands. My smile was partly for myself, for it was good to know that Charlotte was now where I wanted her, even if it was hard to see for the moment just what use I could make of the initiative which now seemed to be mine.

I slowed down the car as I came to the pond field. A man and a boy were carting rakings to top the stack in the field corner, and I guessed that the man who was raking down the stack was Widger. He, too, was a fine figure, tall and with powerful shoul-ders, and his arms and face were burned near black by the sun. He didn't notice me, and I shouldn't have spoken if he had, for I had more than an idea that May would not mention my visit. What I did think of was what he had been supposed to say about Sivley, that if he turned up in Brazenoak he'd run him out. Hot air, perhaps, and yet who knew? Perhaps Sivley *had* left Bra-zenoak because Widger had threatened him. Perhaps Sivley had told himself that since he now had no home at all, he might as well fulfil his own boast and do in Craigne and Passman, and then do in himself.

For I was now of the strong opinion that Sivley had done himself in. The papers had no news of him, beyond the usual foolish rumours that he had been seen in places whose remote-ness one from another made them cancel themselves out. And if he were alive, I thought to myself, remembering those shoulders and arms of Widger, then it was probably a long way from Brazenoak that Sivley was in hiding.

The morning was still young and so I decided not to stay on for lunch but to get back to town straight away, though what I should do there I had no idea. Spend a bit of time at the club again, perhaps, or watch some cricket and tennis, and I might put in a week-end with my sister. But things didn't quite work out that way. Those were the restless days when Hitler was trying on Poland the same technique that had engulfed the Czechs. Every morning was producing a new crisis, and I for one found it impossible to settle to anything. But I did have the case to think about when I could get my mind off Hitler.

The evening after my return Frank rang up the flat. I was out but he left a message with Palmer, that he'd be seeing me at the garage at nine o'clock on what he was pleased facetiously, or diplomatically, to call St. Ritz's Eve, which was of course the Friday. Meanwhile there was still nothing in the papers about Sivley, except an occasional mention that he was still at large. And there was nothing from Frank about Matthews. That was the really puzzling thing.

And it was the first thing Frank mentioned that Friday night. Matthews had definitely not been on that Ipswich bus; he had not taken the train from the nearest station—and he had not hired a car from any nearby village.

"Queenie must have had him in the car with her that time when Harper saw her," he said. "She's parked him somewhere safe."

"I wouldn't be surprised if he's in Brazenoak itself," I said, and a good many days were to pass before I knew how near the truth I had been.

"Talking of Harper," Frank said, "he and I are buddies. If I stay on, he's going to give me lessons in boxing. And, boy, does he love Queenie!"

"We've got an asset in Harper if we know how to use him," I said, and again I didn't know how near I was to the truth.

"Oh, and another curious thing," Frank was going on. "I dropped into the private bar the other night for my usual friendly one, and Widger was there with several of the village big shots. You remember Widger? Husband of May Bullen that was. Well, they were having an argument about Sivley and I chipped in to keep the game going. Widger was saying nothing and looking as if he was the real wise guy if only he took the trouble to open his mouth. We went on arguing and I said Sivley might still be in Brazenoak. One man said the police were watching his mother's cottage day and night. Either that or something else was too much for Widger and he couldn't keep his mouth shut any longer. 'He ain't in this village,' he said. 'How do you know?' I came at him. 'A lot'd like to know that,' he said. He's a surly devil, by the way. 'A lot'd like to know that, but you can take it from me he'll never be seen in Brazenoak again. Nor yet anywhere else.' I stared and we all stared. Then he finished his beer, said good night and out he went. I asked the company what he'd meant and they said—I haven't quite got the dialect—that they reckoned he'd just been a talkin'. And what do you make of that?"

"Damn little," I said. "If he'd been talking about Matthews I'd have been more interested."

His face fell.

"Come on," I said. "Let's go and get a drink. And tell me the latest about Queenie."

He said she was living just the quiet life she'd announced, and that was a fact we both found highly significant.

"All she's been doing is making the rounds of the stores," Frank said. "When I got in touch with Smith this evening he told me he'd seen more knicks and camisoles this week than'd stock Solomon's harem."

"I reckon Joe's turning in his grave," I said. Then I thought I'd tell him about the mirror, and over our second round of drinks I let him know the dirty trick Queenie had played.

"If she's got the mirror in the new flat, I might be able to do something," he said. "We've someone planted there who can give her rooms the once-over."

"I'll drift round some of the nearby antique shops to-morrow. I want something to do. This case is working out all wrong," I said. "Here's me spending my capital for you to have a damn good time, and I've nothing to do to pass the time away."

He grinned. "Well, Queenie's bill will reach you to-morrow morning. There'll be a job for you, inspecting the items. But don't forward it on to her before Monday. I want her to have a good time to-morrow. Poor soul, she needs some sympathy."

"Sympathy, hell."

"Yes," he said. "Sympathy. How'd you like to have been a mother for three weeks and then be told it was all a mistake."

The bill arrived next morning and I re-posted it the same night. My afternoon had been spent in the antique shops but I heard nothing about the mirror I'd regarded as mine. On the Sunday morning Frank rang to say there was no sign of it at the flat. I could see his grin as he said he'd had a great time with Queenie.

"Dancing till three," he said, "out in the long grass at a Palais de Danse. Saw the lady home and didn't even go in for a kipper. Just off now to Brazenoak. Any fresh orders?"

Only the old ones, I said, and he was telling me it was a shame to take my money. He did add that his girl's Nosey Parker of the illustrated had a certain photograph and thought she could do something with it.

The tempo slackened still more. Nothing about Sivley and nothing about Matthews, and, what was more important, nothing noteworthy about Charlotte Craigne. On the Wednesday evening Frank rang me from the Oak.

"Some good news for you," he said. "Nosey's tracked down the photograph."

"Good for Nosey, then," I said.

"It was published in *Haut Ton*. Don't know if you've seen it, but it's a very Ritzy and expensive illustrated. Junior turns out to be the son of the Hon. Marigold Menham, and heir to the Wessborn title. Nosey says you can get a reproduction of any picture in *Haut Ton* by sending so much to their special department. They make packets out of it, she says. And that's how Queenie gave birth to Junior."

"My God, we've got her!" I said, and almost added Harper's pet name. "To clinch it, you'd better get a record of the transaction at the *Haut Ton* department."

"It might be risky work," he said, "but I'll see what can be done. And mightn't we recall our Austrian man? We seem to have all we want."

"Might as well cut down unnecessary expenses. I sent your people a cheque, by the way, and I've sent the bill to Queenie. The next thing is to collect her cheque. I'll make an excuse to see her if she doesn't send me it. But I'm most damnably grateful to you, Frank. You've put in some fine work."

"All part of the Prince and Holloway service," he told me. "But I'm glad that part has turned out so well. And, honestly, Mr. Travers, don't you think I'm wasting my time here? Absolutely nothing doing except picking up gossip. Queenie's coming down on Friday, but what can I do with her?"

"Have her watched every minute," I said. "Put a special man on, especially at night." Then I thought of something else. "Any chance of having a look in her bedroom before she comes down, in case that mirror's there?"

He said he'd have a try. Mrs. Day might be induced to show an interested American over the house.

"As for leaving Brazenoak, you stay put," I said. "I've got a hunch you're in the right place. No news of Matthews?"

"Devil a sound."

"Well, keep your ear to the ground. And, once more, thanks enormously. I beg your pardon; thanks a million."

I suppose I ought to have been elated that that blackmail scheme had been finally uncovered. I tried forcing myself to be, and even then I couldn't manage it, for deep down somewhere was a tremendous uneasiness. This is how I began to see things.

The blackmailing of myself had served its purpose and Charlotte would probably be highly amused if I confronted her with the full exposure. She wouldn't even trouble to deny the trick she had played on me. And why? Because, as I must repeat, *the purpose of that scheme had been achieved*, and now she had no more use for me than last year's hat.

Now follow the argument carefully. Frank's theory, and subsequently mine, was that she was working with Sivley and had been a party to the deaths of her husband and stepfather. Therefore, if Charlotte could afford to dispense with me—and remember she had not rung me up since I returned to town—she must be absolutely sure that Sivley would never be caught, and could never testify against her. In other words, it looked as if we could never pin anything on her. It also explained why she had told the truth for once when she announced that she would have a quiet time in town. Why shouldn't she have a quiet time when she had nothing to fear!

But I am an obstinate sort of person. Far more cunning ones than even Charlotte Craigne had slipped up, I told myself, and began a methodical review of the whole affair with the hope of finding some such slip. After a laborious hour I was left with two things. The disappearance of Matthews was the only tangible thing with which we might connect her. The other seemed at first more promising, but when I got to grips with it, it petered out to nothing. It was this, that Charlotte Craigne had taken me to Trimport so that I—a person of repute with the police—could prove if necessary that she had had nothing whatsoever to do with the deaths of her husband and stepfather.

There everything worked in, and perhaps you see how. She had never been suspected. Because of my statement and her own—and the two dovetailed—there had never been the slightest suspicion of any implication on her part. All the police had given was sympathy. I repeat again: the object of getting me to Trimport had been achieved and she knew she was henceforth safe.

But was she? What had she been doing during that considerable time when I was absent with Mason and the others on Trimport beach? I doubt if she could have got back to Brazenoak and returned, for that would have been incredibly risky, both for a mad drive in those narrow lanes, and because of my possible return at any moment. But mightn't she have aided Sivley's getaway? Mightn't she have done other things of which I couldn't at the moment think?

I told you that second idea was very nebulous, but there it is. And the whole thing was very disquieting. Sivley must have left the country, I thought, or else Charlotte must have met him in town. And she hadn't met him unless she was too clever for Smith, and personally I was betting on Smith. And generally I was getting bored to tears in town, what with the depressing news in the papers and being alone and getting no new hunches about Charlotte Craigne. And then on the Friday morning she actually rang me up.

"How are you, darling? I've been frightfully busy, but I'm simply conscience-smitten at not having seen you."

"I'm pretty fit," I said. "And you're having a good time, are you?"

"You sound very gloomy, darling? What's worrying you?"

"I don't know," I mumbled. "All these crises get one down."

She laughed. "Cheer up, darling, there won't be a war. The papers say there won't. Besides, I met an awfully important person the other day, and he's positive. And sorry I must fly now, darling. Just running down to Brazenoak. All that tiresome business for the executors."

Remember how sure she was about there being no war. It may come in handy when you start putting things together.

I didn't know it, but my brief leisure was almost at an end, and the second phase of the action was about to begin. Ten minutes or so after I had hung up, the telephone bell went again. Who should it be but George Wharton.

"So you're having a nice quiet holiday," he said, after the politer preliminaries. "Nothing to do with yourself."

"Haven't I earned a holiday," I demanded aggressively.

He ignored that. "Still, I'm glad you're free. I told the Powers-that-Be that I thought you'd be available."

"Available for what?"

"A real nice job," he said wheedlingly. "Practically all beer and skittles—especially for you. A few days at a certain country spot, with a nice little pub as headquarters."

You see how the crafty old hellion swindled me? Lured me into saying I had nothing to do, and then sprang the trap.

"To do what?" I asked none too pleasantly.

"The county people are worried about not getting their hands on a certain Mr. S., and they've put everything in our hands. This evening suit you for going down there?"

"My car or yours?"

"You don't get me in that hell-waggon," he chuckled. "Perhaps we'd better go independently. We might want to use both cars."

"I still don't see what use I'm going to be," I protested, though I was pleased enough at the prospect. "Unless you want me to crack your quips on."

"But my dear fellow! You'll be every possible use. Weren't you on the spot, and don't you know everybody?"

"Right-ho, George," I said, and tried to make it wearily. "I'll get down just before dinner. And the drinks are on you."

You see why I was pleased? George represented supreme authority. While Frank and I could do little about those two ideas of mine, it would be very different if I could just hint about Matthews to him, and that Charlotte Craigne had been alone for best part of an hour. Wharton would worry the guts out of those two ideas like a pup with a shoe, and he'd have everything behind him.

I thought I'd wait till lunch-time before ringing up Frank, and then it so happened that he rang me instead.

"Glad you were in," he said. "I've found the mirror!"

"The devil you have!"

"Yes. I worked that gag I thought of and we arrived at Queenie's bedroom. I admired the view and Mrs. D. told me the two wardrobes were locked—I had admired one of them—and that Queenie had given strict orders nothing was to be touched till she came down again. I'd left my camera downstairs purposely, and I said I ought to take a picture of the view from the window. 'Don't you bother, sir,' says Mrs. D., and goes down for the camera. I tried some keys on a wardrobe and, boy, did I get a kick when I saw that mirror! Tucked away behind some frillies."

"Fine work, that," I said. "No danger of Mrs D. letting on you were in there?"

"Never a bit. Didn't I say Queenie had given strict orders? Mrs. D. wouldn't let her know."

"Any chance of getting hold of the mirror?"

"Any chance?" He snorted. "You give the word, Mr. Travers, and I'll have it the first night after Queenie goes—if it's still there."

"I don't know," I said. "A bit too risky perhaps. I'll talk about it later. And you're not lunching with Queenie then?"

"Going to tea," he said. "Still some strawberries in the Manor gardens."

"Then save some for the Oak," I said. "I'm coming down for dinner to-night."

When I told him about Wharton he gave a cynical chuckle. I had a very early tea, with no strawberries, and at four o'clock was on my way. Though I didn't see it in quite that way, the second phase had begun.

III
—AND COMES OUT HERE

CHAPTER XI
THE OLD FIRM

WHARTON AND I reached the Oak within five minutes of each other, which means that I almost caught him up. He had booked rooms for us both, and it didn't feel too bad to be staying at that excellent pub at the public expense. Of Frank there was no sign and I guessed he was having a long session at the Manor. George and I had a clean up and then drinks in his room to wash the dust from our gullets, and in that half-hour before dinner he told me a good many things. He admitted that they weren't his own, but reports he'd collated from Venter and the Trimport police. This is what the official sleuths had so far unearthed.

Sivley had taken a tiny bungalow at Trimport, giving the name of Shipleigh. The bungalow had been advertised unfurnished, in the local papers, and the estate agent's young clerk—it was a small, two-man firm—recognised Sivley from his photograph. A quarter's rent had been paid in advance and the key handed over, and that was on the morning after the day of Sivley's departure from Brazenoak.

Sivley had come by motor-bike, though the clerk had only heard it and not seen it. No finger-prints were found in the bungalow, except one of Sivley's on a dirty tin plate off which he had doubtless had a meal, but there were marks of his motor-bike tyres in the sand outside the back door, and some drops of oil. The bungalow had no neighbours within two hundred yards. Both it and they were comparatively secluded being set in the woody scrub with which all that hinterland abounds, but this particular bungalow was of a type that Trimport strongly resented, with flimsy walls and pink asbestos tiles. It lay in that hinterland exactly a hundred and fifty yards back from the beach and to the west, which was handy for the getaway. As for the weapon Sivley used, it needn't have been a rifle of large calibre since he had been lucky enough to hit his man either in the heart or *near it*. Nor need he have been a particularly good shot, for Craigne had presented a magnificent target. No empty cartridge case had been found.

There was also no sound of his motor-bike leaving. Perhaps he had parked it a little distance along the road, which would have been somewhere not too far from my car, and I pricked my ears at that, remembering how Charlotte Craigne had been alone for well over half an hour. In any case, Wharton said, Trimport was a great place for motor-bikes. All the young pip-squeaks in the place were always dashing about on them, and generally with wenches on the pillions. Moreover, when Sivley made his getaway all eyes were still on Craigne's boat, and hardly anyone realised a shot had been fired.

Wharton said, too, that there had been a tip that Sivley might be with Rogerley; in fact he admitted that Mr. Franks had put the idea in his mind. But Rogerley's place had been watched and nothing had happened. As for why the trainer had come to Brazenoak, and at a busy time in the racing season, the reason was given that he had hoped to find Craigne there. Craigne owed him a considerable sum of money, and since the winnings from the first faked telegram had never been recovered, Rogerley hoped Craigne would be in the funds. And if Craigne himself wasn't there, then he made no bones about admitting that he'd intended to approach Craigne's wife or his stepfather-in-law.

"I saw him myself about that," Wharton said. "He was a liar. I saw it in every word he said. But what's the use? I can't prove it."

There was no need for me to mention Matthews, for George mentioned him himself as an inheritance from Venter. Venter had even got Mrs. Craigne to send on the actual note that Matthews had written.

"You and I might do worse than go to the Manor after dinner and try to check up on the signature," George said.

"But who could have forged it?" I asked with a fine assumption of indignation. "Surely you don't suspect Mrs. Craigne?"

"Of course not," George said, and didn't rise to the hint. "But it's an essential document, isn't it? It's got to be certified as genuine."

He then told me that Matthews hadn't gone to his usual spot in the Isle of Wight, and was then demanding why he should have gone there. That was a sideways cut at me for having suggested it to Venter. Then he admitted that the note read far more as if Matthews were suffering from delusions.

"I made that suggestion too," I said. "Now I come to think of it, however, I'm of the opinion that if he had a breakdown it was an uncommonly sudden one. The brain doesn't snap in an afternoon."

"Then where is he?" Wharton demanded with utter unreasonableness.

"Ask me another," I said, and suddenly I knew that I might have said "Probably dead!" For if Matthews had seen Charlotte Craigne and Sivley, then his life wouldn't have been worth a lot. Probably Charlotte set Sivley on him. After two killings Sivley wouldn't scruple about a third. Mind you, that was a tremendous idea, and at the moment it merely flashed through my mind, though I thought about it a lot in the course of the next few hours. What I then hoped was that Wharton would hit on the same idea. If only the body of the butler could be found, then he might work back to Sivley and even to Charlotte Craigne.

I think that was really why I didn't hint to him about her having been alone near that bungalow for quite a time on that fatal Saturday morning. Also it was my new policy not to know too much about anything, or before I was aware of it I'd be giving myself away.

"What do you think about that?" Wharton was saying.

"About what?" I said, and pulled myself together.

"Why about seeing old Mrs. Sivley?"

"A very good idea," I said. "But didn't I hear the gong go? I don't know about you, but I could eat a couple of meals."

As we got up to go I was telling him about Widger, giving it of course as village gossip. George grunted, but halted nevertheless on the stairs to make a note in his book. When he got to the lobby, there was Frank. He could assume quite a dignity when he liked, and now there was something exquisitely natural in his surprise at the sight of Wharton and me, his smile, and the quiet way his hand went out.

"My, my, my! Two excellent surprises! How are you, sir? And you, Mr. Travers."

Wharton's face was beaming too. I never knew him cotton on so quickly to anyone before. Maybe he thought he was being friendly on behalf of the British Isles.

"Have a drink," Frank said. "What shall it be?"

"We've just had our ration," I told him. "But you join us at dinner. Mrs. Porter will fix a table for three."

"How much longer are you staying here, Mr. Franks?" asked Wharton as the first course arrived.

"That's hard to say, Superintendent," Frank began. Wharton held up a warning hand.

"Mr. Wharton down here. I don't want to broadcast what I'm here for."

"Mr. Franks is a man of discretion," I put in. "I expect between ourselves, he's a pretty shrewd idea what we're here for."

"I guess I'm not going to let that part of it interest me," Frank said. "You two gentlemen have been mighty good to me in one way and another, and I guess it's your company I'm interested in, not your business. All the same," and he smiled ruefully, "I reckon I ought to have had more sense. You see, I always wanted to be a detective myself."

Wharton was politely amused.

"Yes, sir," Frank went on. "I guess you two gentlemen will find this amusing, but I once took a mighty expensive correspondence course in the arts of detection." The smile became more rueful. "Guess we've all felt in need of a hobby, only mine was a bit more . . ." He evidently couldn't find the word. "Guess I've got myself all balled up."

"You people in the States are ahead of us in a lot of things," Wharton said generously, "and the art of detection's one of them. Rather a high-flown title for a job like mine."

"Look here, George," I said, as if suddenly inspired. "Why shouldn't we make use of Mr. Franks? Diplomatically, I mean. He's the most popular man in these parts nowadays, and especially well in with everybody at the Manor. A great friend of Mrs. Craigne, for instance."

Wharton was actually looking interested.

"I guess that's some kind of flattery," Frank said with the same rueful smile. "I admit I had tea with Mrs. Craigne this afternoon, and I've just seen her on her way back to town, but that doesn't qualify me for Mr. Travers' nice remarks. But thanks for the publicity, Mr. Travers."

"Mrs. Craigne was at the Manor?" Wharton asked.

"Just a quick visit," Frank said. "A few personal belongings she wanted to get to her flat in town."

"You'll be interested to hear that Mr. Franks may be having boxing lessons from Harper," I told Wharton.

"Another hobby?" asked Wharton.

"Not exactly. I laze about here and I eat and drink and I ride everywhere. That doesn't do a man's figure much good. But I reckon these lessons will have to be postponed. A day or two and I'll be humping my pack. There's a whole lot more of this country I want to see before I sail for home."

Wharton, patriotic to the point of jingoism, was promptly advising on what to see. I said he'd left out Canterbury. The first place I'd take any stranger to was Canterbury, I said, with its superb evocation of our history. The argument got a bit warm, and it was still on after coffee, and then Wharton happened to notice the time and began getting to his feet.

"A little job I must do at the Manor. I don't know if you two gentlemen would care for a stroll and a look round the gardens?"

He went up to his room to fetch something. Frank whispered to me that Queenie had probably taken the mirror to town, for she had brought a very large trunk with her and it had gone back in the car. If I liked he'd break in that night and find out. He had a key to the study, he said.

"Wait a minute," I said. "I've got an idea."

It was a tremendous idea, for all at once it had come to me just why Charlotte Craigne had taken that mirror. So I sprinted up the stairs and came down again on Wharton's heels. When we were nearing the Manor I ventured to make a suggestion.

"Would you mind, George, if I showed Mr. Franks the study? He tells me he's never seen inside, and he might like to visit the actual site of a murder."

Frank said he didn't want to mess up Wharton's arrangements. Wharton, in excellent spirits that evening, said he'd have shown Franks round if he wasn't going to be busy. And when we got to the house he had a word with Mrs. Day about us before he went off to check up on the Matthews signature.

The study part of the house was incredibly quiet, with only the faint sound of a wireless programme coming from the servants' quarters. There was just the danger that someone might appear from the middle passage that led backwards from the main corridor, but I was more anxious about Wharton, the craftiness of whose mind one could never fathom. Maybe he guessed I was up to something which I had no particular wish for him to know, and in that case he'd probably appear when least wanted.

"We've got to work quick," I told Frank. "If he pops in at the wrong moment, then I shall have to tell him about the mirror."

He wondered what I was talking about, and I could only explain as I went along. Out of the big inner pocket of the tweed sports coat I produced a goodish-sized shaving mirror. The print was stood on the floor and with a piece of string I'd had sense enough to bring, I hung my mirror where the Adam mirror had been. Then we both had a look inside it.

"I get you," Frank said. "Looks as if we've got something here."

Even in that small mirror we could see clearly the side door of the study, and through it to the shrubbery beyond the tiny width of lawn. That was enough for us and in a moment or two we had the print back on the wall and the shaving mirror was in my pocket.

"Let's get out round the gardens where we can talk," I said. "You're supposed to have seen the study if Wharton asks questions."

We found a useful spot where a seat was recessed into a yew hedge, and if Wharton came along we were obviously admiring the view across the valley.

"Funny how I should miss that point about your mirror," Frank said ruefully.

"I missed it myself," I said, "but it's clear enough now. It's one of the things we can be dead sure of from now on. Matthews saw something in that mirror. What, we don't know, and it's no use guessing. My own idea is," I said, eating my own words, "that Queenie must have had an appointment at some time or other with Sivley in that handy bit of shrubbery, probably when Joe was watching cricket at Trimport. You can get to it by the back way from the garage without being seen in the house. That was what the old boy couldn't understand after the murder, and what he wanted to ask me about. He probably thought I could give some explanation. Queenie overheard him talking to me, and when I'd gone she got him in a corner and wheedled or threatened everything out of him. She pitched him some yarn about going somewhere with her that night, where he'd hear some astounding revelations that'd ease his mind. That sounds wild, but it's good enough as a makeshift. She imposed secrecy on him, she typed the letter and added his signature, and she met him at some quiet spot in her car. As we know, he'd have done anything for her and she could twist him round her finger. Where she was concerned he'd be as credulous as a kid with a bedtime story."

"And where's she parked him?"

"Parked him?" I said, and my lip rather curled.

He gave me a look, and then gave a low whistle. "I get you. She got in touch with Sivley that same night and Sivley did the old fellow in."

"You've got it," I said. "And, by God, she's going to swing for it."

"Yes, but she had it pinned on her," he said, and shook his head. "It'd take ten thousand men to begin searching this countryside for newly turned earth, and dragging ponds."

"I know," I said. "All the same there're ways and means. I've got one or two in my mind now. For instance, you must tell Wharton that our mention of Harper to-night made you recall something. You've been upset about Matthews like everyone else connected with this place, and you wondered if there was any connection with a remark Harper had let fall about seeing Queenie's car that night. If necessary you can bring it all out as an instance of what a liar Harper is. You think out your own approach. All I'm interested in is getting Wharton interested, and let me tell you this. Once he gets his teeth into anything, he'll never let go. If Matthews is to be found, he'll find him, even if he has to mobilise an army corps."

"When do I start talking? On the way back?"

"The sooner the better," I said. "And one other thing, this time at Queenie's end. You've got to disappear out of her young life sooner or later, haven't you? I mean, you can't let that Hollywood hooey get so far as quitting her at the dock side. And another thing. If Wharton, or ourselves, should uncover anything and she thinks this country a bit too unhealthy, she may decide to leave. Also my idea is that she may be leaving pretty soon. She was always one to do things and funk the consequences, and I'll bet she's wishing she could be somewhere where there weren't so many reminders. That's why she's got an advance from the executors and has been splashing the money on clothes. She's thinking about impressing Hollywood—and you, too, perhaps."

"I'm inoculated," he said, and gave his cynical smile.

"Well, here's the line of talk I'd like you to hand out," I went on. "If you can think of a better, then use it without reference to me. You tell her you've been ordered by your firm, or whoever it is you work for, to go to Russia to confer with some of their film people. You're sorry you won't be able to accompany her to Hollywood, but you're doing the next best thing. Then you can give her letters of introduction to any goddam people you can think of."

He leaned forward, grinning as his hand patted my knee.

"Brother, I'm ahead of you. I knew I'd have to break away sooner or later so this very afternoon I began a few preliminaries. Nothing that'll cramp your scheme. I told her, for instance, in my modest way, that I didn't know so many people in Hollywood. 'Hollywood's a mighty big place,' I said, and then let on that besides Chaplin and Garbo and Crosby and Gable, and Gary Cooper slightly, and one or two producers, I knew very few people at all. Did she swallow that, hook, line, and sinker or did she? She was all over me. But for that swell girl of mine I wouldn't be here talking to you now."

"And the fact that I'm supposed to be employing you," I added, dryly. "But there's your new assignment—"

He was sniffing. "Wharton's coming from windward. That's his pipe."

Wharton it was, and he found us gloating over that valley view.

Frank had suggested that we should walk home by way of the Lapwings, for there was little difference in distance. I guessed he was making a perfect excuse to speak of Harper again, and Wharton gave him the opening he wanted by supposing that Harper was still at the pub. Frank said Harper had told him he'd be there for months at least, and then added that Harper was such a deplorable liar that one couldn't take all he said for gospel.

"What lie has he told you?" Wharton was asking at once, but as if only politely interested.

Frank gave the one instance, asking Wharton not to mention his own name. He knew it was a lie, he said, because Mrs. Craigne had herself assured him that she hadn't been out of the Manor grounds that Saturday night.

When we got near the pub Wharton said roguishly that we two topers had only lured him that way because we wanted a drink. He'd join us later, he said, but now he was so near Harper's headquarters he might as well have a word with him. So we went into the pub, and we couldn't do much private talking because there wasn't a private bar and quite a few men were in the tap-room. All seemed to know Frank.

"I ought to go easy on the liquor if I'm doing that little job to-night," he managed to whisper to me.

"That's off," I said. "Far better let her be caught red-handed with that mirror when the time comes."

"Well, here's how," he said, and raised his tankard. "And, Gawd, what a magnificent liar a certain somebody is."

I was thinking to myself it wouldn't be a bad idea to write down every single statement Charlotte Craigne had made, reverse it, and see what the results were. But she wasn't so much a magnificent liar as a lucky liar. Take that mirror. I knew she was lying about it, but I never guessed she'd taken it because of what poor old Matthews had told her he'd seen in it.

Frank was talking farming to one of the locals, and doing it very well. I was squinting out of the window and wondering what George was saying to Harper and why he was such a devil of a time about it. When at last he came in he didn't look in too good a temper, but, toper or not, he made no reservations when I ordered a pint tankard.

When we got out of the pub on the way back he began letting off steam.

"That Harper's certainly a liar, Mr. Franks, and he's a foul-mouthed one too. When he began talking about Mrs. Craigne I soon shut his mouth for him."

"What'd he say?" I asked.

"Just vague accusations." He snorted. "Eaten up with conceit, that's what he is. But I'll take some of it out of him, or my name's Robinson. I can't think why Passman ever employed him. His heart must have got the better of his head."

"I think I have an idea about that," Frank said. "You won't think I'm horning in, Mr. Wharton, but I've got really interested in all that's been going on here."

"Naturally you have," conceded Wharton. "But why do you really think Passman employed him?"

"I guess Harper was a bodyguard. From what I've picked up here and there, Mr. Passman was taking Sivley mighty seriously."

From what Frank had hinted to me before, I knew that now he must have good grounds for the statement. Wharton saw something in it too.

"I don't know that you're not right," he said. "The trouble is there's no one but Passman to prove it. That liar Harper swore it was purely the old chap's generosity." Then he was giving Frank a queer, sideways look. "No use asking you how you found out about Harper?"

"Just a bit of gossip here and another there," Frank said dryly. "I reckon these village lads think I'm a fairly harmless character, Mr. Wharton. Maybe they tell me things they wouldn't tell you."

When we got back to the Oak we lost Wharton again. It was one of those sultry nights when you can't help drinking, so Frank and I had a nightcap, with a hundred up on the dartboard to see who should pay. Just as we finished, George appeared.

"You don't mean to say you play darts with that crook?" he demanded of Frank. "Look at his arms. Why, dammit, he doesn't have to throw. He just leans forward and sticks 'em in."

Before I could think of a retort he was going on.

"But I'll be getting up Wooden Hill. Work to do in the morning. Good night to you, Mr. Franks." The tone changed from the facetious to the mild. "Can you spare me a minute, Mr. Travers? Shan't keep you any longer."

I shook hands ceremoniously with Frank, managed to put across a wink and then followed George up the stairs.

"A nice young fellow that Mr. Franks," George was telling me confidentially as soon as he'd closed the door. "No swank about him either." He gave another nod which struck me as more of a tribute to his own perspicuity than to Frank's merits. "We might be able to make use of him in a quiet way. Not that we want him to know all that's going on.

"I thought I'd ring up Mrs. Craigne," he told me as soon as I was seated, "and I was lucky enough to catch her. Just going to bed, she said."

"She swore blind she didn't have the car out that night?"

"Well, yes, she did," he told me gruffly, not too pleased at having the words taken out of his mouth.

"Then, that's that," I said. "We're back where we started."

"Yes," he said, and pursed his lips and frowned contemplatively. "But I'm just wondering whether I haven't been a bit deceived in that Mrs. Craigne. Harper was positive, and I've seen that car of hers. It's one you can't make a mistake about."

"Then how can you prove she's lying?"

"Dammit, don't keep asking fool questions!" exploded George. He waved his hands about, then began prowling round the room. "It's up to us to do something. We've been called in and we're up for judgment." The tone became more pathetic than wheedling. "And you and I have never made a hash of a case yet."

"Well, not too big a hash," I said.

And then some queer wave of sympathy came over me. There he was, getting out his note-book, and adjusting his spectacles. There he was, the same old lovable George, and before I knew it I was saying the last thing I'd ever intended to say.

"I know you hate theories, George, except when they turn out right, but I wonder if you'd like to listen to an amazing one."

"About what?"

"Listen," I said. "It's a long story but don't interrupt."

So I told him the Sivley theory, making it out to be entirely my own. I gave another thumbnail sketch of Charlotte Craigne and even hinted that we'd been pretty thick in the past, and I showed what she had stood to gain. George held me up while he made notes but he asked never a question.

"Right," he said when he at last closed the book. "Keep all this under your hat. Mind you," he had to add, "I don't say there's anything in it but it's worth trying out."

"How're you going to try it?"

"Pick up something about the movements of her car that night," he said, and I was wondering if he'd be more successful than Frank. Then he let out that he had a chief inspector and another man working at Trimport, and they'd now be brought to Brazenoak. The ultimate objective was the finding of Matthews's body.

"You get off to bed now," he told me. "I've got some telephoning to do."

I watched him go downstairs and then slipped into Frank's room.

"I may have been a fool," I said, "but I've told Wharton your Sivley theory. Not as your own but as mine."

"Suits me," he said, and grinned.

"He's now gone to telephone," I whispered from the door. "I'll bet he's putting someone on Queenie's tail. What if the somebody spots our friend Smith?"

He grinned again and gave me the thumbs-up sign, and I went off to my uneasy bed. I didn't know if I was glad or sorry I hadn't said a word about that mirror. When I woke in the morning I was glad I'd stopped at what seemed just the right time, for there were things about that mirror which I'd found it hard to explain away.

The morning brought a letter from Bernice. She had read all about the tragedies before my letter reached her, but the interesting thing was that there was no postscript. The one cryptic remark was: "A terrible time for Charlotte! I think she's doing the right thing in going to America."

CHAPTER XII
THE NEW IDEA

WHEN THE MAID brought my morning tea there was a note on the tray, and she said it was from Mr. Franks. What he was suggesting was a walk before breakfast, and he'd be waiting for me downstairs. My toilet was made in record time, but as only twenty minutes remained before the official hour for the meal, and Wharton would be there on the dot, we strolled across a field-path till we were well out of sight and then did the rest of the constitutional on a stile.

We'd already agreed that now Wharton was making a third, life had considerably more pep, in spite of the riskiness of the double game we were playing. In that cool morning air and clear sunlight it struck me, for instance, that I'd acted a bit precipitately in blurting out Frank's famous theory.

"I think you couldn't have done better," he assured me. "I wouldn't be a yes-man with you, Mr. Travers, and honestly I think you did the very best thing." Then he grinned. "And how am I doing myself?"

"If you mean with Wharton," I said, "then all I can say is you make me blush. In the cause of duty Wharton's the most accomplished liar I know, and I'm not too bad at times myself, but you've got us both stone cold. By the way, that information you offered Wharton about Harper having been Passman's bodyguard; was that genuine?"

"Harper let it slip himself," he said. "Honestly I believe I've got him where he'd tell me anything, and he let this out when we were talking about boxing lessons and he wanted to convince me what a hell of a lad he was. And I'll tell you something that proves it. Harper went to see old Mrs. Sivley to try to fix up lodgings with her, didn't he, because he'd heard Sivley had gone away. That was all boloney. What he went for was to find out if Sivley *had* gone and when he was due back. That's why old man Passman wasn't being guarded on the Saturday morning."

"Maybe you're right," I said. "But that's the sort of dope to hand out to Wharton. Anything that's ostensibly gossip."

"That's how I'd worked things out," he said. "No intrusion. Just sit back and let him make the moves, and you supply a little occasional publicity."

Then I was asking when he proposed to see Charlotte Craigne again, and again he was saying there oughtn't to be any rush. The Monday mightn't be too early, and he'd ring her up on the Sunday morning. He gave me a roguish look as he told me she had a telephone alongside her bed.

"Then you'd better get those Hollywood letters of introduction written," I suggested.

"As a matter of fact I've got three or four written," he said, and then was giving me a quizzical sort of look. "I don't think you're too whole-heartedly in that scheme after all." He saw my questioning look and shrugged his shoulders. "Just something in your tone."

"There's none of that about me," I said. "Playing the game is a good old British term but it doesn't apply to rogues. Wharton licked all that out of me years ago. But you got me wrong. I didn't sound so enthusiastic about the scheme, perhaps, because I saw things like this. If she ever gets to Hollywood, it means she'll have swung clear. We've got to pin something on her long before she gets there. Your letters of introduction are merely to suggest to her that if she wants to bolt, there's a heaven-sent place to bolt to. If we don't pin anything on her before she bolts, at least we shall know where to look for her when we do find something."

"Gosh, it's a pity," he said, and smiled dreamily. "Can't you see her arriving in Hollywood and presenting those letters!"

"It's past eight o'clock," I said, "and what I can see is George Wharton fuming because we're keeping him from his ham and eggs."

George was at the pub door inhaling the morning air, and he was unusually happy for so early an hour. At breakfast he and Frank talked about America, with never a mention of the business we were all there for, at least, till the very end of the meal.

Then he pulled Frank's leg by referring to 'us detectives.' Before I could guess that the quip had purpose, the purpose was revealed.

"And that reminds me. Looking through some notes this morning; I see that the local police report that wherever they made inquiries about Matthews, somebody else had been there before them."

The statement was accompanied by an arch look. My face flushed, but George wasn't looking at me. Frank flushed too. I don't know if he had the gift of producing a blush at will, but if he hadn't he turned that one to good account, and he was looking as much of a fool as possible.

"Sorry, Mr. Wharton, but I guess that was me."

"You!" said Wharton with a deceptive mildness.

"Sure," said Frank and began a modest explanation. Mrs. Craigne, as he'd explained, had been anxious about Matthews, and he'd promised to make inquiries, and the Eddie Franks who'd once taken a diploma in the arts of detection had tried to do the job in the professional manner. He'd even made himself a false moustache, and had tried to talk like the English dude of vaudeville.

"Well, I'm damned!" Wharton said, and then guffawed. Frank looked as if his feelings were on the verge of being hurt, and George patted him on the shoulders.

George wanted me in his room after breakfast and the first thing he told me was that he was flabbergasted when that Mr. Franks had said what he had.

"I was only trying to pull his leg," George said plaintively, and then gave what I always called his Colosseum smile—that of a lion who had snapped at and missed a particularly succulent Christian. "When Venter told me about someone else making inquiries I thought I was on to something."

"You can laugh at Franks all you like," I said, "but he strikes me as the sort of man who'd never be likely to make a fool of himself. But there was something I was going to ask you, George. Are you having Mrs. Craigne watched?"

George pursed his lips. "Don't think it's wise just yet. We've got to get something definite pinned on her first. Theories are no damn good." That was for my benefit, in case the theory turned out to be a dud. "That's why I'm concentrating on the Matthews job."

We both concentrated on it for the next half-hour. I did say that I'd thought he'd intended to see Mrs. Sivley, but he waved that aside. He didn't tell me, by the way, just what Harper told him, and I had to gather that for myself as we went along. I did soon realise that when he'd made out to Frank and me that he'd been furious with Harper, that had been one of his little duplicities.

This is what we worked out first. Harper's evidence was that at ten minutes past ten on that Saturday night he'd seen Charlotte Craigne's car. It was a full moon that night, and so it had never really got dark, and the particular quality of the light tallied with Harper's admission that he'd seen the car but not its driver. As for the exact time, which was the thing that mattered, Harper said he knew it because he had strolled out for a breath of fresh air soon after closing time at the Lapwings.

"Now for the other end," Wharton said. "Mrs. Day has been questioned again, and the maid who saw Matthews, and they put it as at about ten when Matthews went. The trouble is that I daren't question Mrs. Day too closely myself as to when Mrs. Craigne came downstairs with that note, but everything I got last night makes the time roughly eleven o'clock. Nobody, of course, heard Mrs. Craigne's car come back. She simply went the back way to the garage. And nobody would hear her go upstairs because nobody but Matthews was supposed to be in the family part of the house. Matthews would have to lock up, and nobody knew just then that he'd gone and wasn't coming back. What we must assume is that it was at about a quarter to eleven when the car got back. Say ten to if you like. That makes it forty minutes roughly that she was out. If she went straight there and back, that's twenty minutes' driving. Now let's look at this large-scale map. How far would she drive in twenty minutes?"

"Where do you think she'd drive to?" I asked, not wishing to give away what Harper had told me about Breddley Hall and the old flame. Then George was letting out that Harper had told him just what he'd told me.

I had to shake my head at the suggestion of Breddley.

"The lanes are terrors that way," I said. "After all the place is only a hamlet. There's nothing much there but the Hall. Ten miles in twenty minutes in those lanes is incredible, especially as it wouldn't have been twenty minutes. After all she had to do something when she got to the journey's end. She couldn't have turned Matthews out, and driven straight back. Besides, she needn't have gone towards Breddley after all. Just look here on the map. A mile after the Lapwings there's a side lane. It circles round to the Ipswich Road."

That left us where we started from. George said that in any case he'd put his two men on the Breddley lanes first, in case the car had been seen there. I didn't like to say that I didn't think much of the idea. Up to heaven knows what hour on a Saturday night, and a hot one at that, cars would be everywhere on the roads and lanes with their drivers making for the seaside resorts along a forty-mile stretch of coast.

At any rate Wharton went off to do some telephoning which he said should take him only a few minutes, and then we might see Sivley's mother. While I was waiting I kept thinking of that Matthews business, and when I was gravelled for ideas I changed over to Harper about whom we'd been talking too. Then suddenly a most startling idea presented itself. At the moment I thought it one of the most apposite I'd ever had. There *was* a way, it seemed to me, to make Charlotte Craigne incriminate herself. Frank would have to carry it through and it would be both tricky and dangerous, and we'd both have to put ourselves into the hands of Harper. So dangerous was it, in fact, that before Harper could be approached it looked as if I'd have to find some hold over him, to bring him to the scratch and as a guarantee that he'd keep his mouth shut both then and ever after.

The more I thought of that scheme the more I liked it, and the more dangerous it seemed. Skating over thin ice was nothing to it. The one person who must never know a thing was Wharton, and not a word would I say to Frank till the preliminaries had all been worked out. And then I was asking myself what there was that I could use to terrify Harper. Somewhere there must be something I could use as a threat, and I was almost annoyed with Wharton that he should be carting me off to Sivley's mother instead of leaving me in the pub to think things out. A lot we should learn from Mrs. Sivley, I thought disparagingly, after she'd already had the five wits harried out of her by Venter. But there I was wrong, for we did learn something, and it was a something without which we—which is Frank and I—would never have rounded off that case.

Wharton said he had deliberately chosen ten o'clock as the best time for that Saturday morning call, but I wasn't sufficiently interested to ask why that particular time should be so essential. All the same he took the short cut through the churchyard which brought us to the cottage door and round to the back without meeting a soul.

Charlotte had described Mrs. Sivley as an old hag. Perhaps she wasn't quite in the Pond class, though Charlotte herself had never made the grade for that last lucrative reward of the unblemished complexion. But Sivley's mother looked quite a respectable old lady to me; about the late sixties in age, shortish and dumpy, and quiet-spoken. Wharton would always boast of his skill with women witnesses, and I don't think I have seen his technique work more brazenly or with better success than with Mrs. Sivley.

When we came round the corner to the back garden she was shaking a heavy rug, for instance.

"Come, come, that's a bit too heavy for you, Mrs. Sivley," smiled Wharton, and took the rug from her and waved a hand to me, while she stared dumbfounded. Maybe she thought we were advertising vacuum cleaners or something, for her face registered approval while we two shook that cursed rug with its perfectly abominable dust.

"That's better," pronounced Wharton. "Where shall we put it, Mrs. Sivley?"

"Here, sir, in the kitchen," she said, and as soon as we entered: "Was there anything you might be wanting?"

"Well, yes," said Wharton, taking a chair and waving a hand at one for me. "Just a little chat. Don't be alarmed, Mrs. Sivley. I don't know that it isn't more of a gossip. Now this is me."

He was handing over his credentials, and while she was looking at them and puzzling her wits, Wharton was adjusting his antiquated spectacles. From the chin up he looked like a prosperous and benevolent gnome.

"Are you from the police, sir?"

"In a way, yes," he told her mysteriously, and put the wallet in his pocket again. "But the last thing I want to do is worry you. And I'm here to see you're not worried any more."

He glared at me as if I'd been the villain of that piece, and then his tone took on an unctuousness.

"This has been a bad business for a highly respected woman like you, Mrs. Sivley. Some say children are a blessing." He let out a sigh. "They're the ones who don't know."

"Indeed they don't, sir," she said, and was shaking her head. "But you've got children of your own, that's plain. I only had the one."

"Well, whatever they do we're still their parents," Wharton said heavily. "You and I are not excused from that. But your boy wasn't so much to blame perhaps as people think. He got into the hands of rascals, Mrs. Sivley. Cunning rascals."

Her head was shaking again. "It's a comfort to hear that, sir. All the same, sir, I've finished with him now, as I told the other police gentleman that came. Cheating people is one thing, I said, but murder's another, no matter how you're driven. For driven he was, sir, you can be sure of that. He wasn't in his right mind. He couldn't have been. He was like my poor sister who was put away."

"You're probably right," Wharton told her consolingly. "And when he went away that night you had no idea whatever where he was going, or why."

"No, sir, God's my witness."

I thought for a moment she was going to cry. Then she looked at Wharton, her old eyes softening.

"All the police aren't like you, sir. I'll tell you something, sir, that I didn't tell them, nor wouldn't have told, the way they kept shouting things at me till I didn't know where I was. As soon as my poor boy came home, sir, I got into my head that he was going away somewhere because of how restless he was."

"Just a moment, Mrs. Sivley. He didn't come straight home here. To the best of my knowledge it was three days before he came here. I think he spent those three days in London. All we know is that he took the train from Chelmsford to Liverpool Street. I just tell you that in case you didn't know it."

"Some of it, I didn't know, sir. All I knew was that he had something on his mind and I guessed he was going away again. And he hadn't no need, sir. This was his home, till he got something to do, and I wasn't left without a penny, sir, even if he hadn't anything much. But I didn't say anything to him, sir, and then it all came out that very afternoon when he went; when that boy of Widger's brought a note."

"Widgers?" asked Wharton, who must have remembered what I'd told him.

"Don Widger," she said. "Henry Widger's son that now have Pennygate. Him that married May Bullen that was." She broke off here to give a sad reminiscent shake of the head. "There's a hussy for you if there ever was one. Said it was my boy who got her into trouble. Then why didn't she ever get an order out against him?"

Wharton shook his head. I cut in with a question.

"As it wasn't your son, Mrs. Sivley, who got her into trouble, I suppose you couldn't tell us who it actually was? You never heard your son accuse anybody?"

"No. sir, I didn't."

"It couldn't have been Mr. Rupert Craigne, for instance?"

She stared at me. A shake of the head and then she went on with her story, which was all 'I said' and 'he said' and only the thread of it ran in my mind while I thought back. Perhaps it had been ridiculous to suggest that Craigne was the father of May Bullen's child, but had he been, then there was a fascinating prospect, Craigne bribing Sivley to take on the paternity; Widger learning the truth and shooting Craigne, and then completing the job on Passman to throw suspicion on Sivley. After all, everyone knew that nobody but Sivley could have killed both Craigne and Passman. A fascinating theory, I repeat, if I hadn't happened to know that Widger had been haymaking all that Saturday.

In a moment I was picking up the thread of what Mrs. Sivley was telling Wharton. Widger's messenger had said there was no reply to the note. Sivley read it, his mother watching anxiously, and then he threw it contemptuously into the kitchen fire. "I hope he won't think I'm going away because of him," he said with a sneer. "I'm going in any case. And I'm coming back, and no Widger's going to stop me. And when I come back I can buy up Widger, lock, stock and barrel."

Mrs. Sivley asked where he'd get all that money from at which he was hinting. His reply, cryptic though it was, was illuminating. "Just on my travels." That was all, for then he went upstairs. His mother called up that tea was ready, and he asked her to bring him up a cup. He wasn't hungry, he said, and didn't want anything to eat. When she went up she noticed nothing different about the room. In spite of his orders she brought up a piece of cake which he ate when she'd gone.

She was shelling peas at the kitchen table when he came down with the small handbag.

"Good bye, mother," he said. "See you again, soon."

"Pat," she said, "I wish you'd tell me where you're going. Is it after a job? You were bragging, weren't you, when you were talking about all that money. You always was a one to talk big."

He laughed and told her she'd see.

"When are you coming back?" she said. "You ought to let me know."

"When?" he said, and thought for a bit. His lips were moving as if he was calculating something. "About Tuesday, I reckon. Perhaps Monday night."

Then he gave her a quick kiss and was gone. Her lips trembled as she told us that, and Wharton was quickly patting her gently on the shoulder.

"I know, I know," he told her. "But he may come back yet, you never know. And just one little thing more, Mrs. Sivley, and then we'll be going. Did he ever mention Mr. Rogerley to you?"

After a moment's thought she said she had told the other police gentleman about Rogerley, how he had come to the cottage and asked to see Sivley, and was very upset because he was away, and nevertheless wouldn't leave any message. Wharton pressed his original question and she admitted that she hadn't been asked it before. As far as she remembered, her son had mentioned Rogerley only once. She didn't know racing terms but what she said amounted to this. Sivley had been looking at the morning paper and be remarked casually that Rogerley had a couple of runners.

"Hope he brings off a double," he said. "Wouldn't do me any harm either."

That was all he learned, and it seemed to me to be plenty. Wharton had made no comments till we were going through the churchyard again.

"What d'you think of her as a witness?"

"A very reliable one," I told him. "I think it'd be hard for her to tell a lie."

"Let's sit down here," he said. "The seats are hard but it's cool."

Everything has to have a first time, and that was the first time I'd discussed a murder case in a church porch. But perhaps I shouldn't have referred to a discussion, for it was George who did the talking. It always was a fault of his, it seems to me, to let temporary sentiment sway him, and not to be sufficiently fastidious in his selection of vital points. Because he liked the old lady, for instance, and had seen her trembling lip, he let his sympathy include Sivley himself. The stress, it seemed to me, should have been on the fact that Sivley had lied to his mother about May Bullen's child, and if he deceived his mother once, he could do so again. In other words, everything he did and said that afternoon might have been acting and deceit.

"Well," he said, and with a pretended sympathy for myself, "that theory of yours doesn't look any too promising. In fact it looks as if what we've just heard has knocked the stuffing clean out of it."

I merely nodded.

"Sivley's intentions that day, there's the point. Right up to the moment he left he insisted he was coming back. He said he was going to travel, and he bought a motor-bike at Ipswich to prove it. That'd be cheaper than rail. It'd cost him a couple of gallons of petrol to where he had to go, and back."

"You know where he was going?"

He looked surprised. "Yes, don't you? Why, dammit, I as good as told you. To see Rogerley, that's where he was going."

"Yes, but why?"

He snorted impatiently. "Sometimes I wonder if you're losing your touch. Wasn't there a scheme for Rogerley to open a branch swindle in Hampshire? Wasn't it so secret that we didn't learn about it till a few weeks ago? But Sivley must have known about it." He held up an impatient hand. "No, don't ask me how I know that. It has to be right, and it is right. Otherwise, why did Rogerley come down here to Sivley's home as soon as Sivley came out? Why, to keep his mouth shut, of course. And now do you see where Sivley was going? He was going to blackmail Rogerley. That's where his money was coming from. Rogerley got off at that trial. Would he have got off if we'd known then what we know now? Of course he wouldn't. That'd have been the little thing that was needed to tip the scales."

That was all news to me and it was news that made me almost leap off that hard seat. I made no comment on George's disclosures for I was far too busy with my own quick thoughts. Do you see what that news meant to me? Well, you will later, but in the meanwhile I can say that it gave me the very thing I might have hunted for and never found—a hold over Harper.

"Mind you," George was going on, "it's still up to us to find out what made Sivley change his mind after he got to Ipswich. My own idea is that he saw Craigne in Ipswich, purely by chance. Craigne must have had his headquarters at Ipswich. Trimport would have been too dangerous. I mean, he wanted that Saturday speechifying to be a surprise."

"Very likely," I put in, just to show I was still there.

"That's how Sivley learned about what Craigne was going to do at Trimport. I'd say Sivley tried to get money out of him. Maybe Craigne was the father of that child after all. Then they quarrelled, and parted. Sivley brooded, then worked out his scheme. We needn't go into details, but after he'd done Craigne in, then his brain snapped. He went balmy, like that aunt of his, and all his brain told him was to finish the job and kill Passman. How's that strike you?"

"As theories go it's as good as any," I said. To tell the truth I was not sorry he was abandoning Frank's famous theory. Frank and I could now get to work on it with clear consciences, not that Frank had any conscience in the matter. But if it hadn't been for Frank I'd certainly have done a considerable deal of arguing. It would have been my duty to argue if only as Wharton's very humble subsidiary, and there'd certainly have been plenty to argue about, for his own theory was as full of holes as Gruyère cheese.

He got up to go, and as I wriggled and winced while the circulation returned, he began talking about Charlotte Craigne. He was ever so slightly patronising, and when he said there weren't any Messalinas and Lucrezia Borgias about nowadays. I did do a bit of arguing.

"Don't let that rubbish about class confuse you," I told him. "The Kipling tag's still true. Women are sisters under the skin, and I've known pure-bred Siamese cats that could scratch better than the old roof-prowler."

"But murdering her own husband!"

"What about the Thompson-Bywaters case?" I fired at him. "You'll say the woman there only killed by suggestion. But isn't that the case against Mrs. C.? She suggested things to Sivley.

And," I went on, "that's why Matthews is the key point. While we may never prove the suggestions to Sivley—unless Sivley is caught and can be made talk—we can prove something by following up the Matthews end, especially if we find his body."

No more was said because we were approaching the pub. I had seen Frank heading out from the porch and now he was coming to meet us.

"I've been looking around for you, Mr. Wharton," he said. "Porter's got a telegram or message or something."

Off hurried Wharton. Frank gave me a wink.

"It's a telephone message from Trimport. A new witness they'd like him to see. And what were you two doing in the old church porch?"

I ordered a couple of beers to be sent outside to the garden, and when they came, I told him about the hour we'd spent. Before I'd finished, Wharton came bustling out with the news that he was off to Trimport.

"No need for you to come," he told me. "I ought to be back well before tea-time."

"Mr. Wharton always calculates time in terms of meals," I told Frank.

Wharton protested vigorously. No man thought less about food and drink, he said, and when I said I'd have to drink the tankard I saw coming for him, he dug Frank in the ribs and said that was different.

"The old boy's in good form this morning," Frank told me when George's car had at last moved off. "What about you and me having another beer?"

"Oh, no, we don't," I said. "You and I have got a job of work to do, and we've got to work damn' fast. You and I are going to find out if Queenie really had a hand in disposing of Matthews."

He gave me that look of cynical amusement. "And all before Wharton gets back?"

"More or less," I said, and perfectly seriously.

"A pretty tall order," he told me. "What've we got? Three hours, perhaps, and you're going to pin Matthews on Queenie." He grinned. "Suppose you wouldn't like to tell me how?"

"Why not?" I said. "If she killed Matthews, then she wouldn't baulk at killing someone else. We're going to give her the opportunity!"

CHAPTER XIII
WE GET TO WORK

WE HAD LUNCH up in Frank's room and, as it was a cold one, we got it earlier.

"All the better Wharton turning up his nose at your scheme," I told Frank.

"If he has," Frank said. "Maybe it's all camouflage."

"I think we can trust him this time," I said, "even if he is as crafty as a zoo full of monkeys. Your friend Queenie must have impressed him. I believe he's rather ashamed of himself now for ever having had a suspicion of her. What he refuses to get into his head is what I've hinted at, and one hint's usually enough. Queenie was a desperate woman. Do you know what Passman actually allowed her a year?"

"Don't know."

"Five hundred a year, and the way she threw it about wouldn't make it last very long, especially if she was keeping Rupert going as well. I needn't tell you the two most powerful motives in crime," I went on. "As the holder of a diploma in the art of detection you know they're love and greed, even if the love was for herself."

"That wasn't a bad crack about the diploma," he told me. "But what's this about getting somebody murdered?"

"You listen carefully," I said. "I may have to be a bit long-winded but I want you with me. If Wharton's dropped Queenie, then he won't be having her watched. That means we won't have to dodge his men as well as dodging her. That's going to be all to the good, as you'll see.

"And now this scheme of ours. The only way to get at her is through Matthews. Did she or did she not get Matthews made away with? Is she capable of doing it? Once we're sure of that, then we can work back with twice the confidence. You and I think she wouldn't have scrupled about having him done in. Her scheme had come off and then Matthews had to poke his nose in, and he was killed because he knew too much. That's so, isn't it?"

He nodded.

"Matthews was disposed of," I went on, "and she could breathe again. At this moment she's feeling on top of the world because she knows his body won't be found. And that's where we now step in. We produce a Matthews the Second. Someone who also knows too much. We're going to shatter Queenie's serenity. Until that someone's removed she'll be in as much danger as ever. That someone is Harper."

"Yes," he said, and frowned. "I think I'm beginning to see."

"Harper will attempt to blackmail her," I went on. "If she attempts to kill him, then we know she killed Matthews. She may even try to have him disposed of in the same way as Matthews. *She may in that way actually lead us to Matthews!*"

"A damn' good scheme," he said. "I wish I'd thought of it myself."

"Well, you're the one who's going to be in sole charge of it," I assured him. "Harper'll act under your orders."

"That's the weak spot—Harper. He's not gifted with too many brains. And do you think he can be trusted?"

"I've got Harper where we want him," I said. "As for the rest, it'll be up to you to coach him till he's pat. But I'm not worrying about all that. What I'm wondering is this. Can you get a dictaphone installed in Queenie's room."

He gave a low whistle. "I don't know. It might be managed. It may cost a bit in backsheesh."

"Never mind that," I said. "I'm in this so far and I'm going through with it, otherwise there's no guarantee that I shan't have that damnable woman round my neck for the rest of my life. Let's assume, then, that you ring her to-morrow morning and say you'll be seeing her on the Monday. Ask her to tea or dinner somewhere, and get the dictaphone fixed while she's out with you. Harper will go to town with you to-morrow evening, and you can park him at a suitable hotel, and get his part re-hearsed. Then he can call on Queenie on the Tuesday morning."

"I'll do my best," he said. "And when do we see Harper?"

"The minute this meal's over."

"And just one other thing before I forget it. Do I still give Queenie the letters of introduction?"

"You certainly do," I said. "We're going to work a Hitler stunt; one of these wars of nerves. If she loses her nerve and bolts, we'll know where she's bolting to."

The meal was practically over and he asked no more questions till we were actually on the way to the Lapwings. Then he was wanting to know how he was going to be explained away to Harper.

"You keep your ears open and you'll hear," I said. "I'm going to get Harper to come to that shed place where he saw me before, and you can get between the side and the hedge where you'll catch every word. Then at a suitable moment I'll call you in."

I think Harper knew from the gravity of my looks that what I wanted that confidential chat for was something likely to be unpleasant for himself. He was a simple soul, as Frank had said, and his thoughts could be read. Maybe that was why his physique and a certain showy skill had never been enough to carry him through against an opponent who had brains as well as brawn.

"I've really come here to help you, Harper," I began. "I'm sorry for you in many ways. I think you got into the hands of clever crooks. And, of course, you had to pay for what you did. But my view is that once a man's paid, he shouldn't be victim-ised. You've got a chance to go straight again, haven't you?"

"Yes, sir," he said, and was nervously moistening his lips.

"Well, I'm here as your friend," I went on. "Something has come to light that's going to land you in very serious trouble. There's just a bit of hope for you, that nobody else knows about it but me. There's just the chance that I may save you, but it'll depend on your making a clean breast of things, and doing what I tell you."

He was puzzling his wits, wondering what I was driving at. I shed a little more light.

"A man can't be tried twice for the same identical crime," I said. "But he can be tried for another crime of an exactly similar kind. Now do you understand?"

Something was dawning on him. He gave a look, then his eyes turned away.

"Look at me, Harper," I said, "and God help you if you don't tell me the truth. If you do, then I'll do my best to get you clear. You saw Rogerley when he was down here, didn't you?"

"Well, yes. Perhaps I did, sir."

I waved an impatient hand. "No hesitation, or I'm finished with you. Perhaps you'd rather talk to Superintendent Wharton. Or to a magistrate."

"Then I did see him, sir."

"He came to see Sivley and he came to see you," I said, and wagged a finger at him. "He wanted to keep your mouths shut about a certain scheme that would have been in operation if your main scheme hadn't been found out. That's so, isn't it?"

"Well . . . yes, sir. Only I don't know what he did with Sivley."

"How much did he give you?"

He licked his lips and looked away again.

"Not much, sir," he said after a moment or two. "Twenty-five pounds to be exact."

"I see," I said, and nodded heavily. "For twenty-five pounds you made yourself an accessory to a swindle. You accepted money to keep your mouth shut. To defeat the ends of justice, as they say. If it gets out, then what'll you get? Another six months, perhaps. Who knows."

It was rather painful listening to his protestations. He had meant nothing wrong. No one had been more surprised than he when Rogerley had offered him money.

"He insisted on a receipt?"

"Yes, sir, I gave him a receipt. We faked it as if he was paying me back what he'd borrowed."

I clicked my tongue. "As if a judge wouldn't see through that." Then I was heaving a sigh. "Well, Harper, what's it going to be?

I think I can get you out of this scrape, but by God if you open your mouth to a living soul, even to Superintendent Wharton if he questions you, then I'm through with you. Are you prepared to do what I suggest, or not?"

He was prepared to do anything. I think he'd have black-jacked Wharton if I'd suggested it.

What I did was to spin a highly coloured yarn, full of intriguing vagueness and mysterious allusions. Harper didn't know all that was behind that swindling scheme, I said. Naturally he wouldn't be told everything, but only just enough to string him along. Harper would be surprised, for instance, to learn that the swindle was being operated in the States, and that some of his old confederates were mixed up with that too. What was more, some people were now suspected whose names had never come out. Suppose Mrs. Craigne, for instance, had been involved in things. Suppose she'd been responsible for the American end.

"You're no friend of hers," I said. "Provided your own name could be kept out of it, you'd do anything to get her in the dock."

"By God, I would that, sir!"

"Right," I said. "And now here's another bit of news that will surprise you."

And so to Frank. That American gentleman staying at the Oak was also a friend of Harper's, I said, and wished to keep him out of trouble. He'd been looking forward to taking boxing lessons, for instance, and I knew he'd be upset if he had to leave Brazenoak before they could begin. But the American gentleman wasn't quite what everyone thought, I said. Suppose he was an American investigator specially sent over to inquire into Mrs. Craigne's connections with those American crooks.

"Now then," I said. "It's Mr. Franks you'll have to work with, and he'll tell you what he wants you to do. All I can tell you is that it's to do with the disappearance of Matthews. We think Mrs. Craigne knows something about it."

"That was a funny business, sir," he began assuring me. I held up a warning finger.

"Mr. Franks should be here by now," I said. "I asked him to come along. But don't forget what I told you. If you don't want to see the inside of a gaol again, keep your mouth shut and do as you're told."

I looked cautiously out as Frank made an even more cautious withdrawal from the thick hedge. Then I was hurrying back to the Oak in case Wharton had returned.

It was Frank who came back first. Everything had gone satisfactorily with Harper, he said, but certain modifications were necessary in the plan. To keep his mouth shut for another twenty-four hours at the Lapwings might be too great a strain on him, and so he was taking him to town that evening. Harper was giving out that he was going up to town to have a confidential interview with a member of the Boxing Board of Control.

"Harper suggested that himself," he said. "He's too good a liar for my liking. That's why I'd rather have him where I can keep an eye on him. It may mean putting everything forward by a day."

I said I thought that would be an excellent thing. When Frank went to tell Mrs Porter and to pack a bag, I was very pleased indeed about being a day ahead of the original scheme, for as the begetter of the scheme I was impatient for things to happen. And the sooner something did happen, the better for my pocket. And that reminded me. I'd never had Charlotte Craigne's cheque, and I might do worse than give her a reminder. And then somehow I balked at the idea. A hint, if the opportunity presented itself, but hardly a reminder. To have scruples where Charlotte Craigne was concerned seemed more than quixotic and yet I couldn't help having scruples about pestering her for that money. After all, one doesn't charge the condemned man with the price of the rope.

Just as Frank and I were sitting down to an early tea, Wharton appeared, and he was in a wicked temper. An afternoon wasted, he said, and all for a fool of a woman who'd claimed to have seen Sivley in Trimport the previous afternoon, whereas the Sivley of her meddling imagination had turned out to be a tramp.

"What you'd call a hobo," he told Frank, and then was cooling off at the sight of new-laid eggs. "Might as well have a spot of tea myself. But you're a bit early, aren't you?"

Frank explained that he'd been called to town and was leaving almost at once. He hoped to be back on the Wednesday, though only for a day or two.

"I suppose the Yard haven't called you in by any chance?" Wharton asked with elephantine humour.

"I guess not," Frank said, and grinned a bit sheepishly.

"That leg-pull's getting a bit stale, George," I said.

"That reminds me," he said. "I happened to be doing a bit of inquiry work on my own this afternoon and checking up on certain information, and what do you think? Somebody else besides the police has been making inquiries out that way about Sivley."

The look he gave Frank hadn't quite enough pertness.

"Not guilty, your honour," Frank told him. "I owned up to that Matthews business but I give my word, Mr. Wharton, that I've never asked a question about Sivley."

"Just pulling your leg again," Wharton told him with a chuckle. "All the same it's extraordinarily queer. Even before we started out after Sivley, someone was ahead of us."

"You needn't gloat at me, George," I said. "I've got a first-class alibi."

"Dammit! Can't a man make a remark without being taken seriously?" He'd have rumbled on, but his two eggs happened to appear. "And so you're spending a few days in town, Mr. Franks. A pity I shan't be there, or I'd have taken you round the Yard."

"Some other time," Frank said, and was getting up from the table. "But I'm mighty grateful to you all the same. And now if you two gentlemen will excuse me I'll be getting on my way."

"What did you think of that business of Sivley?" Wharton asked me as soon as he'd gone.

I could only shrug my shoulders.

"It's one of the most curious things I've come up against in this case," he was going on.

"Surely the most curious thing is that Sivley's still at large," I said.

George said I was being too impatient. People had been at large longer than Sivley, but the hunt was about to be intensified. I'd finished my tea, so I thought it best to leave him to his. At any moment the questions might become even more awkward.

At about five o'clock we drove some six miles towards Bredley and met the Inspector in charge of inquiries. Neither he nor his man had unearthed any news about a car on that vital Saturday night, and so the four of us went into a huddle over the large-scale map. Certain ponds, two gravel pits and one stone pit were selected for examination, since they lay by the roadside. By the time Wharton and I got back to the Oak, it was nearly nine o'clock. A letter from Bernice was by my plate when I came down to the belated meal.

It had followed hard on the heels of her previous one, and was asking if I'd mind too much if she stayed on for another week, since the people she was with had changed their plans. There was only an indirect reference to Charlotte Craigne. Had I actually got that lovely mirror I'd mentioned, or would there be an auction at the Manor and was I hoping to buy it then. I wrote by return that by all means she was to stay on, for I'd been rather uneasy at the thought of her return before the Charlotte Craigne business was definitely cleared up. A nice impasse I'd have been in if Bernice had come back to discover, perhaps, that I was still only too interested in Charlotte Craigne.

On the Sunday morning George and I were again on the Breddley road, leading a hand in the search. We'd taken cold lunch with us, and after the meal we shifted ground to the road that circled towards Ipswich, and spent an unprofitable afternoon and early evening. I wasn't worrying about missing anything from Frank. Nothing could have happened as yet, and we'd agreed that when there was anything to report he'd ring me at nine o'clock on the particular night.

So to the Monday, and another full day looking for the body of Matthews. I think Wharton began to realise it was a hopeless sort of quest, for he got a bit querulous towards evening. I was in a dither myself, wondering if Frank would be ringing me that night, and what it was that he'd have to report. As nine o'clock drew near I had to keep a tight hold over myself. Then I had a brainwave and managed to get George involved in a game of darts with some of the local experts, and no sooner did I see him settled down to it than Mrs. Porter was telling me I was wanted on the phone.

"That you, uncle?" he said. "Harold here."

"Uncle Tom speaking," I said. "But the line's clear. I've parked our friend Super. . . . And what's the news? Good?"

"Couldn't be better," he said. "I'd put the two disks on if I could but you'll have to hear them later."

He kept his information very much guarded, but it wasn't hard for me to gather what had happened. But since I'm writing in retrospect, and a few days later was to hear the disks that recorded the conversations, I can add details which I didn't know that evening.

Harper presented himself at the flat at about ten o'clock on the Monday morning. Charlotte was amazed to see him. Asked what he wanted. Harper replied that he was in a serious fix and had to put his hands on a hundred pounds at very short notice. She said nothing, but you can imagine her regarding him with an amused contempt. Then he added that he could think of no one who could lend him the money but Mrs. Craigne.

"My dear good man," she said with a sneering laugh, "what on earth makes you think I should lend you a hundred pounds?"

Frank must have coached him again and again for there was a perfection in the doggedness of his tone.

"I don't see why you shouldn't, Mrs. Craigne. I've been a very good friend to you."

"A friend to me!"

"Yes," he went on. "The police have been making inquiries everywhere about Matthews and where he went to that Saturday night. I might have told them a lot of things."

"Indeed? And what might you have told them?"

"About seeing you go out in your car, and Matthews with you."

I imagine then she got to her feet with the pose of a tragedy queen.

"My dear man, you must be mad. The police know I never left the Manor grounds that night." There was a moment or two of silence, and then the tone altered. "This is blackmail. The best thing I can do is ring up the police."

"Very well, madam," he said resignedly. "But if you do there's one thing you ought to know. I wasn't alone when I saw you with Matthews. I've got a witness. He doesn't know it was Matthews because he hadn't seen him before, but he can describe him to the police if I ask him."

"You're mad," she said again, but you could detect a faint anxiety. "You and your witness! It's sheer blackmail, Harper, and I'm not the sort to be blackmailed. If you're genuinely in trouble I can let you have a little money. Ten pounds, say. But it's not because of what you've said. Another threat of that sort and I'll immediately get in touch with the police. The penalties for blackmail are pretty severe."

"Well, I'll take the ten pounds," Harper said, "but it's no real use to me, and that's a fact. You'll have to make it more."

"Have to?" she asked dangerously.

"Well, it's for your own good."

"I'm giving you the ten pounds because I don't want any bother. I've had enough worry lately as it is. In fact, if you could find Matthews for me, I'd be only too pleased to give you a hundred pounds. Here you are. Here's your money."

"Ten pounds is no use to me."

"Don't be foolish," she told him. "But what I will do is think it over. If you can really convince me that you need the money, then I may possibly advance it to you. Come back and see me to-morrow."

There was a mumble which was partly his thanks and partly an inaudible question.

"To-morrow morning, at about this time," she told him. "But don't rely on anything. I shall have a lot of questions to ask."

"And that's that," Frank was telling me over the 'phone. "Except for one highly suggestive thing. Half an hour later she went out and towards the suburbs. In Hammersmith Broadway she found a chemist's shop and bought something to kill wasps."

"Good God!" I said. "Have you got Harper warned?"

"He's wise to her all right," he said. "And that's all for now. I might be with you some time to-morrow afternoon."

I was more scared about Harper than gratified at what Frank had found out. Then I had another idea which was almost as disturbing. Perhaps the cyanide was for herself, and yet it couldn't be, for she was expecting Harper in the morning. And one thing she would certainly have to do, and Frank knew it just as well as I, and that was to get in touch with Sivley.

The following morning George and I were out again, but I had taken the precaution of saying that I would have to get back to the inn for lunch, as I was expecting a private call. It was actually about two o'clock when I did get back to the Oak, and it was only half an hour later when Frank arrived. He'd had a snack at a road-house, he said, and so we went straight up to his room.

"That woman's desperate," he said. "You were right. We can't prove it, but she tried to do Harper in."

"Get on with it, man," I told him impatiently.

"You'll hear it all on the disk," he said, "but he kept the appointment and I'd primed him carefully. She asked him why he wanted the money and he spun her a yarn about training expenses for a fight. Said if he didn't take the chance he'd never get another.

"Then she talked to him like a mother. Said how wrong it was of him to tell such a wicked story, and how she would lend him the money because she knew Mr. Passman would have wished it. Then she held the cheque tantalisingly in her hand, and asked him to own up that he'd invented it all. He stuck to his ground and she shifted hers. He might have made a mistake himself, she said, and indeed he must have done, for the police knew she'd never been out of the house and gardens that night; but that tale about a witness must be a deliberate fabrication.

"Now I'd instructed Harper to hedge a bit once he'd got the cheque in his hands, and he did so. All he now claimed was that he could get a witness if he wanted one, and from that he wouldn't budge. Then she wrote a receipt and made him sign it. I'd anticipated that, and it had all about Harper's training expenses in it.

"But this is the part. While Harper was reading it and signing it, she went out of the room. When she came back she had a little tray with a drink on it. 'Now you must have a drink, Harper, to show there's no ill-feeling.' 'Oh, but this is something different,' she said. 'Something special I brought back from France.' But he wouldn't touch it. Said he was grateful and so on, and then out he went. He daren't look at her, but I guess she was looking pretty murderous. I'd told him, by the way, to cash the cheque at once, and he did. In other words, she didn't dare stop it. I've just brought him back with me to the Lapwings. Told him to cling on to the hundred and keep his mouth shut, and I said he needn't worry about the receipt she held."

I couldn't say anything for a moment or two, for I'd never taken quite seriously the hint that she might even try a new murder. When I did speak I had several questions.

"If she'd killed him, how would she have disposed of the body?"

"Got it into one of those big trunks of hers," he said, "and had the porter get it down to the Rolls. Maybe she was in touch with Sivley to meet her somewhere on the road."

"Did Smith see her telephone?"

"You've got to leave a lot to chance," he said. "When she goes into one of the big stores, for instance, it's best to keep tag on back and front entrances. A man could lose her once she's inside, even if she weren't trying to drop him. And naturally she didn't use the central 'phone at the block of flats because they have an exchange check on all calls."

"The whole thing makes me shudder," I said. "But how'd you get on with her personally?"

There was no smile on his face as he said he'd given her the Hollywood introductions. He'd also rung her up at about eleven that morning to say he'd been called unexpectedly back to Brazenoak, but hoped to be seeing her again soon. He also said he would put in the post that night some of the pictures he'd taken at the Manor.

"You're looking very worried," he said. "Aren't you satisfied with the way things have worked out?"

I patted him on the back.

"If you were the sort who want praise I could give you plenty. But I am worried. We're dead sure now it was she who disposed of Matthews, or got Sivley to do it, and everything's telling me we ought to let Wharton know. And yet we can't. There'd be the hell of a strafe if we did."

"Let things be for a day or two," he said. "That's my hunch. Something's going to happen. I can feel it, just as these Brazenoak grandpops can feel rain."

His hunch was right, though the rain was nearer than he'd thought. That very night things began to happen, and one of them was something that neither he nor I had had the sense to anticipate.

CHAPTER XIV
THINGS HAPPEN

I WONDER IF YOU have ever realized the difficulties of deduction and experienced the alternate optimisms and glooms that possess any seeker after truth. Something at one moment seems crystal clear for you have based it on unassailable premises. Then something goes wrong with a premise and the structure collapses, and all the mental processes must be gone through again. And you, in this story, are better off than I was. You are being told only the essentials. We had a score of unessentials that might have been vital.

While I was having a bath before dinner I began to have doubts of that very kind, and no sooner had I dressed than I went into Frank's room. He was a leisurely dresser, perhaps because he still saw something worth looking at in the mirror.

"Suppose we're all wrong about Queenie?" I asked. "Suppose that loan to Harper was a perfectly genuine one. Suppose that drink she offered him was a genuine one too."

"And suppose she didn't buy any cyanide," he told me, still adjusting his hair in the glass.

"Yes, but suppose she wanted that for herself in case anything happened. Harper was a danger signal, you know."

"You leave everything to Harold," he told me with a grin. "Wait till you listen to those disks. There're all sorts of little subleties that tell a whole lot." Then he was giving me his old cynical look. "You're not suggesting that Queenie wouldn't have been capable of poisoning Harper?"

"I think she's capable of anything under the sun," I said whole-heartedly. "She's cashed in on big stakes, and she'll fight like a wild cat to keep other people's hands off."

"Is this the first time she's really had big money?"

"Now I come to think of it, it is," I said. "She was brought up in a shiftless sort of set. Her father was the kind who bilks every tradesman he can and only pays when he knows he damn well must. The Manor was mortgaged up to the last penny and it was always a mystery to me how they all kept out of the bankruptcy court. Even when Queenie married Craigne the money wasn't a lump sum. It was what he earned as he went along, and what with racing and entertaining and keeping this place and that going, his income was mortgaged for months ahead."

"Ah, well," he said, and took my arm. "Let's give it a rest. Wonder what's happened to the old war-horse."

Wharton came in while we were having a short drink and he looked tired and dispirited. I went back upstairs with him and he told me he was thinking of abandoning that search for Matthews. Every likely spot had been tried and all there seemed to do was to wait till Sivley was apprehended.

"You get on with your dinner," he told me. "I mayn't be down for some time yet."

"We'll wait for you," I said. "And cheer up, George. Something's going to happen. I can feel it in my bones."

"Let's hope you're right," he said, but looked as gloomy as before. I left him to it and went down to Frank.

"We shall have to hand Wharton out something," I said. "He's as miserable as hell."

"There's no dope we can hand him," Frank said. "If only we could find real justification for that Harper business, then we might. As it is, we're liable to six months apiece for unlawful entry and God knows what."

We took two more drinks into the lounge and waited for Wharton. Frank told me bluntly that I was as bad as Wharton, and the quicker I snapped out of it, the quicker my brain would start functioning again. I didn't argue with his logic. What was wrong with my brain was that it was too fertile in ideas.

"That mirror up there," he suddenly said, and I'm sure it was only to get me off the case. "Is it a valuable one?"

"It's a reproduction," I told him, "and not too good a one at that."

We were sitting facing the empty fireplace, back to the open end of the room, and as I looked at the mirror I saw Mrs. Porter approaching, or rather, about to approach. She had a curious trick, by the way: that of rubbing or flicking her nose with the back of a finger as if disposing of an Eskimo's tear. She did that twice while I watched her amusedly, and she also patted her hair. Then she came in, and with a little cough to call attention to the fact.

"Was you two gentlemen waiting for Mr. Wharton?"

"Who's taking my name in vain?" came Wharton's voice from the lobby.

"I'm sure I beg your pardon, sir," Mrs. Porter told him with a titter. "But your dinner's ready, sir, if you are."

Off we went to get it, and the thought of it put something else out of my mind. In that one minute, floating above me in space and with only a hand needed to reach up and grasp it, was the solution to everything that was worrying me, and it was to be a good many hours and after a considerable deal more of worry before I was to have that chance again.

* * * * *

Wharton said he was going to take things easy that night. His brain was tired and his feet were tired and he was proposing to rest both in the private bar. I left him there looking like a latter-day Dr. Johnson, discussing war prospects with the local worthies. Frank had suggested we should take a short stroll and then play darts, but I couldn't find him. Then Mrs. Porter told me he was at the telephone.

It was about five minutes before he turned up, and as he made no mention of what had kept him I guessed it was some private call. But no sooner were we over the stile to the inn paddock than he was giving me his old cynical smile.

"Well, didn't I tell you something was going to happen? That was Queenie on the 'phone.

"Yes," he went on. "Harper's certainly put the wind up Queenie. Guess what she's doing."

"Coming down here," I said.

"Going to America, and straight away!"

"But she mustn't!" I said, and then realised how footling the remark was. "We've just got to get hold of something. Anything so long as we can keep her here." Then I gave him a look. "You're not pulling my leg?"

"My God, no!" he said. "You ought to have heard her. 'So frightfully sorry, Frankie darling'—that's what she calls me now—'but I've really got to get away for a long rest. My dear, I've simply got to.' I said why didn't she come down here, thinking we could keep an eye on her. Then she said she'd suddenly made up her mind to go to some friends in New York, and then on to Hollywood, taking those too, too marvellous introductions I'd given her. She might even be going sometime this week, she said. It all depended on whether she could get everything ready. I said could I see her off, and then she started to make difficulties. Everything would be so hurried, and she couldn't be able to let me know in time, and it was perfectly sweet of me and she'd be seeing me in Hollywood. Oh yes, and she said she'd like to go over on the *Queen Mary*."

"If she said that," I said, "then you bet your life she's intending to go over on a cattle boat." Then I was clicking my tongue exasperatedly. "But honestly, Frank, we've got to do something. If we can't do anything else we'll have to frame her. We simply can't let her get out of the country."

"There's no immediate worry," he assured me. "But I'll get hold of Smith, if you like, and tell him to put an extra outdoor man on her tail. She'll have to buy her ticket somewhere. We ought to know what boat she's crossing on, and when."

"That won't be much good to us when she's gone," I said impatiently. I could kick myself now when I think of the dither I was in.

"You've only got to give me the word," he said, "and I'll nip up to town and keep an eye on things."

"We can't keep explaining your disappearances to Wharton," I said. "Besides, it'd be too risky. That goddam diploma of yours didn't take account of Queenie."

"That's better," he told me with a grin. Funny relations, you may think, between the detective and the gent who was hiring him, but Frank and I had come to be more like Uncle Tom and Harold than the original script had provided for.

We went back to the Oak and he managed to get in touch with the beetle-browed Smith.

"No more panic," he told me. "Smith's well on the job. Did I tell you he's got the flat above hers? And spending half the day with his ear on the floor."

I hope Frank didn't hear my groan. Smith in a five hundred a year flat, and I still hadn't done anything about that cheque from Charlotte Craigne.

It was cool after the day's sultriness, and Frank and I sat on the oak seat beneath the elm. A lovely English kind of smell was coming with the dew from a bed of stocks beneath the bar window, and we were snuffing the air, and saying the same old things about only the fools living in towns. Wharton was still enthroned in the private bar and occasionally we heard his voice or a hearty guffaw.

A man on a bicycle loomed up out of the dusk. As he dismounted he caught sight of us, and recognised Frank, for as he came across he was flicking the peak of his cap.

"Evenin', sir. Been a bit of an accident or somethin' up at the Lapwings, so they tell me. Harper's gone and shot himself or somethin'." I still remember those clipped g's and the slight sing-song of the Suffolk dialect.

"Good God!" Frank said, and forgot all about accent. "When was this?"

"Just now, so they reckon, sir. But I don't know no more about it than what I've heard."

Frank gave me a look, then was taking the handle-bar of the bicycle.

"You lend me your bicycle. Mr. Travers, you take Baker to the bar and give him a drink. Harper was a friend of mine. Guess I'm going to find out what's happened."

Another couple of seconds and he'd disappeared. As I led the way to the bar I didn't know if I was on my head or my heels. Nothing made sense, was all that ran through my brain. Harper couldn't possibly have shot himself.

"Who gave the news, Baker?" I asked.

"That boy of Jim Taylor's," he said. "Perhaps the young devil was tellin' me lies."

"You keep it to yourself for the present," I advised him. "Mr. Franks will let us know when he comes back. You never know what lies people will start."

He reckoned that was so. I stood him a pint tankard and had a half one myself, and while I was asking him about local crops, I was thinking about Harper. I knew perfectly well why Frank had hurried to the Lapwings—to get there before Wharton heard the news. Maybe it hadn't been an accident, and if Wharton asked questions, then Harper would have to be provided with answers. And I was thinking of a dozen other things at the same time. Of all the incongruous things, I thought of Widger, who sent Sivley a note to quit the parish, and who'd been so confident of his own brute strength as to boast in that very pub that Sivley would never be seen there again. I wondered if it was Harper by any chance who'd got May Bullen into trouble; I wondered what Frank was telling Harper, and what Wharton would do when he knew.

That latter was a moment not to be long delayed. Into the bar came another man, full of the news. This time it was that someone had shot at Harper, and he reckoned it was somebody who'd been taking a shot at a rabbit and got Harper instead. Porter, who was serving in that bar, at once went through to the private bar. I was in a panic, then I said to Baker: "What about going up to the Lapwings? We can fetch your bicycle at the same time."

He drained his tankard and off we went. It was ten minutes to closing time, but behind us we could hear voices already outside the pub, which showed that the news had got round. Then a hundred yards along the road Frank came pedalling up. He gave Baker the bicycle, and a bob tip, and enough news to satisfy him, and then was motioning me back among the trees.

"Someone had a shot at Harper," he told me. "Got him in the shoulder. A rifle bullet, but he'll be all right. The doctor's just taking him off to the hospital."

"Has he any idea who did it?"

"He heard a car drive off just after the crack. It must have been Sivley. Queenie put him up to it."

"Where'd it happen?"

"About a hundred yards down the road from the pub. A local man—he's with the local policeman now—says he was coming towards the pub when a stranger put his head out of a car by the side of the road and asked if he'd tell Harper he was wanted. He says he didn't see the man very well because it was dusk, and he didn't recognise his voice, but he got the idea he was a parson. Harper got the message, and as he was coming towards the car he got the bullet. It knocked him plumb flat, and when he sort of got himself in one piece again, the car'd gone."

"You and I'd better go along," I said. "Wharton may think we were still on that walk of ours."

So we set off. Frank told me he'd had a word with Harper, who could be trusted to say he'd no idea who'd fired the shot. Then there was a toot behind us, and the lights of a car.

"Where are you two off to?" came Wharton's voice.

"Just heard some yarn about Harper," I said. "We thought of going to verify it."

There was only a hundred yards to go and we were there by the time he'd drawn up his car. Quite a few people were standing about outside, and Wharton was making for the nearest group.

"Let's get off back, Frank," I said. "I've got an idea."

He made a grimace but followed me nevertheless.

"It'll be all right with Wharton," I said. "We can say the excitement all seemed to be over, and we knew he'd tell us anything there was to tell. But what I want to know is if you've any pull with any of the news agencies?"

"You want me to rush the news to town?"

"Something of the sort," I said. "But have you any pull?"

He thought for a bit, and then said he didn't know. If it was urgent, then he knew a man whose name he could make use of. He might even have to pretend he was that man, and fake his voice.

"I think it's damnably urgent," I said. "What I want you to do is to get the news to any agency where it'll be at once distributed. Say Harper was attacked by an unknown man a few minutes ago and that he's since died. There'll be no time for them to check up."

"My God! you're asking something!" I could hear his grin. "But what's the idea behind it?"

"It's a million to one Queenie put Sivley up to the shooting." I said. "Harper fell, and when they read the morning papers they'll know he's dead. Queenie will be easy once more in her mind and she won't be so eager to bolt. Anything to keep her in England a few more days."

"And what about when the disclaimer comes in the afternoon editions?"

My stride had automatically been lengthening, and I had to slow down for him to get abreast again.

"Maybe she doesn't read the afternoon editions. Even if she does, it may make her change her plans."

At the Oak he let my importunities get the better of his judgment and went to the telephone. When he came back he was looking somewhat rueful.

"There'll be a fiver on the bill for this," he told me. "I won't tell you who it is I've just been impersonating, but your eyes'd pop out if I did."

We waited and waited for Wharton to return and at half-past eleven Frank said he'd be getting up to bed. I sat on, and a quarter of an hour later Wharton appeared. He said he'd been to the hospital, which was eight miles away, to get a statement from Harper. The house was dead quiet, and even on the upstair landing you couldn't hear a snore. Wharton had part of a bottle of whisky in his room and said he wanted a stiff one. I had one too, for my throat was like a lime-kiln with the smoking Frank and I had done while we were waiting.

The first thing he told me was that Harper was going on well, and he didn't know why they hadn't left him at the Lapwings. I could have told him something about that. Frank had reached the Lapwings while the doctor was debating the point, and something he'd put in had turned the scale. As Frank told me, if it was Sivley who'd done the shooting, then he might have another go, but he'd never have the nerve to make an attempt in the town hospital. I saw things the other way and said it was a pity Harper hadn't been left at the Lapwings as bait.

"Who do you think did the shooting?" I asked George.

"Don't know," he said. "The old fool who took the message to the pub couldn't tell me a thing. Take the car. All he knows is that it was a car. Didn't know if it was blue or black. Said it wasn't exactly big and it wasn't exactly little. And I couldn't get any more out of him about the man. He still reckons—as he put it—he was oldish, and a parson, just because he had an educated voice probably and something white round his neck."

"It couldn't have been Sivley?" I suggested.

"What grudge has he got against Harper?"

"If Sivley's a candidate for Broadmoor as you once thought, then reasons wouldn't matter," I said. "He may be just running amok."

Wharton shook his head. "I keep telling myself it wasn't Sivley. Fate couldn't have played me a dirty trick like that: me sitting here and Sivley just up the road. But what I'd like is for you to see what you can find out. I'm going to town in the morning. About time I talked things over with the Powers-that-Be."

"Well, I'll do my best," I said, and with never a blush. "But what about the bullet? What was the calibre?"

"The bullet went clean through," Wharton said. "That'll be one of your jobs, to see if you can find it."

"Some hope," I said dryly. "I'd rather look for a very small needle in a couple of dozen hay-stacks."

Then I thought of something. It was information I definitely needed, and it would be giving George a hint of which he might after all make use.

"When you're in town, George. I wish you'd do something for me. Find out what sum of money the executors advanced to Mrs. Craigne."

He gave me a peering look. "Still on that hunt, are you?"

"I've still got it in mind," I told him. "But you'll try to find out for me?"

He gave me another of his peering looks, then ventured on a chuckle. "As a matter of fact I can tell you now. She was advanced half the cash bequest." He saw my look and gave another chuckle, or rather it was more of a leer. "Oh, yes. I find things out occasionally. Just as well to know how everything stands."

I think I did blush then, but he noticed nothing. "Twenty-five thousand's a large sum to advance, surely?"

"Not at all," he said. "The will's sound enough, and it's all in the family, so to speak. And I believe Mrs. Craigne told them she might be going abroad at any time to avoid gossip. She was only staying on in case her husband's body was recovered."

He finished his second tot and said he'd be turning in. I had a last question.

"About the bullet, George. The direction will be easier if anyone heard it at the pub."

"At the pub!" George said witheringly. "All they heard was a crack, and then they reckoned it was someone potting at a rabbit."

"And how long do you think you'll be in town?"

"Can't say," he said. "What's to-day? Wednesday?"

"Actually it's an hour into Thursday," I said.

"Thursday—Friday. Maybe I'll be back Friday night."

He gave himself a little self-satisfied nod, and as I went to my room I was telling myself that he'd discovered something. So accustomed had I grown to suspect him of subterfuge that I began thinking over all we'd said, and it seemed to me that he'd divulged uncommonly little. And there was that business of the inquiries he'd made into Charlotte Craigne's affairs, and which I'd forced out of him. In fact, as I lay waiting for sleep I was extremely uneasy in my mind. Something did tell me that George was completely unaware of the dangerous game that Frank and I had been playing, and yet even of that I couldn't be entirely sure. Why, for instance, the sudden decision to return to town? And what conference at the Yard could keep him there till the Friday?

When I woke in the morning the uneasiness was still there, and as soon as Frank and I were off on our usual pre-breakfast stroll, I unburdened my mind.

"What's wrong with you is that you've too much conscience," he told me. "You went into this scrap bare-fisted and now you're worrying about not having the gloves on. Why shouldn't Wharton go to town? We're sitting pretty, aren't we? We've got Harper to ourselves. Smith's watching Queenie."

I was still shaking my head dubiously.

"Snap out of it," he told me with a grin. "Your life's been too respectable, so far. Count your blessings—that's the motto. A fortnight ago you were a father. You might have been heading straight for the divorce court. And what are you now? All nerves and misery, when we two ought to be skipping along this path like a couple of lambs."

"It's all very well for you," I said. "You can drop out of all this and I can't. I'll own up that I'm scared stiff." Then all at once I was polishing my glasses, with: "Oh my hat! I've remembered something else. What a bloody fool I must have been last night to have got you to fake Harper's death."

It was the newspaper-boy on his bicycle that had reminded me of that far-too-hasty bit of foolishness. Frank was calling to the boy who knew us both by sight. We could save him getting off his bicycle again, he said, and we were promptly given the papers for the Oak.

As soon as he'd got round the corner, Frank held up an illustrated. It had twin sets of headlines:

HITLER THREATENS POLES
TROOP MOVEMENTS NEAR FRONTIER

That was the left-hand side. On the other was something that made me wince.

ANOTHER BRAZENOAK MURDER
SIVLEY STRIKES AGAIN?

"My God!" I said. "Wait till Wharton sees these papers."

"He won't—not at the Oak," he told me, and grinned. "He'll be off early. I shan't remember them till he's gone."

"That call you made!" I said. "It can be traced to here."

"I doubt it," he said. "I said I was calling from Ipswich."

I was clicking my tongue all the same. Then I asked if he'd care to tell me whom he'd impersonated.

He grinned cheerfully. "In your present state of nerves you hadn't better know."

"Nerves be damned," I said. "You tell me who it was."

"You sure you want to know?"

Then he said okay, but I'd brought it on myself. "As a matter of fact, it was Wharton."

"Wharton!" I fairly gaped at him. "My God that's dreadful."

"I guessed you'd think so," he said, and still cheerfully. "But it'll only be put down as a hoax."

"Hoax!" I said bitterly. "And what exactly did you tell them?"

"Only that the police wanted the news out at once to help in the apprehension of Sivley, and that's why I, Superintendent

Wharton, was sending it direct. I said my name was on no account to be mentioned."

"Well, that's something," I said. "I know it's all my fault, but, oh, my hat! Fifty million people in the British Isles and you had to choose George Wharton!"

CHAPTER XV
DAY OF CLIMAX

FRANK WAS DEAD RIGHT about Wharton, who positively gulped his breakfast that morning and was away and gone a quarter of an hour after it. Frank said he would run over to the hospital and hear the latest about Harper. I, being left at a loose end, thought I'd draw along to the Lapwings, as they say in Suffolk, and make a pretence of finding that bullet.

I was in no particular hurry, so I took a field-path, and, incredible though it may sound in a place so small as Brazenoak, managed to lose myself so that I came out to the south-east of the Manor. Then I thought I knew where I'd gone wrong, so I turned back, and it was as I was mounting a stile that I caught sight of George Wharton. The staggering thing was where I saw him, for it was through a gap in a poplar-shield hedge and in the Manor gardens. What he had been doing I couldn't for the life of me imagine, but he was hurrying back towards the house, and a man wearing a green baize apron, whom I took to be the head gardener, was with him.

I had been right, then, about George, I told myself; and with a complete disregard of the beam in my eye I felt a grievance that he should be playing some double game of his own. So interested was I that I got down from my stile and moved warily to the cover of the hedge and along it to the north. It must have taken me a good quarter of an hour manoeuvering for position, and then it was all wasted, for when at last I had the Manor and part of the drive under observation, I was merely in time to see George's car moving off. I held my breath to follow the sound of it, and it turned left and was lost in the direction of the main Chelmsford road.

It was no use worrying my wits over George's secretiveness, and I managed to force the uneasiness to the back of my mind, though only through a wincing recalling of that cheerful dressing-down that Frank had given me. Perhaps I *was* meeting troubles half-way, and I could tell myself that George would have to disclose his ideas when he returned from town. What he was up to, in fact, was the verification of something I had missed, and I could hear his triumphant chuckles as he drove the fact home.

I spent the morning in the vicinity of the Lapwings, at least till opening time, and then, under the pretext of listening to local gossip. I treated myself to a pint mug of beer. When I got back to the Oak I asked Mrs. Porter where Mr. Franks was, and she told me he'd just gone out to find me. I stayed put and ten minutes later he was back.

"Just had some news," he told me. "Smith rang up on the off-chance. What do you think's the latest? Queenie's sold the Rolls!"

I'd forgotten that car and how she'd have to sell it if she were going to bolt.

"She took it to a Portland Street firm this morning," Frank went on. "Smith says it looked to him as if they were expecting her, so everything must have been fixed up by letter or 'phone. And she left the car there, and she went straight on to her bank. Then she took a taxi home and she was there when Smith rang."

"Nothing about buying a ticket?"

"I take it, no. Smith didn't say anything. But if you ask me, that's the next item I'm sticking around. Smith might ring me later."

There was a thunderstorm that afternoon, with the rain coming down in sheets, so I had to stick around too. It was slow and trying work, with our ears cocked for the faint sound of the telephone bell, and it was not until just after six o'clock that Smith rang up. I was all on edge till Frank came out of the room. His face was serious, which was one good sign.

"The most astounding thing!" he said, and drew me back into the deserted lounge. "Queenie went to Cook's head office this afternoon and took a ticket—*for The Hague!*"

I was polishing my glasses and blinking away like a drunken owl.

"The Hague!" he said. "And she's leaving Liverpool Street on Saturday morning. They got her a corner seat in a first-class compartment."

"What train?"

"The one that leaves at ten. But what's the idea? It's got me beat."

"Me too," I said, still aimlessly polishing my glasses. "Unless there's some connection with those de Karnovik people."

"I thought of that too," he said. "But there can't be. They're God knows where."

"The Hague!" I said. "Only a fool would go abroad as things are now. Yet I don't know. Some Whitehall Blimp or other told her there wouldn't be war. She wanted to bet me there wouldn't be."

"Don't you think I'd better get back to town?" he said. "I don't like it. She's double-crossed me about Hollywood and she hadn't any reason to, unless she was badly scared."

"Stay on till after dinner," I said. "Smith may have some more news by then. And if you do go, where can I get you?"

"Better ring the firm," he said, and was shaking his head again. "Even that corner seat booking may be a blind. She may be taking some other train."

"Who's panicking now?" I said. "She didn't know she was being tailed. There wasn't anybody she could mislead."

"Yes, but Holland isn't the *Queen Mary*. Once she lands on the Continent, then we're beat." Then he was suddenly tense with a new thought. "I'll bet Sivley's now in The Hague. I'll bet he went there to-day."

"The watch is still on at the ports," I told him. "Let's give it a rest and wait for Smith."

After dinner Frank still waited, and he was rewarded, for Smith rang up soon after eight o'clock. There was no news, he said, except that Queenie had already begun packing.

"Me for packing too, then," Frank said. A quarter of an hour later he had paid his bill and gone. The rain was now a dreary drizzle and without him the house seemed as cheerful as a sepulchre.

But the morning dawned clear again, with trees and grass already an incredible green. A freshness was in the air, and lovely intangible scents of moist earth and growing things, and it was hard to be pessimistic. I shall always remember that morning, and how after breakfast I had schooled myself to a mood of philosophic calm. I can still see the wet on the grass and the oak seat beneath the elm where I had thought of smoking a pipe over the morning papers, and still see myself going back to the lounge and settling into an easy-chair.

There was a faint sound, and in the mirror above the mantelpiece I saw Mrs. Porter. She had a duster in one hand and with the back of a finger of the other she gave a quick rub at her nose. Then she saw my long legs.

"Sorry, sir, I didn't know you were here."

Before I could speak she was gone again. I smiled to myself, and then the smile slowly went. I think my mouth gaped, and I know the paper fell from my lap to the floor for when at last I got to any feet I was treading on it. The next thing I knew was that I was up in my room and why I had come there I had no idea. Then I was prowling round the room, glasses in my hand, and adding this and that together and always finding the answer the same. A lunatic's idea it had been, and then all at once I was smiling to myself as I knew that a lunatic's idea it was, and that I was the lunatic for having missed what had been under my nose.

I hooked my glasses on again, and then was taking the stairs two at a time. In a matter of seconds I was calling the Yard, though it was another fifteen minutes before I was actually speaking to Wharton.

"When were you thinking of coming back here, George?" I asked.

"Probably to-night," he said. "Why?"

"Stay put," I said. "I'll be at the Yard sometime this evening. It's important, George. Don't stir till you've seen me."

"What's the idea?" he was spluttering. "Found something out?"

"I can't tell you over the 'phone," I said, "but I think I'm on to something big."

"How big?" his voice came persistently.

My voice lowered, as if that made any difference.

"Don't ask questions, George, but I think it's the biggest ever. I know the way to get Sivley!"

As I drove up to the Manor I was telling myself that I'd been far too precipitate. All sorts of things might go wrong, and if I'd only had more time I might have found out what had happened to the car from which the shot had been fired, and so got on the trail in a different way.

"I'm leaving Brazenoak now, Mrs. Day," I told the house-keeper, "so I thought I'd come and say good-bye."

"That's very kind of you, sir," she said. "We had that other gentlemen, Mr. Wharton, here yesterday. He said he was going away too."

"What a one he is to ask questions!" I said.

She smiled, but I didn't pursue the subject, although I knew I could have found a clue to what had brought George there that morning.

"We expect the new master very soon now," she said. "And perhaps you'll be coming down again, sir."

"I don't know," I said gloomily. "You never know with strangers. Mr. Passman and I knew each other pretty well. Only the last time I saw him I was pulling his leg about the easy way he took life nowadays. By the way, what time *was* it when he used to have his breakfast?"

"He was down at half-past nine to the minute, sir. I never knew him vary."

"Ah, well," I said heavily. "But you can do something for me before I go. Is there an atlas in the study?"

There was one and I had a look at it. Ipswich was, as I thought, very awkward for Harwich, where Charlotte Craigne would embark for Holland. Colchester was far more handy, and it was no farther from Brazenoak.

I thanked Mrs. Day and said good-bye, then headed the car for Ipswich. There I verified the time of that Saturday morning train, and also discovered that a boat from The Hook met the same train. It also seemed that there was a very good train from Ipswich to catch the boat train at Colchester.

After that I headed north for Trimport, and when I came to the spot where Smith had seen the farm-worker who thought he had seen Sivley sitting at dusk by the roadside, I drew the car in on the grass verge. I knew it was the right spot, because there was the stack at which some tramp had slept that night, and to my left were tracks that led to what had been described as old brickfields, and their ruts were still red from the bricks that had been used for rough metalling.

I made my way through scrub and gorse to the top of the slight rise, and there the old workings were. A dangerous place to be unfenced, I thought, for about an acre of the deep depression was filled with water, and there were other pools now stagnant after the drought. But I didn't stay long, for it was past midday, and I pushed on to Trimport.

I avoided the hotels and had a bread and cheese and beer lunch at a small pub, and afterwards the landlady let me use her room, as I had a letter to write, and she provided me with paper and pen. This is what I concocted, and I addressed the letter to the Police Station at Ipswich. The writing was done with my left hand, and with the tip of the nib only, and I made one or two artistic corrections as if uncertain of my spelling.

Dear Sir.

I feel it my duty to let you know something although my husband would be riled if he found out, and he would give my

Tom a good hiding. My Tom and another boy went wading
as they say in the pond in the old brick-fields at Harley St.
Peter by the main road although warned not to by his father
and me and he come running home and said there was a
man in the pond. A dead man, all naked he said and I boxed
his ears for telling lies but he said it was true. I said not to
tell his father or he'd skin alive. I said, and when I thought
it over I thought I had better write this letter. Hoping I have
done right.

Mrs. B.

I posted that letter in Trimport and then went in search of
Quadling, the fisherman in whose boat Rupert Craigne had met
his end. It took me a long time to run him to earth and at last
I found him painting a boat at the west end of the beach. The
beach, by the way, was as crowded as ever, though there were
few bathers.

Quadling spotted me at once. "Afternoon, sir. Haven't seen
you for quite a time."

"No," I said. "I haven't been this way since the morning Mr.
Craigne was killed."

"A bad business," he said, and shook his head. "But there
you are, sir. It's all forgotten now. I'll lay not one o' them on that
there beach is thinkin' about it. Funny about that Sivley, though.
You'd have thought they'd have caught him afore now?"

"He'll be caught," I said, and made as if to be moving on. "I
was this way and I thought I'd see how you were. By the way,
there was one thing you told me that morning which I've never
understood. Didn't you say Mr. Craigne was wearing a suit? It
didn't look to me like a suit. It looked like a bright green bath-
ing-costume."

He laughed. "You got me all wrong, sir. That was a bath-
ing-costume he had on. What I said was, he came down to the
boat in a suit—well, coat and trousers and a scarf sort of thing. He
got in and took the oars, and then he sort of undressed and then
he chucked the clothes back and hollered to me to keep them."

"And you did?" I asked slyly.

"No such luck, sir," he told me ruefully. "Real class they were, but the police got their hands on them and that's the last of them I've seen. Mind you, sir, he didn't mean at the time that I was to keep them. What he meant was to mind them till he got back."

"What'd you think he was going to do in the boat?"

"Do, sir?" He looked surprised. "Why, row out beyond the bar and do his swimmin' out of the way of the crowd." He shook his head. "A pity he didn't."

I gave him a tip and moved on again. By the time I was back in Trimport itself it was nearly four o'clock. With a drive to town before me I thought I might reasonably treat myself to tea. After that I went to the main post office and rang Frank's firm. I told them it was a matter of extreme urgency that Mr. Tarling should ring me at St. Martin's Chambers at seven o'clock that evening. They assured me it should be done.

The roads are good after Ipswich and I was well on time as I came to the outer suburbs. At a certain police station where I was known I rang the Yard and left a message that I would be with Superintendent Wharton at seven-thirty. At ten minutes to seven I had parked the car and was waiting for Frank's call. It was just before the hour when he rang.

"How are things your end?" I began.

"She's still packing," he said. "Went to the bank this after-noon and straight back in a taxi. About tea-time a woman came in a taxi and went away with a load of second-hand clothes. We checked up on that. Queenie was cashing in on all the stuff she didn't want."

"Listen to this," I said. "I'm going to be on that train to-mor-row morning. Later that evening I shall send you a telephone number. It'll be the station master's office or some such spot where Wharton and I will be watching for Queenie. You'll 'phone me there as soon as she leaves the house, and you'll have some-one—or two—on her tail in case she changes her mind again."

"Okay," he told me snappily. "Anything else?"

"Nothing I can think of," I said. "I'm just seeing Wharton. I didn't tell you that I expect to see Sivley on that train."

"I guessed it," he said. "That's why I wasn't asking questions."

"We've three chances," I said. "If he isn't on the train, then he may be on the boat waiting. If he isn't there, then Queenie will lead Wharton to him on the other side. As soon as anything happens, I'll ring you up."

I had a quick clean up and a short drink, then hopped on a bus which would drop me near the Yard. Wharton was waiting for me in his room.

"What's this about Sivley?" he fired at me as soon as I entered.

"Look here, George," I fired in return. "I'm telling you straight away that I'm playing a hunch. You can either come in or not, but if the hunch doesn't work out right, then don't blame me for trying."

"Dammit, I haven't opened my mouth yet!" he protested.

"I know you haven't," I said. "I merely thought I'd get my position clear first. And don't go asking me questions. I'll answer them when the time comes."

"A hell of a lot of blether," he said. "What's behind it?"

"This," I said. "Franks, who's a great pal of Mrs. Craigne, as you know, happened to let fall that to-morrow morning she's going to the Continent, via The Hague. He discovered it quite by accident, and after she'd told him she was going to America. He was very upset about it because it looked as if she'd been leading him on and then wanted to drop him. I told him he was damn-well rid of her, but I didn't tell him what was fishy about her going abroad."

Wharton peered at me over his spectacles, but said nothing.

"As soon as I heard of it I got busy," I said. "I've discovered she's taking the devil of a lot of luggage. In fact all the signs show she's not intending to come back. I dare say if you asked at her bank you'd learn she's in possession of a pretty big sum of money. And she's sold her car. But the point's this. I've a hunch that Sivley will be on that train. She's going to shepherd him through the cordon in some way. If he isn't on the train, then he'll be on the boat. So I'm going to be on that train."

"But she'll spot you."

"Of course she will," I said. "But it'll be too late. You and I will see to that."

"So you're going to allow me to go, are you?"

"Don't be huffy, George," I said. "You're the very one who has to go. What I suggest is that you get rigged up as a Belgian going back home."

That appealed to him. I haven't mentioned the fact in this book, but George is one of the few Englishmen I know who can be said to speak French like a native. His mother was French, and he's always been very much of a Francophile.

"A man I know in Shaftesbury Avenue might rig me up," he said.

Then we got down to details. I told him I'd induced Franks to let me know when she left her flat for Liverpool Street Station, and I think George imagined Franks would be seeing her off. George said he'd fix everything with the railway people, and he'd have four plain clothes men on the train, two ahead of her compartment and two behind.

"For the love of heaven see they don't look too much like flatties," I said. "The least suspicion and our goose is cooked for good."

George said he'd pick them himself, and then we worked out a system of communication. All the time I could feel him holding himself in, and bursting to know how I'd got that hunch about Sivley. Finally we agreed to meet at Liverpool Street at nine the next morning. If anything happened meanwhile, I should be at the flat from nine o'clock onwards. Palmer wasn't due back from his short holiday till the morning, so I'd feed at an hotel.

I had my meal and when I got back to the flat I poured myself a stiff drink to brace me for the last thing that was left to do. It was a minute or two before I felt equal to dialling Charlotte Craigne's number. She was in, and she recognised my voice from only the hallo.

"It's you, isn't it, Ludo?"

"Ludo, it is," I said.

"Darling, how nice to hear you again! But I thought you were in Brazenoak."

"I've had my small holiday," I said. "Now I've got a job of work to do. I'd have asked you to lunch somewhere to-morrow, but I've got to meet some people."

"I'm frightfully busy, too," she said sorrowfully. "Some other time perhaps. But isn't Bernice due back soon?"

"In a few days," I said. "And that reminds me. Don't think I'm whining, but I tried to be decent over—well, you know what. So tell me the honest-to-God truth. Was that a bluff of yours about a certain . . . a certain boy?"

"Bluff's a horrid word," she said. "But as if I'd deceive you about a thing like that. Besides, I may want you to help me again sometime."

"Over what?"

"Darling, must you always be precise? I was talking figuratively."

"Well, I shall be seeing you sometime," I said. "But for having to meet these people to-morrow I'd have looked you up."

I hung up then. I've often wondered just what I'd have done if she'd been only partly decent or repentant and owned up to that damnable blackmail scheme that had worried me more than I could ever tell. As it was, that short telephone conversation was a kind of tonic. Whatever the next day might bring, I knew I could go through with it.

That night I slept very badly. I had, in fact, the kind of night one gets when having to rise at some unearthly hour, and I doubt if I had more than thirty minutes' continuous sleep. At six o'clock I was up and I took considerable pains over my dressing. Then I had a service breakfast and I lingered that out too, and still there was an hour to go before I was due at Liverpool Street. Then the telephone bell went.

"Harold speaking," the voice said. "A taxi just took some advance luggage. Thought I'd better let you know. Everything set your end?"

"Everything set," I said.

"The best of luck, then," he said. "Don't forget to ring."

Another quarter of an hour and it was time to move off. When I reached Liverpool Street I was ten minutes early, but even then Wharton was there before me.

CHAPTER XVI
FINALE

I CAN HONESTLY SAY that I should never have recognised Wharton if I had not known; indeed the whole of that morning there seemed an unreality in thinking of him as Wharton. Yet his make-up was simple—cheeks padded, moustache waxed back and with the short imperial making a Louis Napoleon effect, hair greyed and shoulders padded almost to a hump so that there was an impression of age. Something had also been done to the corners of his eyes to give a slit effect, and as he was swathed in black clothes in spite of the weather, and wore a flopping black hat, he was the very spit of a prosperous provincial. The padding of the cheeks had given his voice just sufficient change and made it slightly nasal and two or three tones higher.

We waited by the telephone till Frank's message came through. I took the call and there had to be some dissimulation.

"Just left," I said. "Thank you, Frank. We're very grateful to you."

Then his end of the conversation was purely imaginary.

"I rather had an idea you were seeing her off. . . . You don't say! . . . Yes, I'm awfully sorry about that . . . To-night, if you could . . . . I'll get in touch with you later. . . . I see, at the hotel. . . . Yes, I'm sure he would. . . . Well, thanks a lot. See you later. . . . Good-bye."

"He couldn't see her off," I told Wharton, "because he's just had a cable that he's wanted back in America himself. He's coming to see me to say good-bye some time to-night. He hoped to see you too."

"A nice fellow," Wharton said. "I doubt if he'll see much of me to-night, though. Even if this business does pan out right, there's another thing or two I've got to do."

We went on to the upstair restaurant from which there would be an excellent view of the train when it backed in. A liaison man had been posted on the platform, and Wharton's other three men were with us. One was in plus-fours and had a bag of clubs; another was obviously bound for a seaside holiday, and the third was a business man. They were scattered about the room and were having tea or coffee, and Wharton and I were at a window table and were having coffee too. Every time a taxi drew in he produced a pair of opera-glasses, though I thought it would be at least a half-hour's taxi drive from her flat through the dense traffic of the morning. Then the train drew in. Wharton looked at his watch and said it was about time she was arriving. Then almost with the same breath he was saying, "This looks like her now."

I spotted her even with my bat eyes, then we both lost her for a moment or two. But she was only calling another porter, for there was more luggage, both in the taxi and on top. Wharton nodded to one of his men to come across.

"A cock-eyed hat with a white feather thing in it," he said. "Black and white handbag, black frock with a bit of white down the front. Get going, and don't forget the corridor side."

A minute or two later he got up to go too. His bag, suitably labelled, was downstairs, and there was a newspaper he had to buy. I waited till it was five minutes to the hour, then made my way to the barrier, keeping my head well down. Then I shot into the nearest door and began working my way along the corridor. At a spot which seemed well short of where Charlotte Craigne would be, I waited for Wharton's man to contact me. Just before the train moved off he came by me.

"Two carriages after this, and four doors along," he told me as he squeezed past. Then the whistle went. There were the last scurryings in and out, and the slamming of doors, and then an almost imperceptible jerk. We were on our way, and all of us with only three choices, for the three stops were Chelmsford, Colchester and Harwich.

I had expected to be in a state of tremendous excitement, and yet I don't think I had ever been less panicky than I was as

I waited in that corridor till the train should have gone through the tunnels and come out to daylight again. Then at last it was light, and after another minute's wait I made my way forward. The train seemed fairly full, but the firsts would almost certainly have plenty of room. Then suddenly I could see Wharton in his corner corridor seat, back to the engine. The door of the compartment was open, and the seat facing Wharton was empty.

"I beg your pardon," I said, as I kicked against his boot. Then I was smiling apologetically again. "Sorry, but I thought this was a smoking compartment."

As I went to back out I let my eyes meet Charlotte Craigne's. She was terrified; there wasn't any doubt about that. I had to be too concerned with my own surprise to notice hers.

"Good heavens!" I said, and sat down again. "What on earth are you doing here?"

She smiled wanly and I knew she was fighting to pull herself together.

"My dear, it's too dreadful! Just after you rang me last night I was rung up by the police. Poor Rupert's body has been found. And, my dear, where do you think? Near The Hague!"

"You poor soul," I said. "And you're going over to bring him back?"

She shook her head. "I think I shall have him buried there. They told me it could be arranged. But you," she said; "what on earth are you doing here?"

"But I told you," I said. "When I rang you last night; don't you remember? Didn't I say I had to go and meet some people? Just two business acquaintances," I added indifferently. "Two Germans. They're coming from Holland. That will be the same boat that you're crossing on."

"Oh, what a rush!" she said. "My dear, it was a perfect nightmare. Packing half the night and then rushing away this morning."

"You're looking a bit tired," I said. "You'd better get back in your corner and have a wee nap."

She said she probably would. I nodded and smiled as I backed into my own corner. The Belgian gentleman opposite me was reading an overnight French newspaper, but as I forgot myself and instinctively brought out my pipe, he saw the movement.

"It is not a smoking, pliz," he told me in an English I could hardly make out.

I smiled an apology and replaced the pipe.

"*Monsieur ne fume pas,*" I said in my best French.

"*Mais non, monsieur,*" he told me quite amiably. "*Ça dérange l'estomac.*"

I bowed and smiled. He get on with his reading. I caught Charlotte Craigne's eye. She made a moue and I grimaced.

You could feel a difference in the compartment after that. I knew she was no longer mistrusting me, and that comical Belgian was something like a fire at which we warmed our hands. I did a bit of reading, and began an assault on *The Times* crossword, and when I looked at Charlotte Craigne again, she was pretending to be asleep.

The train had long been travelling at speed, and as we neared Chelmsford she made an artistic awakening. I eased over in her direction.

"Shall I order you some coffee? I believe you can get it on this train."

She shook her head.

"That's very sweet of you, my dear, but I don't think I could touch a thing."

"I know," I said sympathetically. Then I glanced back at the Belgian who seemed to be sound asleep, hands clasped across his ample stomach. "Funny old boy! What about your asking him if you may smoke?"

"I don't feel like it this morning," she said. "Perhaps I'll have some coffee after all. This is Chelmsford, isn't it?"

Then she was looking out of the window as the train slowed, and saying that of course it was. I pushed the bell for the attendant, and kept my eye on her all the time. But she didn't seem interested in what was happening on the platforms, and then the Belgian woke up and made an interlude as he too ordered coffee. We all managed to drink it before the train began to rock again. Then I said I'd have a cigarette in the corridor.

When I came back to the compartment the Belgian began a conversation.

"We go fast, eh?" he said, and waved a hand at the landscape that hurtled past.

"Quite a good speed," I said, and then tried my French again. Charlotte spoke French quite well and I knew her ears would be cocked.

"You know England fairly well?" I asked.

"Very little," he said, and shrugged his shoulders. "But my daughter has just married an Englishman and I've spent a few days with them."

"What part of England?" I asked politely.

"In Kent," he said, and added that the country there was very different from Belgium.

"What part of Kent?"

A village near Sittingbourne, he said, and there the brief conversation ended, for he was asking where the lavatory was.

"Not a bad old chap after all." I told Charlotte as soon as he'd gone.

"You speak French quite well," she said. "I'd forgotten it was one of your accomplishments."

But the remark sounded like a forced one, and it seemed to me she was nervous again. From Chelmsford to Colchester is under twenty miles, and in a moment the brakes began to drag as the train slowed.

She drew back to her corner and I nestled back in mine. As the train came to a stop the Belgian appeared again.

My heart had now begun to beat more quickly, but I tried to make my interest in the platform only a perfunctory one. As a matter of fact there was very little to see, at least near our compartment. The only passenger I saw get in was an elderly man with a pronounced stoop, and he looked something of an invalid, for he had a white muffler round his neck and made his way slowly along the corridor with the help of his stick. A porter was following with a small bag.

The train moved off again. I didn't dare look at Charlotte Craigne, and then after a minute or two my heart was beating more steadily.

"Only about another quarter of an hour," I said.

She merely nodded and gave a faint smile. I picked up my magazine and began reading it. A peep at Charlotte showed me she was again pretending to be dozing. I hastily wrote a sentence or two in the margin of the magazine and then gave an exclamation of surprise.

"This is extraordinary!" I told the Belgian in French. "Here are two pictures of the very town where you've been staying!"

I passed him the magazine, open at the place.

"Ah!" he said with quite an excitement, and began telling me about this and that which he recognised. Then suddenly he was on his feet and feeling his pockets. Then came a gasp of dismay.

"My gloves! I've left them in the lavatory!"

Off he went in search of them. I leaned back in my seat, but again I dare not look at Charlotte Craigne. When I did glance her way I could see the estuary, and through the open door came a faint whiff of the sea.

"Soon be there now," I said. "No hurry, though. There's always heaps of time to catch the boat if I remember rightly."

"Heaps," she said, but her fingers were fumbling nervously with her bag.

I leaned back in my corner again, and I was straining my ears to catch a sound, and that was foolish, for the noise of the train made other sounds unheard. Now I could feel my heart thumping against my ribs, and I began taking deep breaths to steady it. Then the brakes began to grip again and the train was imperceptibly slowing. Charlotte Craigne was getting to her feet.

"I think I've just time to powder my nose."

"Heaps of time," I said.

Then it seemed as if I could hear a faint scuffling. Then as I drew in my long legs to let Charlotte pass, the Belgian appeared in the doorway.

"Sit down, Mrs. Craigne," he said, and the voice was Wharton's. "The game's up."

Her mouth gaped foolishly. I was scrambling to my feet. As I backed through the door, Wharton's two men came in.

"Quick! Get hold of her arms!" Wharton was shouting.

I looked back and on the floor was a confused heap. There was a shriek, and the sound of it was so frightening that I found myself moving along the corridor, glasses in my hand. People were standing in doorways, and one or two were trying to pass. Then the train gave a jerk and had stopped. Wharton's bellow was heard.

"Get back there, please! No business of yours, sir. Get back I tell you! There's another door there. Use that."

The shrieking had long since stopped. One of Wharton's men came out to the door and stood on guard. Wharton moved on along the corridor. After what seemed minutes and minutes, I made my way forward too. Charlotte Craigne was still lying on the floor, her body now at full length.

"What's the matter with her?" I found myself asking. "Has she fainted?"

"Too quick for us, sir. Grabbed something out of her bag and swallowed it. Cyanide by the smell of it."

All I could do was nod. Then I was shaking my head and stepping down to the platform. A few yards back was a seat and I made my way to it. My thoughts were a mad whirl and I was suddenly feeling weak at the knees, and I was glad to sit down. The air was cold on my forehead and when I brushed my hand across it, it was damp with sweat.

"Going anywhere, sir?" a porter asked me, but I only shook my head. Where I was going was back to town, and by the train on which I had come. Somehow I knew I must dodge Wharton, and all at once I was making for the train again and bolting the door of a lavatory.

Minutes passed and at last I heard the engine as it went by on its way to back to the train. Then there was a jerk as it joined up again, and after a minute or two I ventured to look out. A porter caught sight of me and came up.

"A gentleman's been looking everywhere for you, sir."

"Where's he now?"

"Gone off in a car, sir. A police van, it was."

The words were more of a question but I didn't rise to it. All I said was that I was going back to town and the gentleman would get in touch with me there. Then I made my way to a compartment; not the one in which I had come, for I'd have smelt that cyanide and thought of too many things. I thought of too many as it was.

I felt hungry when I got back to town, and that was a good sign. I had tea in a little place near Liverpool Street and then took a taxi home. Palmer was there, and he said I was looking tired.

"Anybody ring up for me?" I wanted to know.

Nobody had rung, he said, and then when I was having a clean up, the telephone bell went. Wharton was on the line.

"You're a nice one," he said. "What'd you go back to town for?"

"Just something I had to do," I said lamely.

"And a damn nice trick you played on me," he said. "Letting me think to the very last moment it was Sivley. But how the hell did you know it was Rupert Craigne!"

CHAPTER XVII
FULL CIRCLE

I HAD A LEISURELY DINNER, wrote some rough notes on what I had to tell Wharton, and then rang Frank. He was so eager to know what had happened that it was a minute before we unsorted ourselves. Then he told me he'd seen a sensational report in the evening papers about an arrest in the Brazenoak murders, and was it true.

"It's true enough," I began. "But they haven't got the really ghastly thing. Charlotte Craigne swallowed some cyanide before Wharton's men could grab her."

"You should worry," he told me cynically. "And what about meeting somewhere and you telling me all about it?"

"I'm not going over things twice," I said. "Wharton hopes to be here somewhere round about nine. You're supposed to be sailing for home on Monday, so what about coming round to say good-bye? Not at nine. Make it a quarter to. By the way, Wharton says he's got some surprises up his sleeve for me."

It was well before time when Frank turned up. Even before I'd given him a drink he was wondering how I could tell him all about everything in front of Wharton.

"You won't be here," I said. "I've told Palmer that as soon as Wharton appears, you're going in the kitchen. If the door's ajar you'll hear everything. Listen for a cue when he gets up to go and nip round to the door bell."

"Fine," he said. "But you'll have to skate over some thin ice, won't you?"

"It won't be the first time," I told him. "One thing I'll bet you a couple of dinners on. Wharton'll claim to have had his eye on Charlotte Craigne all along."

He hadn't the pluck to take me on. Then before we'd time for a second quick one, the lift was heard. Out went the glasses and Frank with them, and when Palmer showed Wharton in, I was dozing in my favourite chair.

"Hallo, George," I said. "You're a bit early. Have a drink."

"It'll have to be a quick one then," he said. "I'm due to start back to Brazenoak in under an hour."

Before Palmer could bring the glasses, he was asking me how I got on to that Rupert Craigne business. I began by telling him about that Adam mirror and the dirty trick I thought Charlotte Craigne had played on me.

"You didn't tell me about that," he told me accusingly.

"I didn't know what it all added up to till just before I rang you up yesterday," I said. "This is how it was. I was sitting in the lounge at the Oak and. I caught sight of Mrs. Porter in the mirror above the mantelpiece. You know that funny little trick she has of rubbing her nose? And you remember the little nervous trick Rupert Craigne had of twitching his neck, and how I called your attention to it when he did it in court at Chelmsford? Well, I began to think about mirrors and tricks, and then I suddenly wondered what Matthews had really seen. It seemed to me that after all he couldn't have seen Charlotte Craigne and Sivley, because he'd have seen that *before* the Saturday. Even when Charlotte Craigne and I got back from Trimport he was reasonably all right. The tremendous fluster only occurred after he'd heard about the death of Rupert Craigne. That made me think further.

"I thought how Rupert Craigne was socially dead and damned. He had to get money to live on, and he wanted to live with his wife. Now one of the complications of this case was that we were dealing with an accomplished and unscrupulous liar in Charlotte Craigne. We didn't know what to credit and what to disbelieve. I thought that when she said she was still mad about Rupert she was naturally telling lies. She wasn't. She was with him up to the hilt. She wanted money and she wanted Rupert, and Passman was in the way. When I knew that I knew that all that window-smashing and haranguing crowds was part of a perfectly organised scheme. It kept the old swindle before the public, and therefore it kept Sivley's threat in everyone's mind. I dare say, by the way, that it was Rupert Craigne who sent the anonymous letters about Passman. The thing is, however, that everyone still knew that if Craigne himself and Passman were killed, then only Sivley could have done it.

"And what I also knew about Rupert Craigne was that in spite of his affectations, he was a very fine actor, and a master of make-up. Even that famous Jupiter make-up was superb, considering what he looked like before. I also remembered that for some weeks Rupert Craigne had been dormant, so this is how I began to work things out. What he did was to make his headquarters at some convenient spot for both Trimport and Brazenoak—say Ipswich or Colchester—and with his beard off and hair dyed black, to build up a wholly new character, whom we can call X. Then at the psychological moment, which was when that cricket week at Trimport was approaching, Charlotte Craigne made her prearranged approaches to me. She wanted me to be a witness to Rupert's death, and because she had an idea that my evidence if required, would carry considerable weight. That same evidence would include her distress, her venomous anger against Sivley, and the putting firmly into my mind the fact that only Sivley could have done it, and finally alibis for both herself and Rupert, in the rare event of police suspicion, for Joe Passman's murder.

"Here's a record of what she told me over the telephone that morning. I'll go into it in detail when I make my full report, but perhaps you can follow it enough to see how all my suspicions began to be confirmed. She said she had got up early—it was about eight o'clock—became Joe might come down at any moment. As a matter of fact he never got down before half-past nine. She urged me to hurry to Brazenoak, and yet she kept me hanging about when I did get there. And why? Because Rupert's stunt was timed for half-past eleven and she didn't want me there before.

"And now as to how Craigne did it. He knew when Sivley was coming out. Sivley went straight to London. Did Craigne meet him there? Or was Charlotte Craigne the go-between? I don't know, but I think it certain that Craigne had Sivley on a string. Maybe he promised him money or a job, and of course he'd try to explain away the double-crossing in the swindling ease. After all, Craigne had been Sivley's employer, and class will always tell. At any rate I'd say that Craigne met Sivley near Trimport and killed him. He stripped the body and then or later he put Sivley's prints on a plate which was to be left in the bungalow. He hid the motor-bike somewhere handy, and next day he was Sivley. As Sivley he hired the bungalow. As for Sivley's body, a search ought to find it somewhere in the neighbourhood."

"That's where I've got a surprise for you," Wharton cut in. "The Ipswich police got an anonymous letter—or as good as anonymous—about a pond in some old brick workings, and what do you think? Sivley's body was found there this very afternoon, and stark naked except for an undervest."

"That's really good news," I said. "Craigne took everything off him, even to the shoes. If you remember, they were exactly the same height and build. But about the rest of it. Craigne fixed it to have a boat ready on the Saturday morning. In his char-

192 | CHRISTOPHER BUSH

acter of X., the man with short black hair and a black jowl and certain other alterations, he came to Trimport by train. Under his clothes he had on a vivid emerald bathing costume. In the woods near where the boat would be, or else in his bungalow, he fixed his golden beard and a golden wig and was once more Rupert Craigne. Once in the boat he threw the clothes back to the boatman. I don't know why he didn't lay them in the boat. Perhaps his idea was to get into the public eye at the earliest moment, but what I do want to impress on you is this. He kept his back turned to the boatman. And why? Because the front of his bathing costume had a slight bulge in it. The bulge was an ordinary dark blue costume, and probably there was also a pistol or some contraption that would make a noise like a gun when you pulled a string. I'd been wondering, by the way, why the rifle with which Sivley was supposed to have shot Craigne was never found, and I also call your attention to something you may not know. The boatman was expecting Craigne to row out beyond the bar so as to take his swim in comparative privacy. That boatman had known Craigne well in the old days, and therefore he knew, what I didn't, that Craigne was an exceptionally good swimmer.

"The rest is easy. Rupert Craigne, as Rupert Craigne, rowed out to beyond the bar, pricked his finger to make a blood spot or two and then began haranguing the crowd. There he was, in that vivid bathing suit and the sun on his gold hair and beard. At a suitable moment he produced the crack of a shot, and that moment was when he saw my car draw up and Charlotte flutter the handkerchief with which she was ready to wipe her eyes. His hands went to his breast, then he fell, and if there was any contraption, he took it into the water with him. Then he swam under water for the edge of the crowd, and while under water he took off the green bathing suit and tucked it inside the breast of the blue one which he'd either put on or which was already under it. As you know, you can keep under water the devil of a time. Inside that blue costume also went the beard and wig. Maybe he put plumpers into his cheeks too, but when he bobbed up, there he was, simply an ordinary bather. Everybody's eyes were on the boat. After that flaming vision of Rupert Craigne who'd he interested in a perfectly ordinary man with short black hair and in a blue suit?"

"All he had to do after that was to make his way to the bungalow, and, remember, with the eyes of every man, woman and child turned towards that boat. In the bungalow he got into Sivley's clothes and off he went on the motor-bike. Now he was Sivley again, and as Sivley he killed Passman. He wanted to be seen as Sivley, and he took care to be seen—at a distance. Probably he scouted round and saw where a gardener was. What he didn't know was that when he was hiding in that shrubbery, Matthews must have seen him, and that would be when Matthews brought the tankard at half-past twelve. Probably Craigne was looking cautiously out of the shrubbery, and had one of those twitching fits. At any rate Matthews spotted him. It puzzled him and it worried him, and then when the news of Craigne's death was received, Matthews knew he'd seen a ghost! Maybe that's what he wanted to tell me that night. He was going to ask me if I believed in ghosts. He wouldn't worry Charlotte Craigne by asking her that.

"When I worked that out I could guess what Charlotte Craigne thought when she wormed out of Matthews what he'd intended to tell me in my private ear. She got in touch with Rupert and I could guess what he thought too. I also remembered how she'd boasted that Matthews would do anything for her, and everyone knew the old chap thought the world of her. She could spin any yarn to him. Maybe she told him that there'd been a mistake about Rupert's death. Rupert was alive and needed help. Any such yarn would have done, and then she picked him up in her car and took him to where Rupert was waiting. I doubt if even Charlotte Craigne had the nerve to see Matthews killed. I'll give her that credit. All the same, the killing was something that had to be done. And that reminds me of something else. She threw a real faint when she was told about Joe's murder. I wondered why and I couldn't make it add up right, for she must have known what Rupert intended. What I think now is that the faint was a genuine collapse. Even a hell-cat like Charlotte Craigne couldn't last out after the strain of what had happened and what she was anticipating.

"As for Rupert, I worked it out that he went back to Ipswich or Colchester as X. Everything had panned out beautifully. The hue and cry was out for Sivley, Charlotte had a good slab of her money, and all there was to do was to make a quiet exit from this country. I think the idea was to cross to the Continent where both would be immediately safe, and so ultimately to either North or South America when everything seemed absolutely safe. But something else happened, and clean out of the blue. Harper saw Charlotte Craigne in her car that night and he tried to put the screw on her. Perhaps you let on to her that Harper was swearing he'd seen her car or she guessed it somehow, but at any rate, there was somebody else to be removed. This time Craigne bungled it. But the pair had the wind up, and the getaway was decided on for Saturday. Craigne, I suppose, had a false passport?"

"In a way, yes," Wharton said. "It was a new one, made out for what you called Mr. X."

"Well, that's roughly that," I said. "I don't think any of us can be blamed for not having rumbled Rupert Craigne. Everything was so obvious in an entirely different way. All that remains now, to clear everything up, is to find poor old Matthews's body."

"Ah!" said Wharton. "I knew I'd have a surprise for you. You aren't the only one who can produce a rabbit out of the hat. I've found his body."

"You have!"

"Oh, yes." He gave himself a nod of approbation. "Mind you, I've had my eye on that Mrs. Craigne. I don't always let out everything I know. I'm like some people; I know when to keep things under my hat. You didn't know that I'd made some more inquiries at the Manor, but this is what I found out. On the Saturday night Mrs. Craigne had a meal in her bedroom, and she had breakfast there the following morning, and lunch the next day. She wouldn't let the maid clean the room up, but said she might be lying down again—of all the cock-and-bull yarns. Also on the Sunday morning she saw the head gardener and had

Mr. Passman's grave dug there and then, and dug deep. It was ready on the Monday morning, for I saw it myself, but after it was dug she had it covered with a tarpaulin to keep any possible rain out. That tarpaulin wasn't removed till just before the coffin was lowered, and none of the gardening or other staff was at the graveside. Now do you see it?"

"I think so," I said.

"Events prove it. She got in touch with her husband, told Matthews some yarn, picked him up in her car and merely circled round the garage again. Then Matthews was taken through the shrubbery to the lower gardens, where Craigne met him. The body was hidden and Craigne spent the night and the next day in her room. Remember that there wouldn't be a soul near those lower gardens on a Sunday night, which was when Matthews's body was put in the grave and some earth on top. At any rate, that's where the body was found this evening."

"You got Home Office permission to remove Joe's coffin?"

"Oh, no. The ground slopes sharply away. We tunnelled underneath. I'm due back there now to finish the job in the early morning."

"Damn good work, George," I said.

"You were in it too," he told me. "Remember what I said at the Oak one day? You and I haven't lost a case yet." Then he was frowning. "Mind you, there are two mighty queer things I can't get to the bottom of. For the life of me I can't work out who it was that was making those inquiries about Sivley."

"I wouldn't worry," I said airily. "Probably it was Rupert Craigne, trying to throw us off the scent."

"Maybe," he said. "But there's something else. You saw the mistake the papers made, saying Harper was dead. Well, what do you think? Damned if they didn't ring me up and ask why *I'd* made the mistake. I, mind you! They swore blind I'd rung some agency or other from Ipswich and said he was dead. I blasted hell out of them. But what do you make of it? Damn funny, isn't it?"

"Probably they got the name wrong," I said. "But wait a minute, though. Why shouldn't it have been Craigne impersonating you? It could have been done, you know. Yours isn't too difficult a voice."

That was a bad brick to drop. George is proud of his resonant baritone, so no wonder he glared.

"But it *could* be done," I insisted. "After all, look at your own magnificent impersonation of that Belgian. Magnificent isn't the word. It was colossal. It was a masterpiece!"

"Well, it served its purpose," he told me with false modesty, and got to his feet. "About time I was getting on my way. You wouldn't like to come down with me?"

"Don't you remember I'm expecting Franks? He's sailing on Monday and is coming round to say good-bye. But why all the hurry? Have another drink before you go."

He said he wouldn't, but I'd made time for Frank. The bell rang and in a minute Palmer was admitting the caller.

"Well," said Frank, smiles wreathing his face, "this is a pleasant surprise!"

"And for me too," Wharton said as he held out his hand. "Mr. Travers tells me you're leaving us."

"What about the three of us having a farewell drink?" I cut in. "You're not in all that hurry, George."

"But I am," he said. "I'm overdue now. You'll excuse me, Mr. Franks, if I hurry away. Duty is duty."

"Sure," said Frank, and held out his hand again. "It's been a great privilege meeting you, Superintendent. Something I shall recall a good many times when I'm back home."

"It's been a pleasure meeting you, sir," Wharton said him. Then he looked at me and sighed heavily. "Well, the best of friends must part, as they say. . . . I wonder."

"Wonder what, George?"

"Well, in the words of the immortal Bard, 'When shall we three meet again?'"

"I guess you're a Shakespearian scholar, sir," Frank said. I daren't look at him, for if I'd caught his eye he'd probably have had the impudence to give me a wink. "Now there's only one quotation I've ever remembered, and it seems to suit this occasion. 'Farewell! Othello's occupation's gone.'"

"Ah! Othello," George said, and gave a reminiscent nod as if his inward eye saw the very stage. A sigh and he was turning to go. "Well, I must be on my way. And I know my own way out."

We saw him to the lift for all that, and we even watched till the top of the lift was out of sight.

"That was a hot one you pulled about Rupert Craigne," Frank told me admiringly as soon as we turned. "And talk about skating over thin ice!"

"Since I've known you I've told more lies than in all the rest of my life," I told him, and I hoped witheringly. "And how you had the nerve to trot out that Othello gag absolutely takes my breath away. You can grin," I said, "but let me drive this into that feather-pated brain of yours. Keep out of Wharton's way if you have any regard for me. If he ever gets an idea of the truth, I'll be eternally damned."

"Very good, sir," he told me amusedly. "We still hope to continue the Prince and Holloway service. And now what about a drink?"

We sat on yarning about Halstead and heaven knows what till best part of midnight. I asked him what job he'd be on next.

"Between you and me," he said, "I may be doing the one thing I've always wanted to do. You think there's going to be a war?"

"I do," I said. "And what's more, I've got a job."

"I'm going to get one too," he said. "As soon as the balloon goes up I'll be doing what I've always wanted to do—drive a tank."

Well, that's that, and the wheel has gone full circle. I've just read through what I've written and I've been wondering if that challenge I threw out was exactly fair. On the whole I think it was. You should have gathered all along that I'd never got that money from Charlotte and that therefore she was in things up to the neck. The rest was adding this and that and getting the right answer, and if you got that answer, well, you were a cleverer one than I.

What about Frank? Well, he did drive a tank. I got in touch with his uncle last night, and he told me Frank was in that retreat to El Alamein, and that was all he knew. But somehow I can't believe he's dead. Missing, if you like, and a prisoner, but not dead. And if he's a prisoner, then he won't be so long, if I know anything about him. With his grin and brazen impudence and low cunning he's probably by this time impersonated an Italian general. Wherever he is, good luck to him, and if he's under the sand, then God rest his cheerful soul.

The mirror? Well, I wish you hadn't asked that question. Maybe Charlotte Craigne did away with it after all. I've never troubled to inquire although I'm pretty sure the executors would have let me have it if it had been found in her wardrobe. But that mirror hanging over my mantelpiece would have been too much of a reminder. Some things in this life are best forgotten, as I hinted to Bernice only this morning.

THE END

Lightning Source UK Ltd.
Milton Keynes UK
UKHW03f0023130918
328781UK00003B/76/P

9 781912 574179